NO
SAVING
THROW

NO
SAVING
THROW

KRISTIN McFARLAND

DIVERSION
BOOKS

Diversion Books
A Division of Diversion Publishing Corp.
443 Park Avenue South, Suite 1004
New York, New York 10016
www.DiversionBooks.com

For more information, email info@diversionbooks.com

Book design by Elyse Strongin, Neuwirth & Associates.

First Diversion Books edition May 2019.
Paperback ISBN: 978-1-63576-582-3
eBook ISBN: 978-1-63576-579-3

Printed in the U.S.A.

1 3 5 7 9 10 8 6 4 2

In loving memory of my mother,

Terry McFarland,

who supported even the wildest of my dreams.

I

"WHAT DO YOU MEAN, a vampire killed him?"

Outside my office door, a swarm of sugar-rushed, Friday-high kids ran by, squealing like Jawas on scrap-metal discount day at the market. High voices chittered, laughter echoed off the walls, and a hormonal funk of excitement hung in the air. Aggravated, I got up and slammed the door. On the other side, a childish voice said, "Oooooh," igniting another eruption of giggles.

On the other end of the line, Cody yammered on, something about aliens and guns and not having any wooden stakes, and the unfairness of it all. I stalked around my cluttered desk and collapsed in my chair, but something sharp jabbed through the smooth fabric of my trousers. I jumped up with an outraged squeak.

"I know!" Cody said. "He was completely out of line!"

"No, that's not—"

"But it's your job to keep the GM running a fair game," he said, acting as if I hadn't spoken. "I put a lot of time and effort into this character, and if he can just erase all that with one lousy night of weak-ass world-building, then he needs to be replaced."

"I'm sorry you feel that way, but I have no control over the Saturday night games." I bent, looking for the source of my rump pain—one of them, anyway; the other one was currently whining on the phone. Something shiny poked out from the crease of the seat. "You'll need to take it up with your troupe if you have a problem." I thrust my hand into the chair and groped around until I pulled out my new nemesis. It was a tiny pewter figurine of a woman in ridiculous armor. She held a spear as long as her body directly butt-ward. I scowled at her and her proudly exposed boobs, then tossed her into the corner with a pitiful metallic clink. "Coming to me is not going to solve anything. I am not your mommy."

He sputtered. "But you own the store. You set up these games—"

"I sponsor them. I don't run them. You're a big boy. Figure it out." I hung up, exasperated, and collapsed into my chair. I sat for only half a moment before I shifted, irritated. I still wore the suit I'd resurrected from my closet, the one I'd bought when I graduated from business school and hadn't replaced in the ensuing decade, and the trousers were giving me terrible wedgies, exactly what I didn't need when I was already uncomfortable.

Wearing clothes from my twenties was definitely a mistake. Letting a spoiled gamer with a chip on his shoulder get to me was a bigger one.

Outside my office door, I heard a chorus of pubescent voices rising in a symphony of excitement—my employees, Hector and Bailey, must have started forming groups for the *Spellcasters* draft. The new decks had arrived that afternoon while I was off pretending to be a grown-up, and the die-hard fans had started trickling in more than an hour ago to wait their turn to build random decks and join a tournament.

Meanwhile, I was trying to remember why I'd ever thought it would be a good idea to compete for grant money to green Independence Square Mall, the building that housed my store, Ten Again. "Write a detailed proposal," they said. "We have money to improve our downtown commercial district, and we want to give it to you!"

It had all seemed so simple back before a proposal had turned into a series of contractor quotes, which in turn became a presentation before the city's small business committee, and then—well, it was best not to think about the rest of it. I glanced down at my straining blouse just to make sure everything was still neatly buttoned away.

All contained. I heaved a sigh of relief mixed with regret. Sure, *now* my wardrobe wanted to behave.

A few moments later, I heard a thump against my door and a shout. Next came frantic knocking and Hector's voice saying, "Autumn, I need you out here."

I closed my eyes briefly, then pulled the suit jacket off the back of my chair. The cashmere was buttery soft in my hands, the navy lining soothing to my overstimulated nerves. I folded the expensive garment, pressed it to my mouth, and screamed. The jacket successfully muffled the sound, and I sighed, relieved. I shook the jacket out and draped it over the back of my chair. It was time to feed the animals.

I opened the door an inch, peeking out cautiously.

Hector Tran, one of my employees, forced the door open more, thrusting one arm through the crack like a cat shut in a bathroom. I took a wary step back. "What?"

"Help me." He pressed his face to the door, eyes wide and glassy. "I can't keep up with them."

I opened the door all the way. "We can do this, Hector. They're just teenagers."

"Not all of them." Hector looked like he wanted to clutch at my shoulders and shake me. "There are grown men out there. One of them is wearing a tie."

"Well, we can handle him, too."

"And Cody called."

"I know. He called me, too. He says you killed his character with a vampire. There are no vampires in space, Hector."

"It wasn't a vampire! It belonged to an alien race that subsists on human fluids, like the vitreous humor and—"

"Ugh." I held up a hand. "I don't care. But it sounds like you made it up specifically to kill him off. I know he's annoying, but you can't treat him like a leper just because he's a pain."

"Me? The other players *asked* me to kill him off. This was the best way I could think of."

I sighed and made exasperated shooing motions with my hands. "Well, think of something better. You're in charge for a reason. Don't make me put Bay on their game."

"Ha. Bay would have killed him in the first week. And not in character."

"Ha yourself. Are you ready to open the boxes?"

"They're already open. The man in the suit opened them with a letter opener. He had it in his sock."

I blinked at that but kept my collected-boss face on. "Well, then, are you ready to start the draft?"

"They were fighting over the cards like dogs. I wasn't sure where to start."

"Well, go, figure it out!" I clapped my hands in his face, shutting him up. He backed slowly out of the office, and I watched as a wave of gamers swallowed him whole, like sharks devouring a sea lion. I shut the door again, panting slightly.

The notes from my presentation lay in a forlorn pile on my desk—all that careful research about solar panels and geothermal heating, a case study of another historic building in White Lake that had been remodeled to modernize its utilities, even a proposed plan from one contractor for installing forced air ventilation. So much work, and it had all ended, as so many things do, not with a bang but with a nervous titter.

But surely they wouldn't drop me from the running. Not for such a stupid thing.

Someone knocked on my door again.

I growled, whipped around, and yanked it open. "What?" I snarled.

My best friend of more than twenty years, Jordan Hansen, took a step back when she saw me. Her shock quickly faded into bemusement as she took in my appearance, and that bemusement rapidly became amusement. She grinned.

"You look like your mom," she said.

"Not. Helping." I grabbed her by the arm and dragged her into the office.

"What is the matter with you? You have, like, a hundred preteens out there, a creepy guy in a suit, and Bay looks like she's about to punch Hector in the face. I didn't bring my riot gear, you know."

I flopped into the chair in front of my desk and put my head in my hands. "I know, I know. I was so not prepared for all of this."

I heard a creak as she perched on my desk. "Prepared for what?"

"Well, I had that big presentation today in front of the Economic Development Commission and the grant coordinators, remember? They're picking the finalists for the grant money this week, so we all had to explain our plans."

"Right."

I glanced up at her. "Well, remember in sixth grade when Angie Tavers stole your clothes from the locker room and you had to make your student council speech wearing your gym shorts and the undershirt you borrowed from me? Well—"

"You did not have to make your presentation with your ass hanging out."

"No, but . . ." I swallowed, words failing me. I lowered my hands from my face and made a cupping motion with my hands, the universal signal for "Honka honka!"

"No."

"Yes." I buried my face in my hands again. "The middle button on my shirt popped open."

"Was it open the whole time?"

I nodded. "The whole time I was talking, there was my cleavage, interrupting. The. Whole. Time."

"And no one told you?"

"Well, Alice was there, and I did think she was fiddling with her sweater a lot, but—no. I didn't know."

It was a measure of our friendship that Jordan didn't immediately break down laughing. Her silence went on for so long, I finally looked up.

She hastily rearranged her face, but I gave her a half-hearted smile. "I know. Go ahead."

She dissolved into giggles, laughing so hard her dark eyes watered and she threatened to slide off the edge of my desk. I shook my head ruefully, knowing we'd been through and would go through worse. We'd been best friends since the fourth grade, forced together by defensive necessity: she was the only black girl in our Wonder Bread school class, and I was the only child of divorce. When my dad married an African American woman from Detroit, well, I was quite the conversation topic. Jordan and I had rescued each other, and we'd been inseparable since then. These days, she was the first black woman on the White Lake Police force—and the irony of that title was one she more than enjoyed pointing out.

But she was the Diana Barry to my Anne Shirley, keeping me grounded when my flights of fancy threatened to drop me to a plummeting death. When she slapped one of her knees unironically, I had to laugh at my involuntary exposure, too.

"I can't believe you made your entire presentation with your tits hanging out."

I shrugged. "It'll teach me for not updating my wardrobe. I almost never have to dress like an adult anymore. But you don't even know the worst part."

"It gets *worse*?"

"Meghan was there to make *her* presentation—and so was Craig."

That clammed her up. "He was not."

"Yep."

She contemplated that for a moment, then shrugged it off. "Well, Meghan can just be jealous, and Craig's seen it all before. You probably did yourself a favor."

That stopped me short. "No. What if—what if they decide they liked me just because I flashed them? Twenty-five thousand dollars in exchange for a little show?"

"Oh, come on. They'll like you because you were good, and because your plan is a million times better than hoity-toity Meghan Bitchface Kountz's."

Bitchface. I snickered, appeased. It was an apt description.

"Fine. You're right." I straightened in my chair. "But I'm still allowed to be mortified. And don't say Bitchface where the kids can hear you."

"Fair enough." She hopped off my desk. "Now stop feeling sorry for yourself—you have a party to throw."

We made it two steps out my door before catastrophe struck.

Well, catastrophe-light. Someone dropped a deck of cards at my feet in a colorful cascade of monsters and spells, and a curly-haired girl pounced on me. Jordan pressed herself against the wall in exaggerated terror while I blew red hair out of my face.

"Autumn!" My assailant hugged me tight. "This is amazing!"

"Hey, Paige." One of my regulars, she'd been visiting the store since she started at the University of Wisconsin-White Lake, and I'd watched her grow from a gawky teenager into a super-hot young woman of legal drinking age who had half the male gamers following her around like trained monkeys.

Two of her entourage were with her now, glaring at each other over the spilled cards. Paige beamed at me and then at them.

"What's with them?" I asked her as the taller guy, Nick—her current boyfriend—stooped, steaming, to pick up the cards. Wes, Paige's *ex*-boyfriend and Nick's best friend, turned back to one of the nearby display tables with a hurt look on his face.

Paige shrugged. "The usual. Fighting over deck size."

She giggled, and I smiled. Nick and Paige had met more than a year ago through one of Hector's RPGs—a game to which Wes had brought Paige on a date: awkward. But since then, the three seemed to have settled into a bizarre, friendly trio, and Paige herself organized the store's bimonthly live action role-playing game in Independence Square Mall.

"It's good to see you guys here tonight. I didn't know if you'd make it, now that you and Nick have both joined the working world and become too important to come to Friday night *Spellcasters*."

Paige stuck her tongue out at me. "Hardly. We're gaming tonight—this was the only Friday this month we could all get together."

"Really?" I frowned. "I didn't have a chance to tell Donald, and the security guard won't know—and I'm already stretching my credibility in the building with all these kids running around after hours."

She opened her mouth, probably to reassure me, but I spotted Hector across the room, waving frantically to me from the register. I sighed, excused myself, and slid through the crowd, making my way over to him. When I reached the counter, he grabbed me and hissed, "He's here."

"Who?"

"Cody!" Hector nodded toward the back door, the one that led into the mall. Cody was leaning against the railing of the steps that led into the sunken shop floor, glowering at the happy customers around him. With his shaved head and round face, he looked like the love child of a troll doll and a jack-o'-lantern but without any cuteness or whimsy. He was in his early twenties, like the rest of the LARPers, but his perpetually angry demeanor made him seem older.

He saw us staring, and Hector grabbed my elbow and turned me away. "Don't look at him!"

I rolled my eyes. "Why, because he'll turn me to stone?"

"How did he get here so fast?" Hector muttered, casting a dark glance over my shoulder. I turned, too, watching the cranky man through the sea of happy kids. "And why is he here, anyway?"

"I don't know, but he's coming over here." I plastered a fake smile on my face as Cody pushed his way through the crowd to meet us at the register. "Do you think if we hide, he'll notice?"

"I don't know, but I'm going to try—"

I caught Hector's shirt before he could slink away. "No. We can handle this. Hello, Cody. We didn't expect to see you so soon."

"I needed to talk to him." He pointed to Hector, his finger trembling. "You need to take it back. Last night's session. What happened was unacceptable."

"Now, Cody," I wheedled. "Hector explained what happened, and I think—"

"He killed my character because he doesn't like me—"

"I'm not the only one," Hector hissed. Cody went red in the face, making him look like a particularly misshapen pomegranate. I elbowed Hector, but there was no stopping him.

"They all want you out, everyone—ask Wes. He's here some-where. They *asked* me to kill you off. If you don't like how I did it, then you can take it up with them."

Cody opened his mouth and closed it again, his face now brick red.

Into the awkward silence that fell, I said, "Not all groups have the right chemistry, Cody, and maybe this one didn't handle it well, but—" He wheeled, marching back into the crowd—going to find Wes, I assumed. I turned to Hector, one hand on my hip. "Really?"

He was red, too, blotches of an angry blush staining his wide cheekbones. "Didn't handle it well? Way to back me up, boss." He said "boss" with an undue amount of venom, I thought, and I felt my own hackles start to rise. Before I could take him to task, though, he stormed off after Cody.

I took a deep breath, counted to three, then smiled at the customer now waiting for me to ring up his purchase. I took the cards he handed me and forced myself to ask about his *Spell-casters* deck.

At times, running a game shop was like herding cats—or maybe herding clowns. Hormonal teenage clowns. Teenage clowns who were way too sensitive about their floppy shoes and bright red noses, and occasionally had fistfights over jug-gling techniques. Usually everyone spent their days having fun, laughing it up, but then one person would say the wrong thing, kill the wrong character, and suddenly it became a seriously freaky horror movie with clowns threatening to murder each other and terrifying the townsfolk.

By the time I was finished with my customer, Hector and Cody were back, Wes in tow, shouting at each other in whispers.

I caught only part of it, but I distinctly heard Hector say, "Rules lawyer!" and Cody say, "Amateur hour!" Wes gave me a sheepish shrug.

I let them go at it until the customers started staring, at which point I picked up the miniature gong we kept beside the register, labeled "Store Owner and Nerf Herder Use Only," and struck it. It was small but loud enough to make them shut up and stare at me. I smiled sweetly at them. "Enough."

"But—"

"But—"

Wes looked like he wanted to make a run for it. A sweet kid with limp brown hair and dark blue eyes, Wes *always* looked like he wanted to make a run for it. He was ridiculously kind-hearted, and I doubted he'd had anything to do with the group's decision to give Cody the boot—I could also see how he'd managed to stay friends with Paige and Nick. The boy made a doormat look like Godric Gryffindor.

I turned my best this-is-serious gaze on him, the weakest one in the herd. "Wes, did the group decide to kick Cody out?"

He scuffed his feet, looking miserable. "Yes."

"Did they ask Hector to kill off Cody's character?"

"Yes."

I turned to Cody. "There you go. I'm sorry it happened, and I'm sorry they handled it so poorly, but you're going to need to settle this with them, not me. Hector did what they wanted, end of story."

Hector started to smirk, so I rounded on him next. "Hector, you should have told the others that they needed to confront Cody themselves. You're a game master, not chair of the popularity club, and as a representative of this store, you should have known better. Apologize, and tell the rest of the group they'll be doing the same."

His face drained of blood, and I couldn't blame him. I felt a tendril of pity creep up, but I quickly squashed it. Discipline needed to be kept, even if I hated doing it, and even if the pouty-faced victim didn't deserve my justice. I was sure the others had plenty of reason to want Cody out of their game, and I could hardly blame them for wanting to avoid confrontation with him.

Hector turned to Cody, fists clenched at his sides. "I . . ." He paused, looking sick, and swallowed. "I'm sorry. I should have handled things better." A long moment passed as they glared at each other in silence. Slowly, as if moving through gelatin, Hector lifted his hand and extended it to Cody.

Cody stared at it as if Hector was offering him a dead fish and not a handshake. He took a step back, and then another. He lifted one arm, his hand clenched, then pointed a finger at Hector. "This isn't over." He turned and pointed to Wes, then, who looked horrified to find himself in the spotlight. "This. Isn't. Over." He repeated the words slowly, biting off each one with such dramatic clip that it would have been funny if it weren't so ridiculous.

He spun on his heel and marched back through the store, departing through the mall entrance. We all turned in unison to watch him, and when the door slammed shut, I saw that half the other customers had looked up from their ongoing *Spellcasters* games to watch the strange drama unfolding at the front of the store. I blinked, then turned back to Hector and Wes. Hector had taken on a greenish tinge, and Wes's mouth hung slightly open, like a child who had seen his parents putting out the Christmas presents that allegedly came from Santa.

"What on earth was that?" a voice said behind me.

I flinched and turned to see Bailey Adorno, my other employee, carrying a tablet and an egg timer, ready to start the draft. Her asymmetrical bob was ruffled, the blue streak in it mussed, and her cheeks were pink.

"You don't want to know," I told her. "What's wrong?"

"Don't freak out," she said.

My blood pressure immediately skyrocketed. "Why?"

"Look who's here." She pointed.

I turned and swore.

Behind me, Hector said, "That's a dollar."

I handed him a twenty and started walking to meet our new guests.

2

TALKING HAPPILY WITH PAIGE and an uncomfortable looking Nick were Craig MacLeod, my high school boyfriend, and his girlfriend, Meghan Kountz, former Queen Bee of White Lake High, classic mean girl, wearer of mascara at the gym, owner of no fewer than five velour tracksuits. Though it had been more than a dozen years since we'd graduated, I hated her with the fiery passion of a thousand exploding suns. If my hatred had physical force, it would incinerate her where she stood, leaving a tiny pile of ash and the piece of ticking steel she called a heart.

Sadly, my power to set people ablaze with my mind had never manifested, or I would have burned her alive the summer we were both eighteen and she slept with Craig while I was off visiting my mom in Madison—breaking my heart, crushing my self-confidence, and stealing one of my oldest friends in one fell swoop.

She still wore the elegant, pale gray suit she'd worn to the meeting earlier, her dark hair twisted and pinned neatly to the back of her fat head. She looked so perfect on Craig's arm while he blasted Paige with the thousand-watt smile that made him one of the most successful real estate agents in town. Once upon a time, I'd played in his sandbox. He was my first crush, my first kiss, my first love.

The first guy I'd cried over.

Now, he was getting married, or so I heard. Paige worked for him, employed part-time as his assistant, and she occasionally reported his doings back to Jordan and me for the necessary mockery. Apparently he'd proposed to Meghan at a restaurant with the ring in a glass of champagne, a dozen roses, and a fistful of other clichés, but I found myself not caring.

Totally not caring.

His future bride owned a store in Independence Square Mall, too, and was competing for the same small business development grant I was. Her plan was to use the grant money to restore the building's historic façade and make it pretty with flowers and bushes and probably some glitter and sequins. My plan was to make it more energy efficient with solar panels and an upgraded climate control system. That was what Craig had chosen for his life: style over substance.

And now he had infiltrated my world again, and I hated myself for resenting the overlap between my teenage self and my adult self.

"Why are *they* here?" Jordan asked, voicing the question my mind was grappling with.

I shrugged, wanting to seem nonchalant. "Her store is upstairs. And Craig was already downtown for the meeting."

"Yeah, but they're *here*. I doubt Craig has played a game since that time you dragged us all to a *Shadowrun* game junior year."

Remembering the look on his face when presented with a character sheet, I snorted. "Yeah, that wasn't so good. Anyway, they probably couldn't pass up an opportunity to gloat over my peep show."

"That dude has a cruel streak in him, showing up with that woman," Jordan said. "I've always said it."

As if he could feel us staring at him, Craig looked up. He smiled and waved at me, and I sighed. "Damn."

"Don't let Hector hear you," Jordan said.

"I paid in advance." I left her behind and wound my way through the crowd to greet them. Craig gave me one of those awkward old-friend hugs, the loose, shoulder-patting kind you give when you don't really want to touch the other person.

"Great party," he said, his voice falsely hearty.

"Thanks," I said, equally hearty. "And thanks for coming!" Almost involuntarily, I glanced at Meghan's left hand. There was a shiny square diamond on her pointy-nailed finger, and I felt my stomach turn over. More than rumor, then. And I still totally did not care. Whatever.

"Great presentation today, by the way," Craig said. He almost sounded sincere.

"Really?"

"Of course," Meghan interjected. She looked at me like I was a sixth grader who'd done an exceptionally good job selling band candy. "Especially under the circumstances. I thought you handled it so gracefully." She wore a sappy-sweet look of admiration so fake I tasted sucralose. She meant my fake laughter when I'd finally realized my predicament. I'd waved my own breasts off as a joke, much to the awkward amusement of the entire City Council.

"Oh, thank you, that's so nice of you to say." I matched her empty verbal calorie for empty verbal calorie. "I thought your presentation was great, too."

I didn't. Preserving the historic façade of Independence Square Mall by installing fake limestone fronts on the newer parts of the building would mean Ten Again would be closed to street traffic for weeks while it underwent the renovation. Naturally, the construction wouldn't affect Meghan's storefront. Hopefully the grant committee would realize how much that could hurt the small businesses it was supposed to help.

Craig grinned at the pair of us. "Donald said things were looking good—of course, he wins either way!"

Donald Wolcott, the building's owner, was also on the grant committee. The words "conflict of interest" weren't exactly at the top of the White Lake City Council's vocabulary list, and Donald ran the Chamber of Commerce, as well. He *would* think things were looking good if he had two chances to give himself the money. What surprised me, though, was that Craig and Donald had been talking about us.

"How do you know Donald?" I asked.

"He bought a building from my boss last year. We met when I was putting the contracts together. Anyway, he has big real estate development plans, and this building is just the first of those plans. I said I could show him some other properties that have done the kinds of rehabilitation you and Meghan are talking about—"

"You thought you could make a big sale, in other words," Jordan cut in. Craig had always been the ultimate salesman, after all. My dad used to say Craig could sell a blank canvas to a blind man and call it art.

Craig looked wounded. "Come on. A man's gotta eat, and anyway, it's in everyone's best interest to improve this old building."

"Uh-huh." Jordan looked dubious.

Craig ignored her. "As I was saying, he's interested in seeing what improvements like the ones you suggest look like. I think we'll go look at that renovated warehouse in the tech park tomorrow—"

"No one cares, Craig," Jordan said.

I froze, torn between laughter and embarrassment at her rudeness. Craig adopted a hurt expression again, but he stopped his sales pitch. "Point is, he's into it."

"Thanks, Craig," I said. "It's good to know."

In truth, I was pretty surprised. Donald was about as tech savvy as a Little House grandpa, but I appreciated the sentiment. If nothing else, Donald could get behind the idea that he—and, I suppose, his tenants—might save a few bucks every month. He made Scrooge McDuck look like a generous gent, so at least my proposal had penny pinching over Meghan's historical preservation plans, which would earn nothing back but sentiment.

Meghan cut in, pretending to make peace. "Donald stopped by Chic after the grant meeting," she purred. "I've been working with him on some other plans for the building, and we meet pretty regularly."

Of course they did. She was practically daring me to ask what their other plans were, but I swallowed my curiosity.

"That's nice," I said. "Maybe he'll stop by—he likes coming to our events."

Truth was, he hated these events, but he felt like showing up reminded everyone who was boss. He'd make an appearance sooner or later.

That reminded me, though—I needed to speak with him. "Actually, I need to call him," I said, interrupting myself. I looked over Craig's shoulder to Paige and Nick. "I need to go let him know you'll be gaming tonight, or he'll sic Max on you again."

Paige's eyes widened. "That old geezer! Some security guard he is. Last time he threatened to call the real cops on us just because José was leaning over the balcony."

"Well, I'll be sure to let him know we have a cop on hand tonight." I elbowed Jordan, and everyone laughed at my weak joke.

"And we," Paige said, turning to Nick, "should get started before it gets too much later."

"Don't have too much fun," I called after them.

I excused myself before any more pitiful attempts at humor turned me into a dorky den mother. Jordan snorted and went back to the front of the store to help Hector with crowd control.

Back in my office, I hurriedly dialed Donald's number. He and his rent-a-cop security team were pretty cool about letting gamers run around the building after hours for live action role-playing, but they understandably needed to know in advance so some well-meaning and clueless security guard didn't call the real cops on a group of people in fantasy costumes. We'd had that happen once, early in our history, and my parents had almost died of embarrassment when the *White Lake Courier* gleefully reported that a werewolf in the employ of Autumn Sinclair had been mistakenly arrested for trespassing.

No need to revisit that fiasco, especially if Max had been after the LARPers again recently.

It took Donald forever to answer his cell phone, and I drummed my fingers on the desk as I waited, irked. When he did answer, he sounded irritated. "Autumn," he said. "How can I help you?"

"Donald, hi," I said, putting on my very best Bambi voice. "I just wanted to let you know that we had a scheduling mix-up, and we're going to have some gamers running around tonight."

"I see." He sounded irritated. "Will they be upstairs? I have a meeting I don't want interrupted."

"Oh!" Odd—Donald normally went home by seven, and it was nearly eight o'clock now. "Ah, if it's a problem, I can have them wrap up by ten."

"No, it's not a problem. Just ask them to keep it down. I'll tell security when I leave."

"Oh—okay. Sorry about this. I'll tell them not to bother anyone."

"It's not a problem. I'll spread the word."

"Thanks."

"You're welcome. Good night." He hung up.

I stared at my phone, surprised. He never responded well to the unexpected, and he never varied his routine. If he was here late, it was something important. I felt a brief flash of panic that I'd forgotten another tenants' meeting, but there was no way this late in the day.

A secret Friday night meeting—how very cloak and dagger. I would never have guessed Donald had it in him.

I shrugged to myself, then dialed the security desk. Max, the elderly night watchman answered. I heaved a small sigh. "Hi, Max."

"Who's this?" he demanded.

"It's Autumn. From Ten Again."

"Oh, hi, Autumn! How are you, hon?"

I raised my voice. "Oh, fine, I—"

"I was just thinking about you this morning. My wife has been watching this weird show with vampires and werewolves and some kind of fairies, and I thought, 'Now, this seems like something Autumn would like,' and then when I asked her the title she couldn't remember, and so I thought I'd maybe just check with you and see—"

I jumped in when he paused for breath. "I'm not sure. Actually, I'm calling because the store is open late tonight, and—"

"Do you have an emergency?"

I rolled my eyes. "Uh, no." I felt more secure just knowing he was downstairs. "I just wanted to let you know we have some gamers in the building tonight."

"Oh, gamers! You know, my great-niece likes games, but I think she's more a fan of those video games, the ones with the little creatures that fight each other? Is that the same? Because I've seen a lot of toys and things that go along with it, and I wondered—"

"Er, no, not really the same." I was glad none of my employees could hear him. "These are more like people in a play running around the building in costume!"

"Yes, I've seen them around." He paused, and I could picture him glaring at some hapless vampire trying desperately to stay in character. "Are they disturbing you?"

"No! I wanted to warn you, so you know they're here."

"Ah, I see. Well, I'll keep an eye on them."

Of course he would. I thanked him and hung up the phone. Donald would explain the situation, too, and hopefully Max would leave the poor LARPers alone. It couldn't be easy to pretend you were a top predator stalking the midnight streets of a vampire-controlled town when Max the security guard tried to tell you about his wife's hemorrhoids.

In the brief semi-silence, I took a deep breath. Bay had left the ledger program open on my computer, and I glanced at it, impressed. Our sales for the day were phenomenal, and the numbers hadn't synced with the register computer since earlier in the evening. I let out a low whistle—we'd made more than double last year's profits for the same day, and half again already over the profits from the last *Spellcasters* release day. It was always a gamble holding big, expensive events like what we were having tonight, but it seemed like the promotion had made a significant difference.

I needed to remember to give both Bay and Hector a serious bonus this year. I spent the next quarter hour looking at the inventory, comparing our orders with what we'd sold, and making mental notes for the next big *Spellcasters* expansion pack release.

If things went well, and I got the grant to green Independence Square Mall, the resulting storm of good PR would help the store even more—and the vote of confidence from city leadership would do more than bring in sales: it would lend the store a legitimacy in the local business community I'd never even dreamed of achieving. Flighty Autumn, who got her MBA and came back to her hometown, against everyone's advice, to open a shop no one thought White Lake needed, would lead her band of geeks to a glorious victory against the naysayers and the wagging tongues.

And maybe, just maybe, people would start to take us seriously as a community and as a political force and, well, as adults.

I let myself indulge in my fantasy for a little while longer, ignoring the increasingly exuberant voices from outside my door. When my phone rang, it was almost eight forty-five. I sucked in a breath, irritated at myself for neglecting Bay and the party for so long. Seeing Paige's number on the screen surprised me since she was usually strict about breaking character during a live action game. "Paige?"

"Autumn." She sounded like she'd been crying.

"Paige, what happened?"

"I—I need your help."

"What is it? Where are you?"

"Downstairs." She sobbed and hung up.

Disturbed, I rose from my chair. I waded into the party-fray, but I didn't get far before my phone rang for a second time. It was Paige again, but when I answered, Nick's voice greeted me.

"It's okay, Autumn," he said, breathless. "You don't need to come."

"What happened?"

"Nothing. Just—a misunderstanding. We'll talk to you later."

"Are you sure?"

He had already hung up. I frowned at my phone, but there was nothing more I could do. I didn't want to go chasing after them when there was nothing wrong, and it was never in my best interest to get involved in private troupe drama. They could sort it out.

Still, Paige was no flake. If she was in trouble, it was serious.

On the other hand, she wasn't alone. Nick could help with whatever it was.

Bay appeared at my elbow, Jordan trailing after. "What's wrong?" Jordan asked.

I glanced down at my phone, then explained. "I'm not sure whether or not I should go after them."

"If it helps you decide, it's time to start moving folks over to the other room for the draft," Bay said.

"Shit," I muttered, glancing at the timey-wimey clock on the wall. A pair of preteens sitting at the table nearby giggled, and I stuck my tongue out at them. Time to put another dollar in the jar. "You're right. Okay. Why don't you gather up everyone who's paid their entrance fee, and I'll get the box of decks—"

"I'll go check on the LARPers," Jordan said.

I rounded on her. "Thank you!" I could have kissed her, but it would have just been awkward, the pair of us being besties and all.

Bay grinned, then started to herd the kids toward the other room, and I darted for the register, where we'd held back a few dozen booster packs of cards for the draft. We wouldn't play tonight, thank goodness, but the draft itself could take hours, and then we had to sort out which deck belonged to which person, organize the decks by the entrant's time slot the next morning, and a thousand other little chores that would culminate in the weekend-long tournament.

My brain went into autopilot as I gathered up the boxes and started to collect the lists of people who had paid their entrance fees. Around me, the tide of gamers eddied toward the back room as Hector and Bay funneled the crowd out of the shop.

Jordan elbowed her way back to the register just as I flipped open my box cutter. I glanced at her, feeling harassed, and stabbed the tape on the box. "Everyone okay?"

"No."

Her voice caught, and I turned. "What is it? What's wrong?"

"There's been—an accident." Her eyes looked wide and red around the rims.

I dropped the knife on the counter. "An accident? Oh my god, what—"

"Downstairs. There's an ambulance. I asked one of the on-duty cops." She swallowed. "Autumn, it doesn't look good. A kid named Wes Bowen was found dead about twenty minutes ago."

A dull ringing filled my ears. "What?" My own voice sounded distant. Twenty minutes—was that when Paige had called me?

"It—" Jordan paused, swallowed, and tried again. "There are wounds on his neck, like something bit him."

"A vampire killed him?" My voice rose, threatening to crack into hysteria as I said the absurd words for the second time that day. I saw, as from a great distance, one of the parents glance at me. I tried to get myself under control. "That's impossible."

"Of course it is. But he fell, too, from that balcony inside the building. They don't know yet which killed him, the fall or the wounds."

"My god." I put a hand to my mouth. Around me, people were staring. Bay appeared over Jordan's shoulder, her pale face swimming in and out of my line of vision. "Jordan, what should I do?"

"I think maybe you'd better clear out your party. They're still downstairs with—well, you know. And they'll likely want to talk to you and your employees."

"Of course." I nodded. My eyes were stinging. Jordan put a hand on my shoulder. I felt her fingers tighten. "I should be there for the others, too."

"The others?"

"The LARPers."

"Okay . . ." Jordan paused, as if nerving herself. "Autumn, this doesn't look good."

"What do you mean?"

"All of it. Hon, think about it. They were playing a violent game of pretend, at night, in public . . . I think you need to be prepared."

"For what?"

"For . . . anything. Things are going to get bad for a little while."

My vision was clearing, and as the mist faded, my thoughts crystallized. "What are you saying? Bad for me? For the gamers? For the shop?"

She hesitated again. "Yes."

"Okay." I nodded, taking control of myself, as if that would make any difference in the next few hours. "I understand."

"I—I probably shouldn't be talking to you anymore. I should go downstairs since I was here. Talk to the other cops, then head to the station."

"Got it. Thanks for—being the one to tell me."

"Of course. I'll call you later."

She pushed her way through the crowd and disappeared.

The party went on. A bubble of silence had welled up around me, and I wondered who had overheard what. Bay clutched my arm.

"Is it true?" Her blue eyes were huge. She'd heard, then.

I turned. Hector was there, too. He spoke before I could. "There are cops in the hallway. Fire trucks outside and an ambulance and—"

"There's—" I swallowed. "There's been an accident," I said, stealing Jordan's polite euphemism. "I think we'd better wrap up here." I lowered my voice to speak to my employees. "The LARPers. I'll explain in a minute. We need to get everyone out, and through the store, not the mall."

"You got it," Bay said. She turned, already working the crowd.

"I'll get the other room." Hector followed her.

I began to move, slowly, feeling as if someone had strapped a dead bird to my back. Wes Bowen, sweet and gentle, friends with Paige and Nick. So unobtrusive I'd hardly seen him when he stood in front of me in my shop. I'd made fun of him to myself, mocking the very gentleness that had kept his friendship with Paige and Nick alive. It was that sweet nature that made him a solid fixture in our store. Who would have been able to kill him?

I felt my stomach heave. I forced myself to swallow and take slow, even breaths. If I lost it now, I'd never find it again, whatever it was, that slender thread that tied me to sanity, tied the shop to respectability. My lips refused to smile, but I did moderate my voice to the polite neutrality employed by shopkeepers everywhere.

"I'm sorry," I said to the person in front of me. "There's been an emergency, and we're going to have to close early."

I said it again, and again, and again. I deflected the questions, offered reassurances, promised things I could never guarantee. Of course we'll reschedule. I'm sure everything will be fine. We'll see you soon.

Bay sent the last holdout into the early March night and locked the door behind him, then turned and leaned against the glass.

She sobbed.

I heard Hector shut the mall door and come down the steps onto the main selling floor. He stood beside me. "What is it?" he asked.

"Wes is dead." My voice echoed in the empty shop.

Hector sucked in a ragged breath, and Bay let her chin fall to her chest.

"I knew—someone. I looked out the window, and I saw the ambulance, but I didn't know who—"

I took Hector's hand to stop him.

Bay looked up. She stared at us, and we stared back.

"What happens now?" she asked.

"I don't know."

For the first time in my shop, in my corner of heaven, I felt frightened. I didn't know. But I would soon.

3

As it turned out, what happened next was an interminable hell of questioning at the police department.

"Let's go through it again," Detective Keller said. Her lined face creased as she rubbed her forehead. My own eyeballs felt coated in sand. "What time did you see him at the store this evening?"

"Between seven and seven thirty, I'd guess."

"And he was involved in some sort of altercation?"

"No, that's not what I said." The detective's eyes flashed, and I strove to regulate my tone. "I said he was present when my employee was arguing with another customer."

"Uh-huh. And this other customer was angry with him?"

Things were not looking good for Cody right now. I stumbled over my earlier statements. "The other customer was angry, but not specifically with Wes . . ."

"Did he tell you this?"

I wanted to ugly cry. "No, he did not."

"And you saw this other customer again tonight, correct?"

"Yes. He was at the release party this evening."

"At the same time Wesley Bowen was—er—gaming in the building."

"I suppose."

"You 'suppose.' Ma'am, was he or was he not in your store while Wesley Bowen was in Independence Square Mall?"

"Yes."

"Thank you." Detective Keller wrote some notes, as if she hadn't already heard me explain this.

"Now, tell me again what happened when Miss Harding called."

"It was about eight forty-five. Paige called to say she needed my help."

"What *exactly* did she say, Miss Sinclair?"

I closed my eyes. "She said, 'I need your help.' And when I asked where she was, she said, 'Downstairs.' And that was it."

When I opened my eyes, the detective was sucking on the end of her pen.

She pulled it from her lips and gestured with it. "And Miss Harding sounded distressed."

"Yes."

"And then Mr. Lawlis called?"

"Yes. He said, 'You don't need to come,' and that there had been a misunderstanding."

"A misunderstanding."

"Yes." Inwardly, I screamed. She acted like everything I said was the most fascinating thing she'd ever heard. And I was fairly certain I'd put Cody, Hector, Paige, and Nick on her pitiful list of suspects. She even acted curious about Max the too-talkative security guard's distrust of the gamers. I felt like the biggest sellout since George Lucas after—well, it was no time for pithy similes.

"Did he sound upset?"

"Ah," I said. I paused. He hadn't sounded tearful, like Paige, but he had sounded flustered. And also friendly? After going over this twice already in one night, I was beginning to doubt my memories. That was why they did it—soon I would crack and tell them whatever they wanted to know, even if I had to make it up. Wasn't that how torture worked? "I'm not sure. He didn't sound happy, but he wasn't as upset as Paige." There. Fairly neutral.

"Your cell phone indicates that this call came in at eight forty-seven."

"Okay," I responded. Detective Keller made another note. They had no time of death yet, that much I knew. All they had was the time of the 911 call.

I shivered, thinking of poor Wes sprawled dead on the floor of the building's lowest level. Five stories of balconies looked down over that central floor, the building's grandest design feature. There was a fountain in the center and an array of small tables and chairs scattered around it. How far had Wes fallen? How had he gotten the puncture wounds on his neck?

My mind raced. Jordan said the first responders had been unable to tell whether it was the fall or the neck wounds that had killed him. Were they thinking my gamers had done it? Silly, stupid Cody with his petty anger over his dismissal from the other LARPing troupe? Skinny Paige and handsome Nick, finally unable to take the lingering presence of Paige's sad-puppy ex? Both theories seemed so flimsy, so pitiful—but

Cody had been there, lurking and shady. I hadn't seen him after he confronted Hector. And Paige's phone call hadn't stopped being weird since she made it.

The door to the little room opened.

It was my dad, oddly dressed in suit trousers and a zip-up fleece jacket. His thinning hair stood on end, and he had forgotten to tuck his belt into one of the loops. My jaw dropped to see him so frazzled.

"Hi, hon," he said. "I'm sorry—it took me forever to convince them that I'm your lawyer. And there's no grounds for keeping you so long." He said this last bit to Detective Keller with a glare, as if he were a hotshot criminal defense lawyer instead of an aging tax attorney.

"Your daughter agreed to cooperate with us." The detective capped her pen, though, knowing a lost cause when she saw one.

I stood to kiss my dad's cheek. "Thanks for springing me." I turned to the detective. "Am I free to go?"

She nodded.

"You know where to reach me if you have any more questions," I said. I felt a little bad about ditching her like this—years of DARE training in elementary school were hard to undo. A part of me still felt like cops were supposed to be my friends. Hell, one of the White Lake cops *was* my best friend, and I knew that the WLPD generally had our best interests at heart.

I let my dad shoo me from the room, guilt's cold fingers brushing my neck.

Jordan stood outside the door, poker-faced. Her expression broke when she saw me, and she gathered me up in a hug. "Oh, Autumn, I'm so, so sorry."

I started to cry. She was the first person to give me space to melt down, and I stood there under the fluorescent lights, sobbing on her shoulder while my dad awkwardly patted my back. "He was such a sweet kid," I said. My voice broke.

Wiping my eyes, I pulled away. "I'm sorry."

"Don't apologize." Jordan's dark eyes glowed with sympathy.

"Right." I looked up at my dad. "Thanks for coming."

"Of course." He squeezed my shoulder. "Let's get out of here. Audrey is worried sick."

Audrey, my stepmom. I was surprised she hadn't beaten down the door.

She was waiting in the lobby, and when she saw me, she rushed forward and hugged me. Over her shoulder, I could see that half the town was there—Bay and Hector, of course; Donald Wolcott, the building owner, looking shell-shocked; Paige's parents, Nick's mom; security guard Max half-asleep on one of the shiny vinyl chairs.

Audrey let me go, and Bay and Hector swarmed me. We gathered in a giant group-hug, Hector and Bay and me soaking up all the love. When we broke apart, Bay had tears running down her cheeks and Hector wiped surreptitiously at his nose. I squeezed their shoulders.

"Thanks for being here, you guys," I said.

Audrey grabbed my face and kissed it. "We were so worried."

I sort of laughed, a half-beaten sound.

"Are you ready to go home?" my dad asked.

Surprised, I said, "My car is in the garage."

"We thought you'd want to stay with us."

"That's really sweet, but I need to go finish closing up the store, and I wanted to talk to Hector and Bay a little." I glanced at them. Bay nodded—she wanted to talk, too. Hector wore a guarded expression.

"Okay," Audrey said. She shot my dad a let-her-live-her-own-life look. "We'll see you tomorrow."

I gave my dad another hug. "Thanks again for busting me out."

"Let us know if you change your mind, and we'll come pick you up," he said, as if I were fourteen and headed to a sleep-over at a new friend's house, not thirty-three and going to my own home.

I collected my people, dragging Jordan with us. Donald stopped me, though, and pulled me aside. "We need to talk. Soon. Let's meet tomorrow."

I nodded.

Back at the store, still brilliantly lit in the silent darkness, I locked the street door while everyone else sat around the register. The early spring night hung clear and starry over the town square. Outside, the lamps of the streetlights cast an old-timey golden glow on the historic storefronts. If I stepped out and craned my head, I could look up the street to see the stark white City Hall building looming ominously over the rest of the square, but I had no desire to step back into the cold.

It could have been a lovely night in the store, cozy and picturesque, but Independence Square Mall was closed for the evening—and for the horrifying special circumstances—while the rest of the square was as busy as it was any normal Friday night. A group of college students walked by the street door, laughing and talking as they headed for one of the trendy downtown bars. A wave of sadness crashed over me. Wes, Nick, and Paige should have been doing just that tonight.

I turned back to the store, my heart heavy.

Bay perched on the counter, Jordan leaned against the wall, and Hector and I pulled up chairs from one of the gaming tables. Someone had left a small Superman sweatshirt on the back of one of the chairs. I felt a pang, seeing it, and folded it. Bay took it from me and placed it in our lost and found tub.

They stared at me.

"What did they ask you?" I asked.

Bay and Hector both opened their mouths, but Jordan spoke first. "You really shouldn't discuss that . . ." She trailed off when I glared at her. Sheepish, she shrugged. "Sorry." She mimed taking a hat off and setting it aside. "Cop hat off now."

"Good. Thank you. What did they ask?"

Bay went first. They made her recount her night, focusing on Paige, Wes, Nick, and the six other gamers who made up the rest of their new *Blood Ties* troupe. They'd also asked about Cody, but Bay hadn't witnessed the earlier argument. "I didn't see him interact with them at all tonight," she added. "He got his cards and was sitting in the corner."

"I didn't see him leave," I said. "Was he still here when— when we got the call?"

Hector and Bay stared at each other, blank. "I didn't see him, either."

"Did they quiz you about that argument?" I asked Hector.

He nodded. "Grilled me. I think they wanted me to say I was pissed, that I killed Wes because he made Cody into a pain in my ass, but I disappointed them." He looked at Jordan. "Like, a dozen kids and their parents saw me in the game room. They'll vouch for me."

Jordan held up her hands. "Don't look at me, man. I'm not on this one."

Hector nodded, satisfied. "Mostly the cops asked me why Cody and Wes were arguing. They also asked why Wes is in the LARPing group, too, if Paige is his ex. They were fixated on that, seemed to think it was weird he'd want to hang out with the girl he used to date and her new boyfriend."

"They know that one isn't live action, right?" I said. "The group that kicked Cody out?"

"Does it make a difference?" Jordan asked.

"Probably. It's . . . less weird to muggles. Anyway, they're completely separate groups, even if they do involve a lot of the same people."

"Huh." The cop look flashed across Jordan's face again as she made a mental note. I patted myself on the back for helping.

"They asked me about Paige and Nick, too," Bay said. "Their mood, why they said they wanted to add a game tonight."

"Why *did* they want to?" I asked.

Bay lifted her hands. "Your guess is as good as mine. All of them were here tonight, though, so it wasn't like Paige and Nick arranged a fake game just to off Wes."

We stared at her, and she clapped her hands to her mouth. "Oh man," she said through her fingers. "That was horrible, I did not—"

I waved her silent. "No worries. We know."

"Who found him?" Hector asked.

I shook my head, and Bay turned her hands up toward the ceiling in a shrug. I looked at Jordan.

"Erm—" She blushed. "I shouldn't."

I tilted my head and *glared*.

"Fine. Whatever. It was one of the store owners."

"Which one?"

"You're not going to like it."

"It was *Meghan*?"

"Yeah."

"Shit." Hector twitched reflexively, and I added, "I am *not* putting a dollar in the jar this time."

They all stared at me while I glared at the wall. Just what I needed—my archenemy finding one of *my* kids dead while playing a game nominally under my supervision. I was screwed. "She made the call?"

"Yeah. She was leaving for the night when she found him."

"What was she doing in the basement?" Hector asked. He had a point—Meghan's store was on the main ground level. Our store was technically in the basement, though we had a street exit, as well.

"I'll ask Craig," I said. "He was here. We'll find out."

"'We?'" Jordan asked.

"Yes, we. We need to know who killed Wes and why. He died on my watch, Jordan."

Her eyes crinkled in sympathy. "This was not your fault. You don't need to atone for it or anything like that—"

"I'm not *atoning* for anything. But this is going to scare people. Come on, a LARPer died with stab wounds in his neck? While playing a vampire game? We'll be very lucky if we don't end up with a *The Dungeon Master* scenario on our hands, but worse, because it looks like someone *else* killed him."

"They haven't ruled it a murder," Jordan interjected.

"Come on," Bay said. "She has a point. At the best of times, people think LARPers are a joke—at the worst, people think they're insane. With someone dead, someone like Wes who was sweet and harmless, they're going to look downright deranged."

Jordan's brow creased.

"We need to do what we can to prevent this from creating an all-out panic about the store and our little family," I said.

Hector looked green around the gills. "I don't think they'll just—let us help."

Bay rolled her eyes. "Of course they won't. But we can Scooby it up. And Jordan will help."

"She will?" Jordan said.

"Yes, you will," I told her. "This is important to you, too. Remember when I used to sneak you fantasy novels because your mom thought they were the devil's handiwork? And Bill from the comic book store had to talk her down when she found your stash? Well, this is that moment all over again. It's my turn to be Bill."

Jordan sighed. "Fine. Where do you want to start?"

I smiled at her. "Thank you." But when I paused to consider her question, I came up blank. We needed suspects, motives, a time line, probably—things that suddenly seemed very real and scary. "Well," I said. "Uh . . . we know Cody is a suspect. And Nick and Paige."

"We want to know how Meghan found him," Hector said.

"Right. And we need to talk to the rest of their troupe. And . . . um . . . Max? The security guard?"

Bay snorted but she nodded agreement. "He may not hear much over his own voice, but he sees quite a bit."

I blinked. "We . . . may need to work on the quips."

"Yeah, okay." Her shoulders slumped.

"I have to talk to Donald tomorrow morning. Which of you two is supposed to open?"

"Me again." Hector grimaced.

"Well, don't come in till noon. I'll delay opening. I think that's fair, given the circumstances."

He moved like he wanted to fist bump me but thought better of it and just twitched in his seat. "Thanks."

I nodded. "So tomorrow afternoon, let's try to find out what Nick and Paige's story is, what the others in the troupe saw, and who Max might have seen in the building."

"What about Cody?" Hector asked. "And Meghan?"

"I can handle Meghan. And Cody . . ." I hesitated. He seemed to be the closest thing the cops had to a suspect, so I didn't want to spook him or piss off Jordan's bosses.

"I'll find out what I can about him," Jordan said, resigned. "I can at least tell you what he told the detective who interviewed him. Unless they think they're actually going to arrest him, in which case I really shouldn't."

"Fair enough. So there we go. It's a start anyway."

"You really think they're going to blame gaming?" Hector asked.

I wanted to say no. I wanted to offer reassurances and kind words, but I knew he was too smart to believe them. On the other hand, he was smart enough to know when I was lying, and he might appreciate the gesture.

"I'm sure we'll be fine," I said. I meant it.

Hector's face twisted into a grim smile.

"In the long run," Bay added.

"Right." I stood and looked from Bay to Hector. "Things might get ugly for a while, but they'll get better. I promise."

I met Jordan's eyes. She looked guarded. She knew I could promise no such thing; she also knew I had no choice but to try. She nodded at me. I had one ally, at least, who understood the stakes . . . and knew how much I had to lose.

4

THE LEAD HEADLINE IN the Saturday edition of the *White Lake Courier* read, "Youth Killed in Bizarre Game Store Murder."

I crumpled the paper up and stuffed it into my backpack before I left my house. I could not let it distract me from my meeting with Donald. I skipped my usual geek attire and dressed in dark jeans and a nice blazer. Even with enough makeup to cover the dark circles beneath my eyes, I looked like crap — but looking good might be worse on a day like today.

I got to the store a little after nine, curious to see whether the other stores in the mall had opened. Most of the lights on the upper floors appeared to be on, but the lowest level was dark, and Ten Again looked abandoned when it should have been bustling. My homemade sign hung sadly askew on the door, explaining our late opening.

As I walked up the sidewalk, I saw that our doorstep was littered with small knickknacks and figurines. Someone had left a tiny candle, burned out, with some flowers and a picture of

Wes. A miniature knight stood next to a *Star Wars* action figure, and someone had scribbled, "We love you, Wes!" on the sidewalk in chalk. There was a pile of dice stacked like a cairn, and a few *Spellcasters* cards were cast to one side.

My breath seemed to come as though through a straw, thin and not enough to lift my lungs. Poor Wes. Overlooked in life, cherished in death. Even if it was too little, too late—which I didn't think it was—it was balm to my battered soul.

Wiping my eyes, I dug in my bag. I knew just the card I would leave for Wes from my own *Spellcasters* deck: Yanil, the Deathless Angel. One of my better cards, but I would give anything for its power to be real. Might as well play it here, on the sidewalk, in the cold, real world, and see what happened.

I fished out the card and palmed it. The little offerings were blocking the door. I wouldn't get rid of them, but I did need to move them. I squatted there on the sidewalk, indifferent to anyone who might see me, and began to scoot the votive candle and toys to rest under the window display. Someone had left a tiny statue of the Virgin Mary. She seemed rather out of place, but when I stood her next to Han Solo, she looked a bit more comfortable.

I almost missed it. As I fanned out the cards others had left so that I could add my own, I noticed one of them: Elyssa, Spirit of Autumn. A gorgeous card but not a rare one. I wondered what significance it had, but then I saw that someone had scratched off the face of the woman in the drawing.

I shuddered. Talk about creepy. Should I take it out? Or was it meant as some sort of commentary on how Wes, sweet but not uncommon, had been scratched out of the world in an act of violent, pointless destruction?

In the end, I left it, deciding that it would be wrong to silence someone's expression of grief, however strange I might find it. I stood, shouldered my bag, and let myself into the store, locking the door behind me.

I left the lights out on the main selling floor but switched on my office lights before I went to peer out into the mall. Ten Again was on the lowest level, down the hall from the central ground floor lobby. The offices and shops on the interior of the lower level, like my spillover gaming room, had no windows, and even though my main store had street access, it was around the corner from the square itself; the spaces were cheaper here, which was why I could afford to rent on the square at all.

We also had less eavesdropping capability here. When I looked down the hallway toward the fountain floor where Wes had been found, I saw nothing and no one—most of the spaces on this level were rented by nonretail businesses, and they were dark and silent on a normal Saturday. I doubted that any of the shops closer to the atrium would want my curious nose poking in their doors so soon after the tragedy.

On a sudden morbid whim, I closed the door to Ten Again, locked it, and strode down the hall and through the deserted atrium, past the dry fountain and the café at the corner of the lobby. The tiny restaurant had pulled its bistro chairs in against its windows. It was closed and dark, like the rest of the shops on this level.

Maintenance had turned off the fountain, and the building was silent, echoing. I stopped in front of the elevator and pressed the call button. I flexed my hands as I waited and glanced over my shoulder. My back felt cold, exposed. When the elevator came, I hit the shiny number five and rode it up to the empty floor from which Wes had probably fallen, the highest spot in the building.

As soon as the elevator doors opened, I went to the gallery railing and looked down. More than fifty feet below, the tiled floor of the basement lobby gleamed back up at me. Yellow police tape still lined the center of the room.

Had Wes fallen to that floor? Had someone dropped him over this railing? I touched the polished wood, chest-high on my five-foot-five frame. It would take strength to throw someone over this railing, and it would take work to fall over it. No, Wes's death had been no accident, and someone really had to have wanted him dead to make it happen. My skin crawled. If the cops were letting anyone think it had been an accident, it was simply to keep panic from driving people out of this building, out of my store. But that would happen anyway.

Regardless of who did it, Wes had died while gaming. He had been here because of that game, and there was every chance that his killer had been here because of it, too. I didn't want to believe it, but if I wanted to protect my store, I had to look at my gamers, my people, with just as much suspicion as the cops would. And that meant looking at them like murderers.

The elevator chimed at having been called away, and I turned to step in before it vanished. It was time to go.

Back in my office, I flopped into my chair, opened my backpack, and drew out my wadded-up copy of the Saturday paper.

The headline practically leapt off the page. "Wes Bowen, 21, was found dead in Independence Square Mall late last night,

White Lake Police said." Donald had to be just *thrilled* that his building made the first sentence; I certainly was at seeing my store's name in the second. "According to Public Information Officer Michael Spitz, Bowen was taking part in a live action role-playing game sponsored by Ten Again, a tabletop gaming store owned by White Lake native Autumn Sinclair. Police are calling the death suspicious, though they have not yet ruled it a murder."

No one was around to demand their dollar. I swore badly enough my mom would have washed out my mouth with soap.

The article went on to talk about Wes's death, his parents, his friends, his associations with the store, and his love of gaming. Naturally, it discussed live action role-playing in a way that made it seem like an outlet for angsty, violent adults rather than just a grown-up game of pretend. I skimmed most of it, not needing the details about how the rest of the world perceived us. I already knew.

I crumpled the paper back up and threw it into the garbage instead of the recycling. That would show the *White Lake Courier*.

It was bad, so bad. In a few hours, the store would open, and we would welcome mourners and buzzards alike. But for now, I was alone with the cards and dice, the books and figurines. I was home, but I felt very alone and very frightened.

Grant money and solar panels, ex-boyfriends and gaming tournaments, all seemed small and distant. I didn't give a crap about the grant right now, and I doubted I had a snowball's chance in hell of getting it after the newspaper article today. Ten Again would be notorious, home of the murder-games, and

Independence Square Mall would be tainted by association. Meghan would thank me for that when she saw me again.

But none of that mattered.

Wes Bowen had died while gaming, and the world would blame the gaming.

Heedless of my carefully applied make-up, I put my head down on my desk and cried.

5

I SPENT MOST OF the day hiding in my office doing routine store tasks, trying to avoid my own thoughts as well as unwanted visitors. When my office door opened abruptly in the afternoon, I jumped.

"They're all here," Bay said. She tilted her head, peering around the office door. "All the LARPers from last night? They're here."

"Oh!" I glanced at the clock. I'd spent most of Saturday afternoon reading the building's energy usage reports for the last year—fascinating stuff—in preparation for making my final presentation to the grant board, should I get the chance.

Which I wouldn't.

They would select the finalists, and I wouldn't be among them. Doing the research was a distraction, nothing more, and all it had given me was a sense of fatality and a nagging tension headache. Put that on a T-shirt.

In the secondary gaming room, Wes's troupe huddled together in a circle of chairs. They looked like a support group meeting, and I supposed they were—survivors, mourners, frightened scapegoats. Hopefully not that last one—I'd do anything to protect them from emotional death at the hands of an angry crowd.

But first I had to prove to myself that they weren't guilty.

Olivia and José, the other two regulars, sat opposite each other, looking at the floor. I glanced at them, but my attention quickly went elsewhere: in the direction of Nick and Paige, who were sitting together, holding hands. Paige stared blankly into space, her face white. Without her usual sparkle, she looked like a different person, older and more serious. My heart sank, seeing her. Last night had changed her. Did she blame herself? Or, worse, did she feel guilt over her ex-boyfriend's death? Had her skinny hands helped pitch Wes's limp form over the balcony?

I swallowed. "Hi, guys," I said in a serious tone that rang false. I dragged a chair over and joined their circle. Hector nodded at me from across the room—he sat a little outside the group, behind Nick and Paige. Not exactly undercover, but I imagined he'd been listening to every word of their conversation from the moment they walked in the door.

"How's everyone doing?" I asked.

A few of them shrugged, and Paige sniffled. Nick looked at me. "How do you think we're doing, Autumn?"

He was in his alpha-male mood, but I could hardly blame him. It was an inane, insensitive question. "I know. I know it's awful, and it's not going to get better for a while."

"What do you mean?" Paige's eyes were bloodshot, swollen half-shut.

"Well, the cops questioned all of you, didn't they? And they're not done."

"I don't know why," Nick said. "It was Cody. You know it was Cody."

"What are you talking about?"

"He came down to yell at us last night when we were trying to play. Stormed up to Wes and started yelling."

"Why Wes in particular?"

Nick shrugged. "Who knows? Freak show. He said something about being a chicken shit."

"He left right after that, though," Olivia said. She was less familiar to me than Paige and Nick. "Went back upstairs after you yelled at him."

"Yeah, *up*stairs. Wes fell."

Olivia clammed up and stared at Nick, looking intimidated. I held up a hand. "Okay, Nick, let's not jump to conclusions. Cody was pissed, but that doesn't mean anything. I think it's more important that we all agree to work together, and to cooperate with the police, so that whoever actually did it is brought to justice. This is not a joke, guys. It's not an exaggeration or a romantic call to arms—this is real life, and someone is going to prison. The cops may not have ruled Wes's death a murder yet, but it looks really bad. I need you guys to tell me what your game was last night. In as much detail as you can manage."

They told me, words pouring out of each of them in turn. It was a convoluted story of the vampire mafia that secretly controlled White Lake, whose shadowy presence lurked behind every government official, whose cold hands could be felt around the neck of the backwater society. It wasn't a bad story, but it seemed out of place in rural White Lake, whose claim to fame was its rapidly growing extension of the University of Wisconsin. And most White Lake townies hated the University folk; the only vampires here, some would say, were the representatives of a gentrifying institution that threatened to commercialize even the quietest parts of White Lake, Wisconsin, population 30,000.

But in these LARPers' world, White Lake was the seat of a vampire queen so old she had watched Rome burn.

Hector yawned. No one could see him but me, and I hid a smile. A part of me envied the gamers. I missed LARPing. Somehow, when I said I wanted to open a game store, no one told me that gaming would take over my life, leaving me zero time for—gaming. Except for the occasional stolen round of *Spellcasters*, I spent all of my time managing now, overseeing the games and never getting to play.

When they finished, I took a deep breath. "So . . . you're all courtiers. And you have warring factions?"

"Right," Paige said. Talking about the game had steadied her. She sniffled, but her voice was clearer than before. "Wes and Nick were working together—I think." Her voice cracked again. "We're not supposed to know, you know?"

Nick wrapped an arm around her shoulder. "I thought Wes was spying on us to tell Olivia and José we were planning to overthrow the queen."

"I . . . see. And the queen is . . . ?"

"NPC." Non-player character. The poor queen never had a chance. I knew how she felt at the moment.

"Of course."

I wondered how much they'd seen the night Wes died. While Meghan had allegedly been the one to find the poor kid and make the 911 call, the resultant chaos would surely have drawn the rest of the gamers down to the basement. They had to know about the neck wounds.

I cleared my throat. "Are you all aware of the, ah, injuries Wes had?"

Olivia looked confused. "He fell—"

"He had puncture wounds on his neck," Nick said bluntly.

She gasped and put a hand to her lips. Her eyes glistened with unshed tears. "Who would do that?"

"Someone who wants people to think one of us did it," Nick said.

His words hung in the air, quivering, The Words That Must Not Be Named. No one wanted to hear it, no one wanted to deal with it, no one even wanted to look at Nick after he said it.

Finally, Hector spoke. "Why do you say that?"

Nick rounded on him. "Didn't you see the newspaper? People think we're freaks, losers, outcasts. Games are violent, and the violence corrupts our brains."

"I think that's video games," I interjected. "And anyway, there's no need to go all Harbinger of Death on us."

"There's not?" Nick said. "I'd think you of all people would be a little less confident in our ability to come out of this without ending up pariahs. You have more to lose, and god knows you're more liable—"

"That's enough," Hector said. Nick fell silent, and they glared at each other.

"Thank you, Hector, but I can take care of myself." I looked at Nick, blocking out Paige's horror-stricken expression, Hector's indignation, Olivia's mortification. "If you think I'm not taking this seriously, Nick, you need to think again. This store is my life. The people who play games in this store are my family. Nothing means more to me than protecting each and every one of you." My voice shook. "My reputation doesn't mean a damn if you guys get hurt playing on my turf, because my only job in this world is to make sure you guys have a safe place to be yourselves. I don't care what people say about me or the store. I don't even care what they say about gamers as a community. All I care about is holding space for you. And I will keep that space safe."

Nick blinked first. I won. "Okay," he said. "I'm sorry."

"Thank you." My hands were shaking, but I didn't want the others to see. I leaned back in my chair and crossed my arms over my chest. "In that case, we need to think. Every one of you needs to figure out when and where you last saw Wes. Who was with him? What was he doing? You—" I pointed to José, the gamer I knew the least, first. "Go."

We went around the circle, each of the gamers sharing little glimpses of Wes's final hours. No one had seen him for at least half an hour before the 911 call. He had parted ways with Olivia, who had been trying (in character) to weasel information out of him, at around eight o'clock to go and use the restroom. I made mental note of that—Max's desk sat directly opposite the public bathrooms in the lobby. That was still about forty-five minutes before he died, though. Where had he gone? And how had he ended up on the fifth floor?

I voiced these questions, and Paige cleared her throat. "I saw him once. After that."

I looked up at her. "You did?"

Nick looked surprised, too. "When?"

"A little after eight. He was upset."

Nick wrapped his arm around her shoulders. "Baby . . ." he said into her ear.

She flinched, but she kept going. "He said he needed to talk to you, Autumn."

Every pair of eyes turned to stare at me. "Me? Why did he need to talk to me?"

"I don't know. He wanted to bail on the game, and I asked him not to." She sobbed. "We argued." She looked desperate. "And Craig's girlfriend, Meghan, the woman with the clothes store, she heard us, I know she did. I'm scared she might think I killed Wes because he wanted to stop playing."

My heart sank. That was exactly what Meghan would think. She was the one who had convinced Craig, ages ago, that gaming was only for weirdos. And this would give her the perfect edge over me for the grant competition. She'd probably tell Craig that his assistant was a murderer, too. While I didn't think Meghan had the balls—or the strength—to kill Wes herself, I had no doubt she would try to pin it on one of my people, even if the pin didn't sink deep enough to draw blood.

"You told this to the police, right?"

Paige nodded. She wiped a tear from her face. "Yes. And I know what they thought."

"Oh?"

"They think I killed him—no one but Nick saw me after that, not until Wes was—was found." She put her hand on Nick's leg, and he took it in his.

Oh. It didn't look good. If it had just been Paige on her own, no one could have believed she had done it. With Nick's help, though—tall, strong, handsome Nick, who had stolen Paige from Wes—well, it was all too believable.

But I'd seen my fair share of *Law & Order* episodes, and I wasn't the only idiot who would say that all the evidence was circumstantial. And the motive just didn't hold up—they killed Wes, after she'd already dumped him, for wanting to bail on a game? If all someone wanted to do was slander gaming, I suppose that argument would work, but it was a long walk for a very stubby ice cream cone.

"You don't need to worry," I lied. "Anyway, you called me right around when Wes died—you couldn't very well be in two places at once, could you?" Paige blanched, and Nick gave me a wild-eyed look. I faltered. "Uh. Unless you called me about this?"

Paige blinked. "Yeah. I was scared."

The others were looking at us curiously, and I could imagine the befuddled expression on my own face. "Okay. Yeah. So, anyway—"

"You called Autumn?" José asked, suspicious.

I felt a bit taken aback. He didn't even know me, and now I was "Autumn," and he was all shocked that people called me. I opened my mouth, but Nick beat me to the punch. "Mind your own business."

"You're quick enough to accuse Cody—"

"I thought we were supposed to be cooperating," Olivia muttered.

"Yeah, come on, guys," I cut in. "There's no need for—"

The door into the hallway opened, and Bay appeared, white-faced. "Um," she said. "The police are here."

I opened my mouth to say, "Do they have a warrant?" but years of training from Jordan told me that getting belligerent wouldn't help anyone. Best to try polite first.

"Oh? Well, welcome," I said as Detective Keller and a man I didn't recognize came in. "How can I help you?"

Detective Keller looked right through me to Nick. "Mr. Lawlis? Would you mind stepping out into the hallway? We'd like a word."

We all turned as one to stare at Nick. He looked green around the gills, but his bravado had not left him. He stood, Paige on his heels. "Am I under arrest?"

The detective's gaze flickered as she looked from Nick to me and back again. "No. But we'd appreciate it if you'd come speak with us all the same." Nick opened his mouth to protest, but the detective barreled on. "Miss Harding, if you'd accompany us, as well."

The threat—even imagined—to Paige was too much for Nick. "No!" he shouted. He exploded into motion, pushing Paige forward as if she had somewhere to run. Instead, she just stumbled over a chair while he dove at the other cop. Paige and the chair hit the ground, and Olivia screamed. The cop caught Nick easily and held him by the collar like a misbehaving kitten. Paige sobbed, making Nick shout louder, and Detective Keller started to yell at Nick in turn.

The LARPers stood, then, too, and Olivia said, "You can't take him! You don't have a warrant!"

"We just want to talk to you, kid," the uniformed cop said to Nick, who flailed, trying to escape.

I sighed, elbowed my way past the struggling tangle of Nick and the cop, stooped, and hoisted Paige back to her feet. I dusted her off, looked straight into her eyes, and said, "Call your mother. Right now."

She nodded as if I'd slapped some sense into her. In a trance-like state, she turned and began walking to the door. Bay wrapped an arm around her shoulders and guided her across the hall. Meanwhile, the cops dragged Nick to his feet. He'd managed to get—or give himself—a bloody nose in the process of his futile struggles, and he looked like quite the hardened criminal as he stared at me, the whites of his eyes wide. "Autumn—"

"Don't," I said, still using my boss voice. "You have to go with them now, whether you want to or not. Don't talk, and when you get to the station, call your parents. They'll take care of the lawyer and everything else."

He nodded.

I felt like an old woman. Paige and Nick were a decade my junior, but I could feel my hairs turning gray as one by one they joined me on my slow march to insanity. The rest of the gamers filed out after Nick and the cops, leaving Hector and me to stand in the wreckage.

"Wow," Hector said.

"Amen."

"Did you see Paige when you asked her about that phone call?"

"Like a deer in headlights."

"No, not that." Hector's eyes met mine, his glinting. "She was squeezing Nick's hand like holding it would keep his words in."

"She wanted to hide the phone call from the others—"

"Yeah, or she wanted to hide something from you."

"Damn it."

Hector held out his hand, palm up.

"And damn you," I added, fishing for my wallet.

6

THE OTHER LARPers EXITED as if escorted by dementors, leaving silence and despair in their wake. Their chatter erupted as soon as they left the store, though, and I knew that the news of Nick's detainment would spread across town in the Sunday papers. When the door closed behind them, Bay let out a long, low whistle.

"Not good," she said.

"Nope." I turned to her. "How are sales today?"

She grimaced. "You won't like it."

I craned my neck to look at the register's screen. When I pulled up the day's totals, my eyes widened. "That bad?"

"Yeah. Just a few more *Spellcasters* sales. Everyone who has come in has wanted to talk or has brought things for, well, you know." She nodded toward the sidewalk.

"Some reporters came by, too," Hector said. Bay elbowed him. He crinkled his nose at her. "She needs to know."

"What?"

Bay sighed. "They were asking about you, about the shop, about the games. They all came by when the police announced that they're officially investigating Wes's death as a murder. I didn't say much—I'm pretty sure they wanted me to say that games lead to Satanism and the occult and the sacrificing of babies."

"Oh, the usual, then."

"The usual."

I hoisted myself onto the counter behind the register. "I assume you told them about the fridge of dead babies in the office?"

"Of course not, but I did offer them a leg from the dead goat we keep in the alley."

"You guys are not nearly as funny as you think you are," Hector said. He turned to Bay. "If you didn't want me to tell her, why are you joking about it?"

"What else are we supposed to do? They'll come by, and they'll write their stories regardless of what we do or say. And anyway, it's funny. They want us to be horrible, youth-corrupting baby killers, and they have no idea what geek culture even means."

"Ugh, don't start on about geek culture. Last time we were here for an hour."

"But it's important to think about our image," Bay said earnestly.

I cut in. "Okay, but let's think about our image later. Thanks for telling me about the reporters. I appreciate the protection, Bay, but I need to know these things. Did you guys send out the email blast about the tournament cancellation?"

They nodded.

"Good. Let's start thinking of some ways we can make up the business. We can reschedule the draft and the tournament, maybe for when the first expansion packs come out, but I think we ought to do something sooner—"

"We should have a memorial," Bay said.

"What?"

"A memorial for Wes. It doesn't need to be super sad or any-thing—more like a wake. People can come, they can swap sto-ries. We'll play some of the games he liked."

"You want to make money off people's grief?" Hector said, sounding sick.

Bay looked appalled. I rushed to her defense. "No, no, it's not like that. It will give people a safe space to mourn, and it'll help them stay confident in the store. If they see it as a sanctuary rather than a threat, they won't be driven away. Plus," I said, my brain running ahead, "we could invite someone from the paper. They'll take some nice, sad photos, and the paper will run them, and people will see how nice and normal we all are."

"That's genius," Bay said.

"Right? And not completely self-serving since it will be for Wes."

"What about Paige and Nick?" Hector asked.

I bit my thumbnail: they were the sticking point. Paige, Nick, and Cody. All suspects, all closely associated with the store. I didn't want to seem heartless, inviting them and ignoring the chance that they had been involved in the death of the kid we all wanted to mourn. On the other hand, it was a tragedy for all the Ten Again community, especially Wes's friends. We needed to honor Wes, and we couldn't let our paranoia turn us against our family.

I dropped my hand back into my lap. "We won't invite them, but if they try to come by, we'll handle it. I don't think any of them would make a scene, but it wouldn't be out of line for us to ask that they leave if anyone gets upset."

"So we'll wing it, then?" Hector said.

"Well, what's your bright idea?" I asked. "They're not, as far as I know, under arrest, any of them. We can't just kick them out. Wes and Nick were best friends. Paige used to date Wes. They have more right to be at his memorial than anyone else does." Unless they killed Wes, in which case letting them in would be a pretty big faux pas on my part.

The store's mall door opened. Donald walked in, his face shiny beneath his balding head, and Meghan trailed in his wake, composed and stylish as ever. She wore a deep purple blouse with a black skirt and high heels that I refused to believe she would wear all day in her stupid fancy store. Her mouth was turned down in a frown, but her eyes were smiling.

"Hi," I said. Time for the meeting Donald had requested, I guessed. And worse, he brought reinforcements. This was turning into the longest, worst Saturday of my entire life. I slid off the counter and went to meet them.

"I just heard that the police are calling the young man's death a murder," Donald said without preamble.

"Yes, I heard." I looked from Donald to Meghan. I could understand why Donald wanted to meet with me, but I couldn't see what role Meghan had to play in it.

Donald saw me staring at her and said, "We saw the police take a young man from this store."

Meghan tilted her head when I glared at her. "So upsetting," she said. "I wasn't too surprised, though. I heard that boy and his girlfriend arguing last night with the boy who died. It doesn't seem good, does it?"

Wait, she'd heard Nick arguing with Wes? "Are you sure that's what you heard?" I asked her. "Because he said—"

"Oh, playing Nancy Drew, are you?" She smiled. "Or would it be that other one, the girl who fights vampires. She had some dorky friends who helped her—"

"Buffy," Hector said helpfully.

I cut in. "What's it to you, anyway, Meghan?"

"Well, the police wanted me to talk to them. It seems I may be the only witness to so much of what happened last night. And then, of course, I found the poor boy—" She broke off and put a hand to her mouth as if overcome by emotion. So fake. Donald put a hand on her shoulder.

"Don't pretend you care," I said.

Donald's eyes widened. "Autumn, that's terrible. Meghan's had a shock—we all have, and we need to support each other right now."

"Uh-huh."

Meghan lifted her head and dabbed artfully at one eye. "Thanks, Donald." She took a step away from him.

"I wanted to talk to you in private, Autumn." Donald glanced at Bay and Hector.

Private—except for Meghan. I had a feeling I wouldn't enjoy this conversation. "Of course," I said in a forced cheerful tone. "Let's go across the hall." I led them back up the short flight of stairs and out the door. As I left, I glanced at Hector and Bay standing together behind the register. Bay gave me an encouraging smile, but Hector looked like he wanted to punch Donald on his reddened nose.

Great. Even my employees thought I was about to get pwned.

In the spillover gaming room, I picked up three of the chairs Nick had upset during his great escape attempt and shoved them close to a table in the center of the room. Meghan and Donald sat together on the same side, facing me like members of a jury. I suspected I wouldn't be getting a fair hearing, but I might be able to get something useful out of it all the same.

"I was surprised to see you at the station so late last night," I said to Donald, fishing.

"Oh? Oh, yes." As if he didn't remember. He glanced sideways at Meghan. "They were asking me about the building's security and access. Things like that."

"You were here late last night, too." I hoped I sounded curious and not accusatory.

"Yes. They wondered if I saw anyone unusual, but, of course, I was in my office. And, anyway, I was gone by eight fifteen. Craig MacLeod and I walked out together. We were talking shop that night." He made a strange motion with his arms, half shrug and half expansive gesture, and glanced at Meghan, who gave him a tight-lipped smile. "And I told them about the building's safety precautions and the waiver your customers sign when they use the building for their games, and all that."

"Right, right," I said, as if I had been through the same discussion with the cops. "Did Max see anyone? You said you were going to talk to him before you left last night. And he has those security cameras . . ."

Donald shifted in his chair. "Ah, yes, well. Those cameras are more of a precaution than anything else."

"What does that mean?" I glanced at Meghan, but she didn't react. She and Donald seemed to be so cozy, she probably already knew about the cameras.

He sighed. "They're not hooked up to anything. Budget cuts, you know—" He waved a hand, then planted it firmly on the table, looking at me squarely. "Businesses are struggling."

"I'm aware." My voice sounded small and stiff.

Donald turned his serious, sympathetic landlord face on me. "Autumn, we need to talk about what's going to happen in the next few weeks."

"What do you mean?"

"Well, the store and the building are already getting a lot of attention. First with the grant business and now with all of this, there's a lot of public interest. And not all of it's positive. Despite what they say, not all publicity is good, and some of it is very bad. We need to protect the interests of the businesses in the building as well as the safety of the customers. And in the meantime, I think we need to do everything to minimize the backlash from this incident."

My jaw dropped at this sudden change of subject. "A boy died, and you're worried about publicity?"

Meghan swooped in. "You know that's not what Donald is saying, Autumn. But the store and the building are going to be the focus of a lot of scrutiny. And it's such an important time, with the grant on the line. This building needs some attention, whether it's the preservation plans I'm advocating or even your remodels. Donald and I were talking, and we're both afraid that the gossip your store is attracting right now might spill over onto the building's reputation."

I wanted to speak, but no words came to mind. I stared at them both, my heart pounding. Donald shrank backward as if he wanted to retract into his shell, but Meghan remained poised and neutral. Too neutral. "What are you suggesting I do?"

"We thought it might be best if you retract your name from the grant application pool."

There it was.

"And what should be my reason?"

"You feel it's inappropriate, given the situation?" Meghan suggested. "It's valid reasoning."

I closed my eyes and took a deep, slow breath. "Look, my plans for the grant are good. The publicity from the grant is all good. I understand why you're worried, but it won't hurt any of us for me to get the money to green the building. It might even help with the bad press—people will remember me, and the store, and the building, for the upgrades. And anyway, they're announcing the finalists on Monday. It may not even matter." I worked very hard to keep the pleading note from my voice. I hadn't realized how badly I wanted that grant until this moment. "Just let me wait until that announcement."

Meghan looked at Donald. "At least say you'll consider it," he said.

"Of course I will. We're all still reeling, but I have plans to make things better. I think we'll have a memorial for Wes next week, and that will do nothing but good for everyone involved." My words ran on, falling like sand from a broken hourglass. Donald looked dismayed.

"Autumn, I don't know—it might be better all around if you just suspend operation until they decide whether those young people taken in today are suspects."

"You want me to close?"

"No, no, I didn't say that. But it might be best—it would give you time to think about the grant, to consider whether or not you want to keep forcing yourself into public notice. Closing temporarily would give everyone some distance."

"Forcing myself into public notice? You think I want all this attention, that I want reporters hanging around, questioning my employees, that I want to be meeting with the City Council every week, that I want to do anything but run my store and give my gamers a safe place to hang?" I stopped, short of breath. My vision had blurred but not with tears. I could practically see the blood boiling beneath my skin.

"Listen to yourself, Autumn," Meghan said in a quiet voice. "You don't even like working for the grant. Why not let it go, save yourself the stress? You're already struggling. No one would blame you."

"You have no idea what the hell you're talking about. You have no right to tell me what to do with my store, to spread rumors and act like you run this place," I snapped at her. "Besides, dropping out of the grant competition has nothing to do with closing my store."

"Now, ladies," Donald said fretfully. "Don't fight. Autumn, we want the best for you and your store. That's the only reason we're suggesting you take a step back."

Wrong. Meghan wanted me out of the running for the grant money to improve her own chances. Donald wanted to protect his checking account. I stood up. "I'll consider it. But I'm not closing—that's not an option. Shutting down would be like admitting I thought the store, the games, had some role in Wes's death, and that's just plain ridiculous. And more than that, this is supposed to be one of our busiest weeks of the year—closing might very well sink me. Shutting down right now would hurt you, too, and open up another vacancy in the building. If you're so worried about making money, you ought to be helping me, not trying to close me down." I paused and looked at Meghan. "And you're right. I don't like the attention, I don't like making the presentations, I don't like any of it. But I believe in my grant application. If I decide it would be for the best to drop out, I will, but I won't do it to make your life easier."

They both stared up at me. Meghan retained her cool, carefully arranged neutrality, but Donald's face had gone red again. I seemed to have that effect on him. He stood. "Autumn, please be reasonable. I understand your position, but I will ask you to consider the situation of everyone else in this building. You're not the only one whose reputation is on the line."

"No, but I seem to be the only one who isn't worried about how a death is going to impact my sales." I'd gone too far, and I knew it as soon as the words came out of my mouth. "I'm sorry, Donald," I said. I wouldn't apologize to Meghan—Donald was genuinely concerned, but Meghan was trying to capitalize on his legitimate fears. "I'll think about it. I swear. I'll take a day to consider, and I'll speak to the committee on Monday. If it seems like I'm out of the running, it won't matter, and if it seems like they would like me to step back, I will." Maybe. I didn't know, actually, but I did need to buy myself some time. If we could prove that the murder had nothing to do with gaming, there would be no need for me to drop out.

But how I was supposed to solve a murder in a day, I had no idea.

Donald seemed to deflate with my apology. "Please consider it. And let me know what you decide about the shop's activities." He hesitated, then added, "If you decide to have a memorial, I would like to be there."

That seemed like a friendly enough gesture. I smiled. "Of course."

I moved to let them both out of the room, my heart still pounding from my small gesture of rebellion. I didn't like confrontation, never had. I wiped my sweaty palms on my jeans before I shook Donald's hand, bidding him farewell. Meghan lingered after him.

"You're making a mistake," she said.

"Thanks for sharing your opinion."

"That boy's death came at exactly the wrong time for you, Autumn. If you had any sense, you'd back down, do what Donald says, and let the publicity blow over. By staying in the running for the grant, you're going to feed the story. I promise you, this will get worse for you."

"Is that a threat?"

She smirked. "Please. I'm just stating the obvious."

"For someone who recently 'had a shock,' you're awfully snide."

"I'm tougher than I look." She turned to go. I let her, seeing no need to drag out our little spat. She *was* tough—tough like patent leather, shiny and impervious.

I went back to the main store, exhausted. There were no customers. Bay and Hector watched me slink over, and Bay offered me a cup of coffee when I slumped into the chair behind the register. I told them what Donald said, about Meghan's threats, about my wild hope of vindicating the store and the other gamers before someone forced me to tuck my tail and hide under the bed.

"So now I have to figure out how to solve a murder in the next thirty-six hours, or I'll end up having to drop out of the grant competition and all this time and effort will have been completely wasted. I get the feeling that Donald will pull some strings and make me close up for a few days if I don't."

"He can't do that!" Bay cried.

"Wait—" Hector said. "You don't have to solve a murder."

"I don't?"

"Nope." He grinned, dark eyes shining. "You don't have to prove someone else is guilty. All you need to do is prove that Paige and Nick, and Cody, I guess, are innocent. That's all our justice system needs. Reasonable doubt."

"That wouldn't get suspicion off the store," I said dubiously.

"No, but it's easier than trying to solve a murder. Just find some way to prove they didn't do it or weren't likely to have done it."

"What if they did do it?" Bay asked.

"If they did, closing up for a week might not be a terrible idea." The words, bitter as burnt tea, spilled out of my mouth before I could stop them.

"No way," Bay said. "If there was a murder because of a game and you close up, you'll never open again."

She had a point. "You're probably right." I groaned. "We're so screwed, but we have to try."

Hector grinned. "I think I know just the people to help."

7

Sunday was usually the day I ran the store alone. It was a short day, not terribly busy, and the atmosphere was laid back. But that particular Sunday, two LARPers and two of the tabletop RPG players from the group that had given Cody the boot showed up at the store promptly at noon, eager for the chance to vindicate their friends—and more than a little titillated at the opportunity to play their greatest roles yet.

"So, what, we're like, investigating the murder now?" José asked Olivia under his breath. "Is this for real?" He sounded excited.

Olivia shushed him. "Autumn will tell us what to do."

Like I had any idea what to do. I silenced them by ringing the gong on the register. They stopped talking and turned to stare at me. My mind went blank, and I stared back, daunted. What on earth was I supposed to do with four gamers, security cameras that recorded nothing, no leads, and one very chatty, very oblivious guard manning the security desk downstairs? Eight expectant eyes gazed up at me, and my mouth went dry.

"You're probably wondering why I've gathered you all here today," I said weakly.

They giggled. From the corner, Hector nodded encouragingly. He had volunteered to come in on his day off, showing far more interest than was probably healthy in our amateur detective project. After some arm-twisting, Jordan had come, too. She refused to say anything about what the police knew or didn't know, though, and insisted she was here in a general advisory capacity. She would tell us what questions to ask but not who to talk to or how to approach them: my own, personal, half-committed Watcher.

Her presence gave me heart.

"Okay," I said, bolstered by Jordan's support. "You all know that the police are suspicious of Paige and Nick, and Cody, too."

"Good riddance," one of the tabletop gamers said. Hector grinned.

"I know, he's not the most likable guy, but he's one of us, so we need to do what we can."

"How are we supposed to solve a murder if they can't?" Olivia jerked her chin toward Jordan.

Before Jordan could get riled, I said, "They can and they will, but it will take time. Today we're just looking for evidence that may help them to solve it—and to prove that Nick, Paige, and Cody are innocent." Hopefully. "We need to know what went down during the night of the game. You guys are going to walk us through that night, step by step, and show us every place where you saw them: Wes, Cody, Nick, and Paige. We need to figure out who was the last person to see him before he died. That means talking to the shop owners; to Max, the security guard; and even finding out if there were any customers here that night. We have to know who was in this building Friday night, where they were, and what they were doing. It's not going to be easy. But if we can find out anything, any tiny piece of information the police might have missed, that will force them to reconsider."

Jordan cut in. "Keep in mind that you guys have zero authority. Most of the people who work in the shops have already been questioned. They may not want to talk to you. Don't make a nuisance of yourselves, or I'll have to act in a more official capacity." Hector made a face at her, but she adopted her most serious-business expression. "I'm not kidding. I'm helping out for the same reason you guys are—I love Autumn and I love this shop. But if you interfere with the official investigation, the police will stop you in whatever way they have to, even if that means putting you in jail. I know you want to help, but you have to protect yourselves and Autumn first. Be very, very careful."

"Okay, Mom," José mumbled.

Jordan glared at him. "Don't mistake me for your mom—I'm much, much worse. I will stop you if I think you're becoming a problem."

Hoping to lighten the mood, I clapped my hands. "Okay, Scoobies. You know what to do. Ask the people in the shops if they're willing to talk. Find out what, if anything, they saw. Find out when they were here. If anyone acts reluctant or cagey, don't press them."

"But tell us they didn't want to talk," Hector said.

"Right," I said. "I'm going to go downstairs first to try to retrace Wes's path. If you saw him Friday night or talked to him, please come with me."

The LARPers formed a small mob around me as I trekked out of the store and up the stairs to the lobby that was the ground floor at the town square entrance. From there, one could look down on the fountain and the tables surrounding it. The elevator rose in a shining column from the bottom level, and Max's security desk stood sentry at one end of the long, narrow space. We should have been at eye level with the fountain's spray up here, but building maintenance hadn't turned it back on yet. Without the pleasant, babbling, ambient noise from the fountain, the lobby was eerily silent. Donald refused to play music in the lobby and hallways, for which I was normally very grateful, but today the silence seemed more creepy than peaceful.

I stared sideways at Max, sizing him up. He sat with a newspaper open in front of him like a deflector shield, but I knew his rheumy eyes kept a vigilant watch on the lobby and the basement spread before him. Mostly his job was to keep homeless folks from setting up camp at the basement tables and to run off teens who loitered, throwing coins and rubbish into the fountain. But he took it seriously, and I knew that if there had been anyone in the building who shouldn't have been, he would have seen them.

"This is a very bad idea," Jordan muttered in my ear as the gamers scattered like ants, mapping out their starting points for the game. Max peered over his paper at them, his eyes narrowed. He was like a caricature of a security guard, and I felt a brief wave of pity for him: the murder had happened on his watch.

"You're probably right," I said to Jordan. "But it's all I have, and I need to do something."

She nodded. I left Max for the moment, figuring he'd be easier to talk to after the crowd had dispersed, and went to speak with the LARPers. José met me by the balcony, his face solemn. "Before we get started, I wanted to say a few quick words to everyone."

Thinking he wanted to say something about Wes or the group's sadness, I nodded, rather touched. He beckoned, and the LARPers gathered around us in a huddle.

"Remember, everyone, that it's going to be more important today than ever to stay in character," he said. I blinked, puzzled, and he continued. "We're retracing our steps from the other night, yes, but we all need to think of ourselves as detectives today, too, especially if we're going to get any answers. Try to see everything you saw the other night, but look at it with fresh eyes. Consider Wes's perspective. Consider a murderer's perspective. Keep your long-term goals in mind, but stay focused on the short-term. Don't make any assumptions about what we know or think we know—remember, you can only see what your character sees. In this case, try to see what an investigator would see. We need to question each other, too, so, just like any time we play, try not to take anything we do today personally."

The others all nodded solemnly, as if this was a familiar pep talk. I felt my jaw drop a little at the sheer madness José was spouting, and I looked at Jordan, standing behind the rest of the group. She rolled her eyes and gave me a "What did you expect?" shrug.

I sighed. "Yes. Well. Uh, thanks José."

He nodded importantly. "This is where we met for the evening."

"Not at the store?"

José shook his head—the group seemed to have elected him leader in Paige's absence. "The lobby is more central."

"Okay. What then?"

He walked me through their assignments. It seemed Nick, Wes, and Paige had vanished immediately for one of the upper levels while José and Olivia, the semi-neutral and undecided parties in their vampire politicking, had remained in the lobby for at least half an hour, putting us at about seven thirty.

Presumably, only Nick and Paige knew where Wes had been during that time.

The next confirmed Wes sighting by someone in the troupe other than Nick and Paige had been Olivia, crossing paths with him on the third floor at around seven forty-five. "What did you say to him?" José asked her.

Olivia folded her arms over her chest. "I asked him whether or not he was helping Alaria and Kelvin overthrow the queen."

In response to the question he read on my face, José said, "That's Paige and Nick."

"Ah."

"Yesterday you said you were interrogating him. What exactly did you do?"

Olivia lifted her chin. She had long, dark hair that spilled down her back when she moved. With her deep purple eye shadow and silver choker, she almost looked the part of the vampire queen herself. "I cornered him against the railing. But I never touched him, and when he said 'pause,' I let him go. He said he needed to use the bathroom." She made a disgusted huffing noise, as if interrupting a fictional interrogation for real life necessities showed great weakness in the line of fire. "He took the stairs, and that's the last time I saw him."

José loomed over her, bad cop stats maxing out like he'd rolled a ten on intimidate. "Are you sure?"

"Yes."

"And you didn't use force—didn't threaten him with your fangs, or talk about feeding on him?"

This took Olivia aback. "Well, I—"

"You did, didn't you?"

"We always threaten force, that's how this game works!" Olivia was near tears.

"Did you threaten to bite him?"

"Yes, I did, okay! But you know I would never do anything to hurt someone in real life. Wes was upset, so I let him go!" Olivia took a step back toward the railing, cornered and upset.

"Easy, José," I said. "Come on."

He gave me a hard look. "We've got to ask the tough questions, Autumn, and if you're not willing to do it, I will."

Shocked, I raised my voice. "Why are you acting like this? Who appointed you investigator, anyway?" José was normally a sweet, quiet guy, and this was a side of him I'd never seen.

"Cut, I think," Jordan said.

I blinked, puzzled by the non sequitur.

José froze. "I'm sorry," he said, uncertain.

I looked at Jordan. "Cut?"

She grinned. "It's a safe word in LARPing. Remember? We used it in our *Shadowrun* days."

It all came rushing back to me. "Oh my god, you're right." I turned back to José. "What the hell?"

He shrugged. "My character has the highest investigate skill level. I have practice. The others thought I should take point."

I glanced at Olivia, and she nodded. I did an actual, real-life facepalm, groaning. "You were seriously . . . role-playing . . . the last twenty minutes when you were walking me through all of this?"

"You know how it is, Autumn. You used to do this stuff." His voice, so cool and hard all afternoon, was suddenly soft and shaky.

That shut me up. He and the others were frightened, grieving. I had asked them to come back to the site of their trauma and reenact the final hours, the final minutes, of their friend's life. Role-playing was a safe space, and José wasn't just pretending to be an investigator—he was pretending to be an earlier, innocent version of himself, even as he was forcing himself to look at his play and his friends with the jaded eye of his critics. My reputation wasn't the only one on the line.

"I am so, so sorry, you guys. I didn't think this through."

"We want to help," Olivia said in a small voice.

"I know you do. But I think maybe we should focus on talking to the people in the stores. The only ones who know where Nick and Paige were are Nick and Paige."

"Maybe the others found out something about Cody," José said hopefully.

"Maybe so. Let's find them."

I led the way to the stairs, Jordan at my side. She didn't say anything, and I knew the words, "I told you so," would never cross her lips, but she had been right to disapprove. Pretending we knew what we were doing, that we would find something the trained professionals had missed, made a mockery of Wes's death. And if Paige and Nick had killed him, we were doing a disservice to his memory. My jaw clenched, the beginnings of a headache threatening to clobber me. I knew I'd have a migraine before the end of the day.

Our "investigation" concluded, we waited on the others back in the lobby, where Paige and Wes had argued. She was the last person to admit to seeing him Friday night, a little after eight. After that, his time was a mystery.

I sauntered over to Max while we waited. "Hey, Max. How's it hanging?"

"Oh, fine, young lady, just fine." He put down his newspaper.

"How's that retirement plan of yours coming?" I asked. Might as well butter him up a little. I slathered on the small-town sweetness.

He beamed at me. "You remembered! Pretty well, thanks. I'm looking at some new investments. I think the missus and me may be able to hang it up for good pretty soon."

"Oh, come on—you know you'll never stop working," I teased. It was true. The man loved his job.

He waved me off. "None of that. I'm thinking I'm just about ready to start taking it a little easier."

"We'd be lost without you," I said. I leaned on his counter. "You practically run this building."

"You're not wrong." He gave me an old-man wink.

I cringed but kept smiling. "Speaking of, that boy who died— you saw him Friday night?" My voice echoed in the too-quiet lobby.

Max nodded. "Yeah. I just wish I'd been at my desk when it happened. I was down the hall—someone said they heard arguing in one of the shops."

My ears perked up. "Down the hall on this floor?" That's where Meghan's shop was, down the hall and at the corner of the building, right on the main street of the square.

"Yep. Nina from the gift shop heard a man and a woman shouting at each other, a real dust-up. She told me as she was leaving for the night. But when I got over there, they'd split. All the shops were dark, no one there."

"Odd."

"Yep."

"Did you happen to see another guy around, with a shaved head like a cartoon thug? He might have seemed cranky." I described Cody the best I could. Max's eyes lit up. "Yeah, him. He was lurking around, real suspicious, around twenty after eight or so. I told him to move on, and he said he was waiting for someone. Eventually he went back upstairs, to your store, I guess. I went upstairs right after, around eight thirty or so, just after Mr. Wolcott and Mr. MacLeod left."

That didn't help at all, except to confirm that Cody had been in the building when Wes was still alive. And apparently he'd been in the lobby when Paige and Wes were fighting. Damn. But I knew now that Craig had left with Donald, not Meghan. That was interesting.

I wondered if Nina from the gift shop had heard Paige and Wes arguing, or if she'd inadvertently witnessed someone else's fight. Meghan had still been here then. But for all I knew, Nina could have heard any pair of the LARPers having an in-character confrontation.

When I turned from Max, the role players who had been interviewing the shopkeepers had appeared, a beaming Hector in tow. I glowered at him.

"You're supposed to be in the shop."

"I put the back in ten sign up—you'll want to hear this," he said. He made a come-closer motion, and the whole seven-person gang leaned in like we were having a pregame huddle.

"We just heard from Nina in the gift shop that Meghan and her boyfriend were arguing the night of the murder."

"Meghan and Craig?" I said, shocked. Jordan and I looked at each other, her surprised face a reflection of mine. "Did she hear what they were fighting about?"

"Apparently, she was trying to get Craig on board with something. Saying things like, 'Can't you see it's in my best interest?' and, 'You never think about what I want.'"

"Good gossip, but it doesn't sound like it's useful to us," Jordan said.

"No, but listen—apparently Craig said something like, 'You make it very clear that you'd do anything to protect your own interests,' and then he stormed off. Nina saw Meghan in her store alone when she—Nina—left, around eight twenty-five. She said Meghan looked pissed."

Understandably. Meghan *would* do anything to protect her own interests, but pointing that out to her seemed to be the height of bad behavior. This explained why Craig had left with Donald. "So we know Meghan was around and in a bad mood."

"Here's the thing, though," Hector said, still looking excited. "We think Wes may have heard what they were arguing about. Nina said she saw him in the stairwell, going up right after the argument. Like he'd been on their floor the whole time."

"She didn't see Wes listening with her own two eyes?" Jordan asked. "It's hearsay at best."

"But we only have to prove that Nick and Paige might not be guilty, right? Not that they're actually, uh, you know." Hector trailed off, uncomfortable.

"It's not a good sign that you're finding it harder to prove they could be innocent than the prosecutor would find it to prove them guilty," Jordan said.

"You have to admit that there's some wiggle room," Hector said defensively.

José chimed in. "I wonder if anyone talked to that woman's boyfriend—Craig, right?"

I looked at Jordan. She shook her head. "If they have, I don't know about it. I'll tell them—"

"No, wait," I said. "I want to talk to him first."

"I don't think that's a good idea," Jordan said.

"I'll keep it casual. I'll just drop by, ask him how Meghan's doing, the usual. She's here today. I could go by his house no problem. We're friends, right?"

Jordan studied my face. "You're insane," she said finally.

I shrugged. "I never claimed otherwise." With that, I turned back to the gamers. "Great work, team," I said. "Let's break for now. If you guys want to keep working, you could draw up a map and timeline of Friday night. Otherwise, I say go home and take a break. You've had a rough weekend."

We split, Hector and me walking back to the store through the mall. He practically pranced up the stairs, he was so pleased with himself. "I'll bet you twenty bucks we could get the cops to think it was Meghan," he said. "She's nuts, I tell you. Remember that time she yelled at us for standing in costume outside her door? She said we were scaring off customers. I could totally see her offing Wes just for getting a glimpse of her life being less than perfect. And it'd be convenient for her, too, wouldn't it? She's the one who's getting Donald to ask you to drop out of the grant competition because of the bad publicity. Psycho prom queen puppet master probably engineered the whole thing. I bet you anything that's what's happening."

I pondered his words. Meghan made Cordelia Chase look easygoing, and she was ambitious on top of that. But would she kill to protect her reputation? Or even to get the grant she so desperately wanted? I doubted it. However, I could definitely see her capitalizing on Wes's death, making the most of a convenient situation and trying to drive me under using the weight of my own troubles. Hector was wrong: she wasn't a psychopath, but she always struck me as a sociopath. Normal people just weren't so—unflappable. She was more of an android than a woman.

We stopped at the door while Hector unlocked it, still chattering about Meghan's possible motives. He fumbled with the lock, then flung the door open in his excitement. The cardboard "back in ten minutes" sign flapped in the door's wake, and something fluttered to the floor.

I bent to pick it up. It was another *Spellcasters* card, the Undead Samurai. The face had been scratched off.

"What's that?" Hector asked, seeing me studying it.

I showed him. "There was another one outside. I guess someone is leaving them for Wes? I'll put it with the others."

Hector looked down at it. "Creepy," he said, echoing my earlier thought.

Creepy was right. I pocketed it. One disturbing memorial token was enough.

8

WHEN I KNOCKED ON Craig's front door early that evening, it occurred to me, too late, that there was a good chance he and Meghan were living together by now. I stared in horror at my knuckles as if I could undo their rapping. But Craig answered the door, and I was released from my need to bend the laws of reality.

"Hey, Autumn," he said, his voice both sorrowful and warm. He had a towel in his hands, as if he'd been drying dishes, and he stuffed it into his back pocket when he saw me. He reached out to draw me into the house, hugging me in the process. I let him do it, hoping to butter him up a little. "I heard, and I wanted to call, but I thought you must be so swamped."

I followed him down his short hallway into the little kitchen. There was no evidence of female occupation. The kitchen was stark, utilitarian, no dishes out, cold and sterile as a Cylon warship. There was a paintbrush in the drying rack, a sealed can of paint on the counter. It was too clean, full of chrome appliances and shining tile, utterly unlike my own house. Craig lived in one of the new developments on the south side of town, where all the houses looked so prim and similar, they might as well have been stamped from a mold. My own house was a little bungalow not far from downtown and the store, a quirky place with arched doorways and slightly uneven wood floors.

At times, it was surreal that the boy I used to make out with outside of homeroom owned a house and washed his own dishes, painted his deck, mowed his lawn. Craig and I had reconnected after I'd finished graduate school and moved back to White Lake. By then, he'd been well established at his real estate agency, successful, prosperous, and more handsome than ever, but we'd managed to rebuild our old friendship.

At thirty-three, I should probably feel less bitterness about the end of a high school relationship. Everything had worked out. After that horrible summer, when Meghan slept with Craig while I was off visiting my mom, I went to UW-Madison, graduated with honors, got my MBA, and came back to open Ten Again. Craig and I stayed friends, and when Meghan returned to White Lake to open Chic, she and I had settled into an amicable mutual dislike, fueled at a distance.

Sometimes it irked me that they'd managed to turn their fling into a long-term relationship while I'd never managed to keep a boyfriend for more than six months. Not that I was complaining. Somehow, every boyfriend I'd had since Craig—including Craig—managed to disappoint. It always seemed better to just date casually, have fun, and call it quits before things got complicated. Love 'em and leave 'em, Jordan said.

Well, most of them I left.

"Thanks, Craig," I said when he pulled out one of the kitchen chairs for me. I sank into it, dropping my bag onto the floor. "It's been a nightmare."

"I couldn't believe it when I read the paper." He stood at the sink, rinsing out a plain stainless steel teakettle and then filling it from the tap. "And now they're saying it's a murder—it's too horrible. Those poor kids."

"You remember when we used to LARP?"

"Yeah." He flashed me a white grin. "You and me and Jordan. And Micah. And who was that guy . . . Man, I'm getting old. I can't remember his name!"

"Stuart," I said. "His name was Stuart. He moved away after junior year."

"Right! Man." Craig put the kettle on and lit the burner. "Seems like ages ago."

"Yeah." I wondered, as a stiff silence fell, how to bring the conversation around to his fight with Meghan. "Mostly I feel bad for the players. They're all in their twenties, and they were all pretty close. What a shock."

"I can't even imagine," Craig agreed. He took a pair of mugs from the cabinet, then leaned against the counter with his arms crossed.

"It must have been pretty awful for Meghan, too." I lowered my eyelids, hoping to seem casual.

"Yeah." I felt him studying me. "She was horrified. She felt guilty, I think, for not being able to do anything."

I'll bet she did, a part of me—the part that wanted Hector to be right—thought. "I feel that way a little, too. Like, if I'd been more attentive, or if I hadn't let them change their night, or a number of things, Wes might still be alive."

"You can't blame yourself."

"Thanks." I half-smiled at him. "That's what I hear."

The kettle began to whistle, and Craig took it off the burner. He poured the tea and sat silently beside me at the table.

I bobbed my bag in the steaming water. "Did she mention if she saw anyone—anything—strange that night? You were there, too—did you see anything?" Maybe if I approached it like I was just conducting a general investigation it wouldn't seem weird to ask about their fight.

"Playing Mulder?"

"Mulder? How *Mulder*?"

"You know. Hunting vampire kids or whatever." He grinned at me like he'd said something funny, and I suddenly felt grateful to Meghan.

I tried to laugh, to butter him up, but it just seemed cruel. I didn't want to argue, though. "Something like that. I want to help. I think the cops suspect some of the other gamers, and that would be the worst. Not just for me and the store, but for everyone involved with Ten Again."

Craig nodded. "I hear you. She did say she heard some of the gamers arguing, but I'm not sure what about. She didn't talk about it much. I left before she did. I was talking to Donald about those properties I told you about."

"Yeah, Max said he saw you two leave."

Craig's brow creased. "Really? Donald went down to the basement when I left. But I guess Max saw him leave after that."

I frowned. "Huh. I wonder what he was doing down there."

"He said something about checking the doors. You know how he is."

"That's for sure." I switched directions, as if mentioning Donald's detour had made me think of it. "How'd Meghan end up in the basement before she left, anyway?"

"You'd have to ask her." He took a sip of his tea and grimaced at the heat.

"Are you guys okay?" I asked. It seemed a reasonable question since he was being cagey.

He raised his eyebrows. "Yeah, why?"

"It just seems like . . . maybe she didn't talk about what happened very much. Or something."

"Would you want to talk about it? She found a dead body."

Probably, and to at least one therapist. "I dunno." I decided to bite the bullet. "A woman in the building told me she heard you guys fighting."

"I see." Craig chuckled. "You can take the girl out of the small town, but you can't take the small town—or the gossip—out of the girl."

I bristled. "What's that supposed to mean?"

"Come on, Autumn. You haven't been the most supportive about me and Meghan."

I shrugged, trying not to feel defensive. "Trying to be friendly. My mistake."

Craig put down his mug and sighed. "Geez, I'm sorry. I'm just a little touchy. We did fight, and now this whole thing has her freaked, and the grant stuff—it's just not a good time." He looked at me, sad. "You're one of the few who gets it right now."

I did get it. I felt it, too, like I had to perform for the city's leadership even when my store was under the worst scrutiny it would ever face. I felt like Jabba's slave girl, dancing on a chain. But I still had hope of breaking free, and Craig didn't seem to realize that his girlfriend was trying to drive a stake into my lead. "Meghan's not making it easy for me."

He snorted. "No. She would never do that. She always gets what she wants, and right now she wants that grant."

And to put me out of business.

"What were you guys fighting about?"

"Oh." He waved a hand. "It was about taxes—and getting married. She wants to file our taxes separately or something, so that it's less complicated. Better deductions I guess."

That seemed pretty flimsy. "Really? Nina said you guys were shouting."

"Yeah. You know how Meghan gets."

I did, but she struck me as irrationally calm, not hysterical. Screaming wasn't in her cold android nature. "I guess so." I toyed with the string on my tea bag. "She came to me today saying I should back out of the grant competition."

"Really?" He didn't sound surprised. "Are you going to?"

"No."

"Good," he said. He smiled. "I think your project would be great for that building."

"Don't tell Meghan."

"Yeah, don't tell her I told you that."

"Scout's honor." I glanced around. "It's weird that we're in your kitchen."

"Why?"

"I don't know. You own a house; you have a kitchen. You cook food here."

"You have a house, a kitchen. I assume you cook."

"Of course I do."

He tilted his head. "Yeah, okay, I see what you mean. It's a little weird. I remember when you couldn't heat up frozen pizza bites."

I snickered. "Yeah. I'm surprised you didn't get food poisoning, eating all that charcoal."

Craig laughed out loud. He stood. "Come on, let's go sit in the living room. It's a little less grown-up."

It wasn't. As I followed him in, mug in hand, I realized Craig *was* grown up. His furniture matched. He had coasters on the tables. The DVDs weren't stacked precariously on the TV stand like at my house. He had become an adult while I was away at school, and our newly rebuilt friendship had formed only a small step stool, giving me mere peeps into the windows of his life. My existence was much easier to see: I worked in the store, and the store was my home. It was an extension of myself. While it reflected my community of gamers, too, it was mine in all ways. My dream, my work, my haven.

If this was Craig's haven, it didn't tell me much. A pile of papers stood on the coffee table—contracts, I thought, and what looked like some development plans. A fat spy novel sat on the couch, surprising me. I didn't think he read much, but the book's spine was broken, and the bookmark sticking up from its battered pages looked well loved. A basket of fashion magazines rested beside one of the armchairs, the lone mark of Meghan's presence.

Craig picked up the book and tossed it onto the coffee table with the papers, then slid a coaster my way. I sank onto the leather couch and wrapped my hands around my mug. "Will you guys live here when you get married?"

Craig glanced at me. "Nah. Meghan wants to find a new house, start fresh together."

I nodded. It made sense, I suppose. And Craig didn't seem to have planted his roots here. When the inevitable stilted silence fell, I glanced around, searching for some way to bring the conversation back around to Friday night and his argument with Meghan. Meghan's presence in the building wasn't terribly suspicious, but their fight still seemed like fertile ground for reasonable doubt. The title of the papers read, "Proposed Development Plan A, Property 8142, White Lake, Wisconsin." Yawn. Craig's firm did that sometimes—bought properties to redevelop.

That raised another question. "What were you doing at the building Friday night, anyway?"

"Hanging out with Meghan." Craig's expression was bland as he sipped his tea.

"Yeah, but you said you've been talking to Donald," I prompted.

"Oh, that." He put his mug down. "Donald came to me when you and Meghan made the semifinalists. He wanted to know how your proposed changes would increase the value of the building."

"Is he looking to sell?" I asked, alarmed.

"Not at the moment, but he is interested in how improvements like yours affect a property's chances in the market. He's looking to invest elsewhere, as well. Lots of investors are interested in those sorts of changes right now."

"How *would* my changes affect a property's chances in the market?"

Craig grinned, in his element. "Well, long-term, they're for the best, but in the short-term, it might raise the price—the value—out of the range investors in a community like White Lake can afford. Like I said, though, in the long-term, green building and utility management will increase the property's marketability. The key is efficiency. Investors want property that can help to sustain itself, especially in a college town, where corporate developers can build new properties more cheaply than they can buy existing ones. A building like Independence Square Mall might not earn back on the initial investment for improvements for many years, meaning it won't become self-sustaining in terms of energy for even longer."

I frowned. "But it would have an immediate improvement in its utility costs, and—"

"I'm talking in sheer dollars, Autumn. That reduction of utility costs won't cover the price of the improvements themselves for several years. It has to earn out before it can actually earn, you see. It's fine for a case like yours, of course, when the property owner isn't putting the money down himself. But for investors buying a building, it makes less sense. There are records of similar sales, both with and without those sort of upgrades—I could have Paige bring you some figures. They might help with your final grant presentations, actually."

I opened my mouth to argue, but at that moment, the door opened. Craig's face went from salesman-friendly to sick in a heartbeat.

"Is that—her—car?" Meghan's voice echoed in the front hallway. "Is she here?"

"Whoops," Craig muttered.

I peeked at the clock on the wall—only four. Chic stayed open till five on Sundays, and Meghan shouldn't have been done at the store yet. I'd been so careful about timing my visit. So much for that. She stormed back to the living room, her high heels loud as a poorly oiled mecha warrior on the hardwood floor. Craig stood, his arms spread defensively. "Meg, she just came here to talk about—"

It was a good thing she didn't let him finish that sentence, because I'm not sure what he would have said. I hadn't given him a reason for my presence.

She stopped in the doorway to the living room and pointed at me over Craig's shoulder. "You," she said. "You bitch, you think you can intimidate me?"

"What the hell?" I stood. "I have no idea what you're talking about."

"Meghan, calm down, Autumn has been right here—"

Meghan stamped her foot. Her cheeks were flushed with anger and the early spring cold. If there'd been a trinket by her, she would have thrown it at me, I felt sure. "But she was there earlier! I saw her!"

"I was where?" I still had no idea what we were talking about.

Meghan changed tactics. "She and her little friends did it, I'll bet anything. I know what you were doing today, poking your nose around, asking questions about me. If you think I'm going to lay off of you because of one sick little diorama, you'd better think again. Never were the brightest, were you?"

Craig looked at me over his shoulder. I shook my head. "I have no idea what's going on."

"Oh yeah?" Meghan flung her purse from her shoulder and began to fish through its depths.

Alarmed, I took a step back. "She doesn't have a gun, does she?" I muttered to Craig.

"No, she does not," he said, but he said it in a warning tone, not a reassuring one. I took another step back.

"I don't have a gun," Meghan gasped. "But I do have a phone." She brandished it, the blank screen reflecting Craig's and my bemused faces. "Here," she mumbled, pulling it back and poking at the touchscreen with a trembling forefinger.

When I took the time to study her, I realized how upset she actually was. Her shirt had come untucked on one side, her skirt had giant creases around the hips, and her usually smooth hair was gathered back into a rumpled ponytail. A streak of something red outlined the slim muscle of her forearm.

"Look," she said, holding the phone up again, an image on its screen.

Craig took it from her and turned to me, studying the image. The palm-sized digital screen showed a photo of a figurine, a gaudily painted plastic medieval princess, the type commonly sold at big box stores, hardware stores, educational stores—and game stores. We had some of them in my store. The toy's head had been cut off, and fake blood—red paint, I guessed, or even costume blood—pooled around her dissected form.

Someone had traced the words, "You're next, bitch," in the puddle.

My mouth dropped open. "What the hell?" I said again.

Meghan pointed at me, and I realized the red on her arm was the paint, smeared when she was cleaning up the mess.

Or doing it herself, a tiny voice in my head said.

"One of your little friends did this. It was on the sidewalk outside my store."

"Come on, Meg, you have no proof—" Craig said.

She ignored him. "I'm next? You know what that means, right? One of her little gamers killed one of their friends, and now they're after me—that gamer probably did something to hurt you, and now that I'm looking like a threat, I'll be taken down, too. Everyone who doesn't like you, one by one, we'll die!"

"You're acting insane," I said, my voice shaky. "No one I know did this, would do this. You want me out of the grant contest so bad, maybe you set it up yourself just to discredit me—"

Whoops. I hadn't meant for that to slip out. Meghan swelled like Violet Beauregarde but without the blueberry tint or winning personality. "I vandalized my own store now? How dare you suggest that I would ever stoop to such a pathetic prank? You—"

"Oh, but it's fine for you to accuse me of harboring a murderer—you'd have accused me directly if Craig hadn't been able to vouch for me!"

"You're only here so you have an alibi. I bet you set the whole thing up."

"Ladies!" Craig said. "Calm down—"

"I'm not the one who needs an alibi. You're the one who found Wes dead. You're the one no one saw right before he died—"

"You think I killed him, you pathetic little—"

"Enough!" Craig shouted. Meghan subsided, panting. I stared at her, my teeth clenched so hard my jaw hurt, my hands curled into fists. Craig turned to look at me. "Autumn, I think you'd better go."

I nodded. One by one, I forced my muscles to relax enough to propel me forward, toward the door, out of this house where

I never should have come. I stopped when I reached Meghan's side in the doorway.

"You reported it?" I asked.

"You bet your ass I did."

"Good. I'm glad. They'll know I had nothing to do with it."

As far as parting shots go, it wasn't a great one, but I took the last word and ran. I had an alibi, and I was sure Hector and Bay had one, as well. I couldn't control the other gamers, even if one of them had done it. Vandalism was beneath them, if not out of the question, and no one but my employees knew Meghan had been threatening me. But having the cops know what happened would serve me well.

The vandalism disturbed me. Either someone had let slip my amateur investigation attempts, or someone else had connected Meghan to all this mess, whatever it meant. That meant the grant competition and the murder weren't so neatly separated as I wanted them to be. Regardless of who had done it, this would mean more publicity, and it wouldn't take a genius to make a connection. Meghan had little in common with the game store beyond our shared roof and the grant competition. It all boiled down to the building.

Of course, the simplest answer was that Nick and Paige had threatened Meghan. Meghan had witnessed Paige fighting with Wes—maybe Paige worried Meghan's testimony would incriminate her. But Wes had had something on Meghan in return. If it had been math, all of the negatives on either side of the equation would have balanced out to zero, but as it was, I felt like the one with nothing.

Meghan's screaming voice echoed in my head as I strode back down to my car, parked in the street. I adjusted my opinion of her as I walked—perhaps she wasn't quite the ice queen we all thought she was. And she certainly wasn't the type to let things go.

Maybe she would kill to get ahead, which would put me in the line of fire. Or maybe I was so unreasonable, so blind to the obvious answer before me, that screaming was the only way to get through to me. And that would mean my gamers, my friends, had committed these crimes.

I wasn't sure which answer I preferred.

9

EARLY MONDAY MORNING, I found myself at City Hall again. The city built its ultra-modern government building about fifteen years prior, and the airy structure had a slick, timeless quality that made it stick out in scruffy downtown White Lake like a Stormtrooper in a sea of Browncoats. Many local businesses had picketed it, saying the new, tall façade ruined the historic "skyline" of the retail district around the square, but the City Council persisted and now people cared just as little about the new hall as they had about the old one.

It was my turn now to try to drag the town of White Lake kicking and screaming into the present, and knowing that in a decade no one would care did not make my task seem any easier.

I wore my normal clothes this time, refusing to pretend to be something I wasn't. Vanessa Cleary, the city councilwoman serving as head of the grant committee, met me in the lobby. Alice, the receptionist, gave me a small smile as she touched the bosom of her rainbow-striped sweater, an eye-searing number worthy of Wesley Crusher, and gave me a thumbs-up. My face flared red, and I glanced reflexively down at my T-shirt, just to double-check. All clear. Alice was an old friend of my family—she babysat me when I was little, and my stepmom did her husband's taxes every year, and while her mood was perpetually as bright as her clothes, she had a sensible head on her shoulders. Apparently I should pay attention when she gives me umpire-style signals.

Donald joined us, puffing and red-nosed from the cold. We said little, and Vanessa led us directly to the conference room where we gave our presentations. The room had been rearranged with three tables forming a U-shape. A woman from the Economic Development Commission met us there, but no one else showed, which was probably a very bad sign.

I took a seat toward the center, and the others arrayed themselves around me like I was chairman of the board. My hands trembled, but I kept my voice and face calm. "Thanks for meeting me so early on a Monday," I said.

"We understand it's been a difficult weekend," Vanessa said. She smiled warmly, surprising me. I would have pegged her as the sternest one of the bunch, but she seemed strangely supportive. "We've all been praying for you and for that boy's family."

Oh. One of *those*. That explained the friendliness. "Thanks. Uh, well, I wanted to talk to you about my application. It's been brought to my attention that it may not be in my—or even the program's—best interest if I continued."

I couldn't read Vanessa's expression. The woman from the EDC nodded as if she agreed with me. She exchanged a look with Donald, whose gaze I avoided. I sighed inwardly at that. I'd hoped for more support—and I'd hoped that more of the committee would have been able to make it.

I launched into my carefully prepared speech. "I wanted to talk to you before I made any decisions. I understand the concerns, but I want to keep my name in the grant pool. This project is very important to me, and I think it's in the building's best interest. Additionally, I think receiving this grant would help the building as a whole—not just my store—recover from this weekend's tragedy. Positive action, and action so beneficial for the community, would help us to shine in a retail market that's struggling, even when customers aren't spooked." I took a deep breath. "I also feel like dropping out of the grant process would seem like an admission of guilt—or worse, like my store and I are being punished for events beyond my control. I know there are rumors about the investigation, but I assure you, I believe in the innocence of my shop's community." I met Vanessa's eyes. "We need this vote of confidence."

A little line appeared between her brows as she considered what I'd said. "Well . . ." she said, drawing out the word. "We haven't announced our finalists yet, but we have been discussing this issue over the weekend."

Uh-oh. I didn't like how that sounded. I rushed ahead. "You should know, the community has rallied around us. Our customers have shown nothing but kindness and affection for us, and even those most impacted by Wes's death have shown tremendous loyalty. People want to help. We're thinking of having a memorial for Wes, and I think that will help to alleviate some of the concerns."

"It's not the death itself that concerns us," the woman from the EDC said. "It's the suspicion around some of the other young people associated with your store."

"There's been no arrest," Vanessa said. I shot her a grateful smile.

"No, but it's still horrifying. The idea that these kids may have . . ." the commissioner trailed off, shaking her head. Apparently the end of her sentence was too horrible to speak. I knew what she thought, though: violent game, violent kids. Fictional vampires, delusional vampire wannabes. My heart sank, but the stereotype was all too familiar. She continued. "And now the vandalism at the store of one of the other contestants—even if you didn't do it, Miss Sinclair," she said, noting my indignation, "it reflects very poorly on the sportsmanship of your employees. You may not have known about it, and maybe it didn't relate to this competition, but it looks like a shameful attempt to intimidate one of your competitors. I'm not accusing you, but associations will be made whether anyone says the words or not."

"I'm asking for the benefit of the doubt," I said. "They're innocent until proven guilty. And either way, it's nothing to do with the store."

The woman glowered at me. She should have been wearing a monocle and twirling a Bond-villain mustache. "As much as you might wish it otherwise, Miss Sinclair, everything that happens to its patrons has to do with the store . . . and the building that houses it."

I glanced at Donald. He shifted in his chair, miserable. This was too much for him, would be too much for any landlord. As president of the Chamber of Commerce, Donald was acutely aware of his prominence in the community. And if Ten Again's troubles reflected on his building, that in turn reflected on him, and the Chamber, and on up the chain of association. White Lake was a veritable fun house of distorted reflections, and public perception was as gullible as any eight-year-old at the carnival.

I might as well have worn a red shirt: I was doomed.

"What do you think, Mr. Wolcott?" Vanessa asked.

Donald clasped his hands on the table, then straightened his fingers and refolded them, over and over. I almost pitied him. "Autumn knows my opinion on it."

"And what is that?" Vanessa asked.

"I, erm," he paused, cleared his throat. "I think it would be better for everyone involved if she withdrew from the competition."

There it was. I heaved a sigh but fixed my face into a mask of neutrality. Dismissed before I could even play. Vanessa sat back in her chair, looking unsurprised but oddly disappointed. She nodded. "I had a feeling you might say that." She looked at me. "Without the consent of the building owner, you would not be able to make any of the changes your plan describes."

"Are you withdrawing your consent, Donald?" I glanced up at him sideways.

He did not meet my gaze. "You know I hate to do it."

I nodded. He probably did, if only because confrontation made him gassy. My throat felt thick. I swallowed, but the lump moved to my stomach where it lay like cold iron, weighting me to this grim reality. "I understand," I said. I didn't.

"I'm sorry, Autumn," Vanessa said. Her eyes told me she meant it.

I smiled weakly. "No, I do understand. And there's always next year, right?" If they got the money again. And if my store survived the next year. I stood. "I want to thank you all for your support so far. This has been an educational project, and I hope someday to put everything I've learned to good use."

I shook their hands in turn and let myself out, my eyes burning. I would not cry, would not, not until I reached the safety of my office. I blinked rapidly as the elevator carried me down, slunk by the front desk, avoiding Alice's questions, and flung open the doors onto the sidewalk. The cold air hit my face like a slap. I gasped, taking my first free breath since I'd walked into City Hall.

My heels rapped a slow cadence on the sidewalk as I made my walk of shame back to the store. My heart hurt. I wanted that grant. It hadn't sunk in just how much I'd wanted it, and not just for myself—for the building, for the environment, and most of all, for my store. If I legitimized myself, just a little, by LARPing the grown-up and heading up this project, that would make my store look amazing. It would show that grown-up gamers weren't just stunted adults with Peter Pan complexes: no, we were intelligent, contributing members of our communities who were willing to work for the future, preserving the world and the environment for later generations. I knew it was true, but it seemed like most of the world—including, too often, my own parents—didn't.

For a minute there, it had seemed like I could do it, like I could belong to both worlds. I could be myself and the person my three parents wanted me to be; I could be a geek and a popular kid; I could be a progressive and at the same time preserve one of the world's greatest traditions. I could satisfy everyone

KRISTIN McFARLAND

who looked at me and wanted to see more than they did. I could make a difference, for myself and for my community.

But now, slacker Autumn was back where she started, and nothing was enough.

Thoroughly sorry for myself by then, I wiped at one persistent tear that had escaped from my lids. The dirty cotton clouds spat snowy rain at me as I made my way back to the store. I felt like I'd been battling upstream for Ten Again my whole life: when I graduated from business school and told my mom—my real mom, not my stepmom—that I wanted to move back to White Lake and open a game store, she'd done everything she could, short of staging an intervention, to stop me. My dad had asked for a formal ten-year business plan before agreeing to cosign a small business loan with me. No one had fully supported me but Jordan.

But I'd gotten it all started, anyway.

I slid to a halt on the slushy sidewalk, stumbling like a poorly trained snowtrooper as I realized something. Never before had I let someone tell me what I could or could not do. This was the first time in my entire career that I'd let others' doubts shape my perception of myself. I'd let them put me in a box, tell me I was just a geek, just a store owner, just a businesswoman. What did I know about green technology? Or helping the environment? Or solving murders? But the truth was, even if I didn't know something outright, I had the wits and the enterprise to go and learn and do and make things happen. I'd proved that time and again in my life. The drive and logic and dedication and wits that got me where I am, that helped me start my business and get my feet under me, those qualities were what qualified me to go for these goals. And that didn't just apply to me.

Every gamer in my community had to be smart, decisive, and creative. That's what mattered: those core things, not the way the world viewed our decisions.

No, I couldn't upgrade Donald's building without his consent. And the grant money was the Economic Development Commission's to distribute as they saw fit. But I needed to run my store and support my community in whatever way *I* saw fit. That was my responsibility, and no one else's.

I would do everything I could to protect the kids who visited my store. There were more important things than letting some petty little bureaucrats pat me on the head and tell me I was doing good things for the team. *They* were not my team. Their opinion did not matter. I had to look out for the best interests of my community, my gamers, and my employees, and while the grant was the best way to do that, I'd been willing to pursue it. But now that people were using it as an excuse to judge me, to judge the kids in my store, well, it damn well wasn't worth the effort, whatever anyone on the City Council said.

I started walking again, the tears dried on my face. I had work to do. I needed to focus on keeping my store afloat and my customers feeling safe and happy. And there was no way they could feel safe until we knew who had killed Wes, and why.

10

I KNEW THREE THINGS. Firstly, a gamer had died. Secondly, suspicion had landed squarely on his fellow gamers. Thirdly, someone wanted to scare or look like they had scared Meghan. I could guess at a few other things: whoever had done it was connected to me, the store, or the grant. I was the only common denominator. Maybe Meghan had killed Wes for witnessing her fight with Craig. Maybe Cody had killed Wes and was trying to make the store look bad because things hadn't gone his way. Or maybe, worst of all, Paige and Nick had killed Wes and then blackmailed Meghan to keep silent after she heard their fight.

I needed to talk to Meghan, but after she'd found that gory little diorama on her doorstep, I doubted she would have anything to do with me. Maybe if she knew I was no longer her competitor she'd be more willing to have a conversation. I wanted to believe the murder had something to do with the grant, I really did. Unfortunately, Wes himself had no connection— other than me—to the process. But unless he had managed to witness some secret dealings of the City Council in Independence Square between eight fifteen and eight thirty, the only additional possible connection to the grant was Meghan.

It still didn't add up—a portion of the evening was missing, for everyone involved. Paige and Nick could vouch only for each other. The same was true for Craig and Meghan. Donald had left the building but had seen nothing, heard no one—and he'd left after a mysterious errand to the basement. No one knew where Cody had gotten to after Max had seen him in the lobby. The Independence building wasn't that big. The odds had to be down near zero that someone we didn't know had killed Wes. The simplest explanation was the most likely, right? I may not actually be a Sherlock, but I knew that much. That pointed to Nick and Paige, but I wasn't quite ready to give them up for lost.

I redirected my steps from my own store to the building's front door. I needed to talk to Meghan, and that meant cornering her at Chic. I didn't know her hours, but I knew Monday was very often a delivery and inventory day for retail stores. She might just be there, recovering from the weekend. I ducked under the awning, pulled open the door, and strode into Independence Square Mall's main lobby.

At ten thirty on a Monday, it wasn't crowded. The fountain was operating again, so a steady splashing echoed from the exposed brick walls. One of the part-time security guys sat at Max's desk. He nodded to me as I crossed the lobby and headed down the hallway for Meghan's store. There were few customers here this early, but I saw an elderly woman browsing in the gift shop, and a young woman with a baby strapped to her chest waited outside the old-fashioned barber's shop. I caught a glimpse of a man in the chair chatting with the elderly barber. It looked like a scene from a nostalgic TV show, like the Independence Square Mall was the set of some old-timey comedy. Any minute now, a kitten would get stuck in a tree, and there'd be a comedic misunderstanding about who would save it.

Maybe people were right, and Ten Again didn't fit in here. I tried to quell the thought, but no matter what I did, it kept recurring. Donald worried about how we affected his image, and I worried that gamers weren't welcome here. I wasn't ready to give up, not yet, but it seemed like the deck was stacked against me, and the dealer wanted me out.

The little bell on the door to Chic tinkled as I pushed my way in. It was not a clothing store in which I would have chosen to shop. Instead of colorful piles of clothing, it had sleek wooden fixtures, silver trim, and stark, recessed lighting. Few sizes were displayed, and even the headless mannequin standing beside the door, creepy as a *Doctor Who* prop, seemed judgmental.

Meghan wasn't at the counter. One of her employees, a young woman with sleek black hair, came toward me. "Excuse me, ma'am, but you shouldn't be here," she said.

"Excuse me?" I stopped beside the mannequin. "You're kicking me out?"

The girl stopped about ten feet from me, one hand on her cocked hip. She held a cordless phone in her hand. "That's right. I have strict orders from Ms. Kountz to keep you out."

I held up my hands like the cops had a gun trained on me. "I just want to talk to her—"

"She's not here, and, no, I won't take a message. She has nothing to say to you. The police told her not to talk to you, and we're all supposed to report any suspicious visitors."

Well, that was too much. I dropped my hands to my hips. "I'm not a 'suspicious visitor,' I know Meghan, and I work in the building—"

"I know who you are, and you're definitely not supposed to be here. Now, please leave, before I call security."

"What, you're going to call the part-time rent-a-cop? He just saw me, he knows I'm not a vandal."

The girl pressed a button on the phone and lifted it to her ear. "Hello, security?"

"Fine, fine!" I took a step back, then another. The girl hung up the phone, looking smug, and I would have bet good money that she never even dialed. "What's Meghan trying to hide, anyway?" I snapped.

The girl's face reddened. "You have no idea what you're talking about." She started pressing buttons on the phone, and I beat a hasty exit, letting the door slam behind me.

That was odd. I got that Meghan didn't want me around, but I was surprised she'd ordered her employees to shoot me on sight. Maybe she was hiding something, though I couldn't imagine what. I wondered if the girl knew anything about Meghan's arguments with Craig—not that I would be able to get close enough to her to ask any questions.

Freaking small towns. No one trusted anyone enough to just casually open up to a stranger. No matter who you talked to, they knew someone you knew or who knew you. My reputation always preceded me, for better or worse. And in this case, every roll for reputation had a minus-four penalty.

I made my way back toward the lobby, planning to see if Meghan's employee really had called the security desk. If a janitor hadn't come out of the stairwell at the exact moment I passed by, I never would have heard Paige's voice, thick with tears, ringing in the empty stairwell.

I stopped and turned on the spot, startling the janitor. I smiled at him as I pushed by him and kept the door from falling shut. I held it open just wide enough to squeeze through and darted inside.

"I don't want to do this," Paige said below me.

"You know what will happen if we don't. He saw us—he saw the blood." I sucked in my breath, shocked. Something told me they weren't playing a scene now. Nick continued, his voice unmistakable. "He knows. It's enough to land us in jail."

"I don't think he does know—and even if he does, he doesn't know what happened."

"He wasn't dead, Nick," Paige gasped. "Maybe if we had done something else—"

"Shh," Nick said. "You can't go down that road. For now, we just need to be very careful and do what he says."

"What if they arrest us? They think it's us. We shouldn't have called Autumn, and if they knew we were here now, we'd be in even bigger trouble. Maybe we should tell her—" I flinched at my own name, but they were speaking so rapidly I had no time to react.

"That's a bad idea. We don't want to get her in trouble, too."

"What do you think he knows?" Paige whispered.

"Too much. If Autumn knew, though, she would have done something by now."

"If we came forward, maybe he would go to jail."

"For what? He didn't do it. We know he didn't, because he was there—"

"Ugh, fine. I don't want to talk about it anymore." I could picture Paige throwing up her hands. "I wish we'd never gotten involved in this."

They began to move up the stairs. I didn't know if I wanted them to see me, to know I'd overheard their strange conversation. I hardly even knew what I'd heard, and I needed time to process it before I could feel ready to confront them. I leapt up a few stairs, moving with exaggerated care, like a cross between a ninja and a mime, placing my feet so my shoes wouldn't make noise on the ancient flooring. It figured that the one time I managed to be stealthy, no one was there to witness it—though I supposed that was the point.

They departed the stairwell on the main floor, where I'd been standing. When the door shut behind them, I lingered, trying to catch my breath. I hadn't learned anything new, not really, but their secrecy shocked and frightened me. What were they hiding? I knew I should tell someone about their conversation, but I didn't want them to get arrested—and while I didn't think they had killed Wes, that conversation was deeply incriminating.

My mission to talk to Meghan forgotten, I trailed down the steps one by one, looking around me as if the empty stairwell could give me some clue as to the couple's activities. Whatever they were about, they had left no trace of it in the hallway, but I felt a miasma of unpleasantness filling the air where they'd been. I did not want to doubt my people. But they were making it harder and harder to trust them.

I opened the door to the basement and began my bemused, solitary walk back to the store. Should I tell Jordan? Should I *not* tell Jordan in an effort to keep this from the police? Would that get me in trouble? I resisted the urge to beat my head against the wall of the hallway. Down the hall, I could hear the fountain gurgling softly, but this time it failed to calm me.

I should have gone to talk to Meghan. I should never have followed Paige's voice. I should have done anything but try to play investigator. My hands were tied, now—either I was covering up for them, or I was ratting them out. I didn't like either option.

My steps slowed as I reached my own door. There was something lying on the ground outside the door, something that made my breath catch.

Someone had spilled something red outside my door, paint or red corn syrup. A doll or an action figure—I couldn't tell, down the dim hallway—lay in the middle of the puddle, something impaling the join of its head and neck. The *lub-lub-lub* of my heart pounding grew louder as I approached the sticky puddle.

It was an action figure of Princess Leia, her brown hair twisted into buns over her ears, her white dress smeared red. Someone had stuck a broken plastic sword onto her neck with clay or red-colored glue, and her head twisted at an unnatural angle to look over her own shoulder.

There's way too much blood, I thought irrationally.

When I looked up from the twisted little diorama, I saw that someone had painted onto the store's door, *GIVE IT UP, BITCH.*

I stifled a shriek, emitting a squeak instead, like a mouse in a trap. Through the window I could see Bay standing at the register, sorting through a stack of invoices for an order that had come in while I was off eavesdropping on Nick and Paige.

She had no idea what had happened right outside our door. I didn't know whether to be frightened by or grateful for her ignorance.

Had Nick and Paige done this? My stomach churned at the thought. Was this what Paige hadn't wanted to do? I had heard them arguing in a stairwell mere yards from my store, and, from the sound of it, they were concealing evidence. Now here was proof someone didn't want me looking into the murder—

Unless it was someone who didn't want me in the grant competition, someone who didn't yet know that I'd been kicked out. Someone like Meghan, who wasn't in her store. That would add up if she'd been the culprit of the vandalism at her own store, but I had no reason beyond my own wishful thinking to lead me to believe that.

But now the drama had hit close to home. This wasn't just the death of a gamer: this was about me, my store. I realized my hands were shaking, and I felt a little weak in the knees. No one had actively threatened me before, some small, rational part of my brain observed, and I couldn't say the feeling was a good one.

I stepped around the mess and pushed the door open. At the register, Bay looked up. Her eyes widened when she saw me. "Autumn, what's wrong? Did they make you drop out of the grant competition?"

"Yes, but that's—" I broke off, shaking my head. "Was there anyone in here? Did you see anyone?" I started to stride toward her, but a piece of paper on the floor caught my eye. I bent down to pick it up.

It was another *Spellcasters* card, the Queen of the Fey. Her face was scratched off. Someone had tucked her in through the old-fashioned mail slot in the store's mall door. I shuddered but left the card on the ground where it lay. It might have prints on it, and, unfortunately, it was time to report these ghoulish shenanigans.

"What is it?" Bay asked, coming toward me.

"There's been—someone's been outside. There's some vandalism."

"What?" She pushed past me, opened the door, and looked. "Oh my god."

"I know." I pointed to the card. "There's that, too. There's been more than one of these. I don't know if they're related—I thought the cards were for Wes. But now . . ."

"I'll call the cops." Bay started to jog toward the register, but I grabbed her sleeve.

"Wait," I said. I told her what I'd heard, about Paige and Nick. As I spoke, her face creased with worry, her blue eyes narrowing with anger and fear. She looked as troubled as I felt. "If we call the cops about this, I'm going to have to tell them what I heard. I'll be as good as handing them Paige and Nick for Wes's murder, and I still don't think they did it."

She pulled herself free and put her hands on my shoulders. "Autumn, you have to call the cops. This is a threat to you, to the store, and after what has already happened, we can't ignore that. It makes me sick, but if they hurt Wes, and we've been protecting them . . . Well, if the police don't lock them up, they'd better find a safe place to go." She flexed her fingers.

"What do you think Wes 'knew'?" I asked, quoting Paige. "What could he have known that would make me do something if I knew it, too?"

"I have no idea, but we're unqualified to answer that question. I think this is bigger than just a lovers' quarrel, especially if they're threatening you and Meghan now, too. We need to get the cops on this."

I couldn't argue with her no-nonsense pragmatism. I let her go, and she went to make the call.

11

I WATCHED, POWERLESS, AS my life became an episode of a police procedural.

Jordan was on duty, and she came with the beat cops to check out the scene of Princess Leia's murder. Detective Keller trailed behind her like a sullen teen, absorbing everything while simultaneously trying to look cool and uninterested. The cops traipsed back and forth across the hardwood floors, the knight in shining armor guarding the old-fashioned games and some kids' costuming kits, a silent witness to the action. Jordan paused beside me as the others gathered up the action figure, the card, and samples of the fake blood. She looked like she wanted to talk, but words never seemed to come, and she just lurked beside me, unspeaking as the knight.

They ransacked the memorial the others had left for Wes on the front sidewalk. Bay watched with wide eyes, a hand pressed to her mouth, while I stood by and let it happen. Jordan asked, when they started, why I hadn't mentioned the scratched off

Spellcasters cards, and I explained that it hadn't occurred to me that the cards might have some sinister meaning. She gave me a pitying look and handed each of the cards to a gloved officer collecting evidence.

By the time they finished, the shop looked like a crime lab. Uniformed officers dusted for prints by the scene of Princess Leia's demise; others scrutinized the shop for any other stray *Spellcasters* cards, hairs, toenail clippings, or anything else they could use to get DNA from the mystery vandals. The size and quantity of dust bunnies they uncovered beneath some of the racks made me realize I needed to establish stricter cleaning-at-close policies with my employees, but now didn't seem like the time to mention it.

They insisted I come down to the station, and I felt as if I were being packed up and carted away like just another piece of evidence. Bay came, too, and we locked up the store during business hours yet again. Monday afternoon wasn't exactly a busy time, but it was still cutting into my business. Pretty soon, Donald would get his wish, and the store would shut down, if only because I couldn't manage to keep my employees in it for more than twenty minutes at a time. That was the least of my worries, however—Detective Keller dragged me back to the little room where she'd first interrogated me, leaving me to stare blankly at myself in the mirror that filled one wall.

Was anyone on the other side of it? Was some poor, under-paid cop staring at me now, wondering if my Starfleet T-shirt had some deeper meaning? I pulled a dreadful face at the mirror, irritated that they hadn't let me put my store back together after their invasion.

As soon as I made the face, the door opened, and I scrambled
to rearrange my expression. Detective Keller looked distinctly
unamused as she came to sit across from me at the table. She
dropped a folder containing a thick stack of papers before her,
just like in the movies. I wondered what they said—I'd never
even had a parking ticket, so she could hardly pretend it was my
criminal record.

"Well, we're seeing a lot of you, aren't we, Miss Sinclair?" she
asked in a fake-cheerful tone.

"Yep. Can't stay away."

"Were you aware this is the second act of vandalism we've
seen in your building in as many days?"

I leaned back in my chair like Han Solo in the cantina,
striving for indifference.

"I'd heard something to that effect, yes." I wished I had a
cigarette or something, some cool tic to underline my studied
devil-may-care attitude. This day had gone from crap to shit
really fast, and I might as well play the part of the hardened
criminal. My sense of humor had died with that action figure's
dignity. My chair wobbled a little as my confidence ebbed.

"Yes, we had another similar scene at the store called Chic,"
the detective said as if I hadn't spoken. She opened her folder
and drew out a photo like the one I'd seen on Meghan's phone,
showing the medieval princess's drawn and quartered form.
I supposed I was lucky, meriting Princess Leia rather than
generic damsel in distress. That was comforting, in a really
sick sort of way.

Detective Keller had understated the "similarity." The scene
at Meghan's was exactly like what I'd found, right down to the
corn-syrupy blood and the wording of the message. Whoever

was insulting us wasn't very creative in their derogatory terms for "woman." The blood looked a lot like what high school productions and—alas—LARPers might use for prop wounds. That didn't look good for Nick and Paige.

I thumped the legs of my chair back down and grimaced at the photo. "Yes, I've seen it."

"You have?" Detective Keller asked, excited.

"Meghan showed me a picture."

"I see." She scribbled something on a notepad. "Had you ever seen anything like this before?"

"Murdered action figures? No. The blood looks like stage blood to me, but that's not a huge leap. And as for the *Spellcasters* cards, no, I've never seen anyone do that before. Those cards are collectible, so I meet more people who keep them wrapped in plastic than people who would ever deface them."

"Your attitude is very . . . nonchalant."

Oh, she was playing good cop, being my counselor and not my confessor. "I'm sorry," I said. I almost was. "This has been a rough day already, and levity is my coping mechanism. I'm worried about my store and my employees. Whoever did this set it up without Bay—Bailey Adorno, that is, my employee— ever realizing they were there. It's frightening, because it's probably someone we know who has permission to be in the building."

The detective wrote all this down, then looked up at me, her expression serious. "I understand that in addition to the vandalism, you wanted to report some suspicious behavior."

I sighed, feeling like a narc. "Yeah, that." I told her about Nick and Paige's conversation, repeating it as near word-for-word as I could.

She listened intently, writing nothing down, which gave me the bad feeling I'd be telling the story several more times over the next hour. "You never saw them?" she asked.

"No." For better or worse, my ninja act had kept me from ever seeing their faces—or whether they carried buckets of fake blood and a sheaf of damaged *Spellcasters* cards.

"And, in your opinion, they suggested they had something to hide?"

"Yes."

"Did you get any sense of what they thought Wesley might have been hiding? Since they seemed to think knowing that information might have driven you to act?"

"Not a clue."

"Do you have any guesses?"

"No," I said. "I have no idea what they meant."

Detective Keller frowned. "Let's talk about that phone call Miss Harding and Mr. Lawlis made to you the night of the murder."

"What about it?"

"Miss Harding said she needed your help."

"Yes."

"And shortly after, Mr. Lawlis said it was all just a misunderstanding."

"Yes . . ." I didn't like the turn this had taken, but I was the victim this time, and I needed the cops on my side.

"Do you think it's possible, Miss Sinclair, that Miss Harding called you after realizing Mr. Lawlis had killed Wesley Bowen? And she wanted your help?"

Clearly, good cop had gone home for the night. I pulled back from the table. "Wait, what? No—is this a trial? Because

I thought this was about the vandalism at my store. I'm trying to help here."

Detective Keller smiled and stood up. She linked her hands behind her back and leaned casually over the table. "Of course you are," she said in a patronizing tone that made my attitude go from sour to downright curdled. "Earlier today, you said Miss Harding told Mr. Lawlis she, quote, 'Didn't want to do this.' Do you think 'this,' might have been hiding their guilt? Are these acts of vandalism a way of threatening the people who might have known about their guilt?"

"No, I—I have no idea. You know I can't answer that," I snapped.

She drummed on her chin with one finger, as if thinking. "Is that because you've been helping them to hide the evidence of their guilt?" She dropped her hand, all pretense of consideration gone.

"I am not answering that," I said. I wasn't a complete idiot.

"Your store sells stage blood, Miss Sinclair," she said, taking a sudden left.

I blinked, stunned—we did, in stupid little costume kits in the kids' section. She actually managed to surprise a real answer out of me this time. "Not the kind that would make pints of liquid fake blood, like the person who vandalized my store used. The stuff we sell is just for accent, for kids or—" Or LARPers.

The detective smiled, like she knew the end of that sentence. "Did you threaten Meghan Kountz, Miss Sinclair?"

"Excuse me?"

"Answer the question."

"Absolutely not," I said, fuming. This was too far. "I want a lawyer. I will not speak any more until I've had access to a phone." I folded my arms across my chest, as if that would keep the words in.

"I understand you and Miss Kountz have been longtime competitors, and now there's this grant contest you two have been involved in. Miss Kountz said you were asked by your landlord yesterday to drop out of the race—she was worried that the vandalism might have been an act of aggression by you or your employees, meant as revenge for that request. But now—" Detective Keller leaned over me, murmuring in my ear. "I wonder if maybe it wasn't just revenge for that— maybe you know some of your friends killed Wesley Bowen, and you've been helping them cover it up. Maybe you're trying to pin the murder on Miss Kountz just because she has things you want."

I scooted my chair an inch away, trying to get out from under her Ronan the Accuser glare.

"She has your ex-boyfriend. A successful store in the same building as you. She's your top competitor for the grant money. Maybe you thought when your gamers came to you for help, it was the perfect opportunity to help yourself and them at the same time. If you raised suspicions about her role in the murder, you would get everything you wanted. She heard your friends arguing that night, you know. She's a key witness. They—and you—would have every reason to slander her." She dragged one of the other chairs over next to me and sat down, like we were pals sitting in the park. "Aiding and abetting is a serious crime, you know. We're aware of your attempts to 'investigate' this crime yourself, and interfering with a legitimate police investigation is also a serious crime. But if you wanted to tell us what happened, we'd be much easier on you—if you just help us to arrest Mr. Lawlis and Miss Harding, we will be much more forgiving of your role in all this."

I sucked in a breath through my nose, still refusing to speak. I had not expected this interview to go like this, had not anticipated any of this. I had to admit, it didn't look good. I hadn't bungled the police investigation like Jordan feared I would, but I had bungled my own alibi and visible innocence.

Fortunately, a dozen people could attest that I'd never left the shop the night Wes died, had seen that I hadn't gone to help Paige and Nick. Unfortunately, there were vast swathes of time when I was at home, alone, and no one could confirm that I wasn't spending those hours sneaking off to conspire with my friends. It was a convenient story, and it would make Detective Keller's job much easier. If I told a nice story about how the horrible gamers had killed Wes and tempted me down the dark path into covering it up, well, there was a neat case and a great headline. They could even make it look like I was an innocent victim, too.

"It doesn't look good if you won't talk to us," Detective Keller said.

I looked over at her. "You're speculating. And you know as well as I do that I shouldn't talk without my lawyer. Now, do I get my phone call, or do you want to keep telling me that story?"

She waved a hand. "Your dad's on his way."

"Does he know you've been detaining me?"

"This isn't Guantanamo Bay, Miss Sinclair. He'll be here any minute."

I shouldn't have gotten involved. Any moron would have been able to tell me that. Jordan already had. At this rate, I was going to end up the Ned Stark of my own fumbling research, unemployed if not decapitated, and the people I loved left to pick up the pieces—literally.

But I wondered why the vandalism at my store had been the tipping point—had something else happened that had suddenly put me under suspicion? Had there been something else at Meghan's store that had led them to believe it was me? I shouldn't have gone there that morning. Her employee had probably called Meghan as soon as I left, and Meghan in turn had called the cops. That made sense: when the new vandalism popped up right around the same time, the cops decided it was time to bring me in, scare me straight.

That totally hangs together, I told myself.

Too bad I didn't believe it.

The door banged open, saving me from any further existential crises of self-doubt. My dad stormed in, angry tax attorney attitude dialed to eleven. You don't mess with Ronald Sinclair or his clients—and his daughter was another matter entirely.

"How long have you detained this woman?" he asked Detective Keller.

"About forty-five minutes," the detective said, unperturbed.

"And do you have any cause for detaining her? A warrant?"

"She came in voluntarily."

"After her store was vandalized—she reported a crime, she didn't commit one." My dad hauled me out of the chair. "Come on, Autumn, this is ridiculous." He pointed a finger at Detective Keller. "I'll be reporting this to your supervisor. You've been interrogating her without a lawyer. You'll be lucky if you're not thrown off this case."

Wow. Thanks, Dad. I trotted after him as he stalked out of the little interrogation room. Detective Keller called over my shoulder, "Don't leave town!" and my father waved a dismissive hand back at her.

He didn't slow as he began walking me back to Independence Square Mall.

"Why were they keeping you?" he asked, his breath puffing in the cold air.

"Uh, they think I've been helping two of the gamers cover up their part in the murder—oh, and that I vandalized Meghan's store to scare her out of the grant running. And maybe to frame her? Detective Keller was pretty unclear."

"Does she think you vandalized your own store?"

"Yep."

"That's an awful lot to prove."

"I know, right?" I took a giant step over a frozen puddle on the sidewalk in front of City Hall. "They've got nothing."

"That's almost certainly true, but they're fishing."

"Why do you think they want to say I'm framing Meghan?"

My dad stopped walking, and I almost ran into him. No one else stood on the sidewalk, and tiny pellets of frozen rain hit our coats. "Why do *you* think they want to say you're framing Meghan?" my dad asked.

"Well, you know, the usual. Old drama, the grant stuff, mutual dislike. Plus, I sell that fake blood in my store. It's convenient."

"What do you know about the vandalism that happened at Meghan's store?" He started walking again, more slowly this time.

"I saw a photo, not much more. There was a broken doll, some fake blood, a message. 'You're next, bitch.' It was pretty similar to what was at my store."

My dad glanced at me. "Uh-huh. And where were you when it happened?"

"That's the trouble—I was at Craig's."

"Craig's—Meghan's Craig?"

"Yep."

"Huh." My dad fell silent, striding past the jewelry store and the big antique store that took up two store fronts on the east side of the square. An old woman passed us, her head wrapped in a flowery scarf that didn't look warm enough by half. Everyone wanted to pretend it was spring, but winter still had us tight in its grip.

"What?" I asked. I was breathless from the cold, from half-jogging to keep up with him, and surprised at his intrepidness: Ronald Sinclair, closet Keith Mars. "What are you thinking?"

"Well, Meghan wouldn't like that, would she?"

"No, but how could she have known?"

"That's the question, isn't it?" We stopped for a crosswalk, watching the traffic whiz by, heading toward campus. "If someone set it up, it's someone who knows a lot about you and Meghan's history. Who would know that but also know your gamers? Who would have a reason to harm one of them?"

"I have no idea. No one could have had any reason to harm Wes. He was the world's most inoffensive kid."

"You think? There was nothing he could have known, nothing he could have seen?"

"I don't know. We haven't been able to account for at least twenty minutes that last night. He did overhear Meghan and Craig arguing. But Craig was with me when Meghan's shop was vandalized. And he was with Donald the night of the murder."

The little green man on our light lit up, and my dad led me across the road at a jog. "What about the gamers? Do any of them know about your rivalry with Meghan?"

"Probably. It's not exactly a secret. Everyone knows about the grant stuff."

We came to a halt on the other side of the intersection, the awning of Independence Square Mall mere yards away. My dad rubbed a hand over his forehead. "I know you don't want to admit it, Autumn, but it might very well have been some of your customers who killed that boy, who have set all of this up. Who else would know what to use? You've been getting cards from some game, right, with the faces scratched off? Those aren't well-known items."

"There wasn't one at Meghan's, though." And maybe *Spellcasters* wasn't well known, but the cards were hardly specialty items: you could buy them at any big box store, even some grocery stores. But they probably looked unusual, even highly specific, to someone who didn't know our world well, to someone like my dad. Or to someone like Meghan.

"Maybe because she wouldn't get it," my dad said, as if on cue.

And I had to admit, maybe he was right—maybe I was looking for a more complicated explanation when logic said the simplest one would do. Maybe Paige and Nick were just guilty, period.

12

BACK AT THE STORE, Bay and Hector were repairing the mess the cops had left when they came to investigate the vandalism. The fake blood was gone, the scrawled words on the door erased. Someone had put Wes's memorial back together, more or less, but it seemed like a mockery now, especially since I knew it had been hiding a threat to me and my store.

Hector wasn't even supposed to be there on a Monday—he had to be skipping class. I put the closed sign in the door and called them both to join me at the register. Bay had filled Hector in on the vandalism, but I told them both about the cops' new suspicions.

"Wait," Hector said. "Those *Spellcasters* cards were supposed to be threats?"

"Apparently. Autumn queen and all."

"So—what, the samurai knight was me?" He snorted. "Dude, I'm not even Japanese. That's so racist."

"Beside the point, Hector," Bay said. She rounded on me. "Does this mean you're a suspect now?"

"Not officially, no. But I'm pretty sure they want me to turn on Nick and Paige. Those two look the most suspicious, and it would get this case off their laps. If they pressure me enough, maybe I'll cave and hand them a real suspect."

"They can't have enough evidence," Bay said. "Especially if they're forcing you to fabricate some."

"What does Jordan have to say about all this?" Hector asked.

"I have no idea. I haven't seen her. But she did warn me not to get involved with the investigation."

"Do you think they're punishing you for it or something?"

"No. Not really. I think they're just desperate for a lead, and Nick and Paige are the best they have."

"What about Cody?" Hector said. "We still have no idea what he was up to that night."

"It's a good point," Bay said.

They both looked at me so hopefully, their young Padawan faces alight with the zeal of the just. They wanted to prove their friends innocent just as much as I had—did—but I was losing hope. A part of me just wanted to give up on finding out anything more about Wes's death, to leave the investigation to the professionals, to focus on keeping the shop in business and nothing more.

Cody was a convenient alternative to the police's theory about Nick and Paige, but I had no idea how we'd learn anything more about his whereabouts without inventing some sort of truth serum to make him fess up.

"If you guys want to talk to him, I say go for it." Couldn't hurt. Probably.

Hector beamed. "Excellent."

Bay was not so easily satisfied. "What are you going to do?"

"Nothing. I'm going to get the store cleaned up, I'm going to call Wes's parents and plan a little memorial party, I'm going to figure out what companies we need reorders from, and then I'm going to pay the electric bill."

"What about the grant?"

I shrugged. "That's done with, unfortunately. I think all I can do for now is try to keep myself out of jail."

"What about our investigation?" Hector asked.

I bit back a snarl. The investigation seemed to be hurting more than it was helping. Our attempts to investigate—so far— had yielded nothing. All we had learned was that two couples had been fighting the night Wes died, and that whoever had committed the murder wasn't afraid to threaten others to cover his tracks.

My despair must have shown on my face because Hector's merriment faded. "You want to give up, don't you?"

"Shut up, Hector," Bay hissed. "She's just having a shit day."

He didn't tell her to put a dollar in the jar. They both stared at me, looking like kids who had seen through the wizard's giant illusion face to the man pulling the levers. My shoulders slumped. "Guys, I just don't see the point anymore. I won't make up a story for the cops, but I think maybe it's time we stop trying to protect Paige and Nick. Wes is dead. We can't change that. And, unfortunately, even if we don't want to believe it, we may have been protecting his killer all this time."

"You don't believe that," Hector said.

"It doesn't matter what I believe. I have to put this store before anything else. If I get in trouble, the store goes down, too. You two would be out of a job, and there would be no game store nearer than Milwaukee. That's not what I want."

"It's not what we want, either," Bay said.

"But—Cody," Hector said. "And Meghan. You know there are other possibilities. It wasn't Paige and Nick."

"If we know it, the cops know it, too," I said. "There must be some reason they think it was Paige and Nick, some piece of evidence or some part of the time line we don't know about. They're not complete idiots, whatever Jordan says about her coworkers sometimes, and we have to trust that they'll do the right thing."

"The grant board didn't do the right thing," Bay said, as if that was evidence that the police also wouldn't do the right thing.

"Maybe not. But I think the jig is up. I'm not sure what else we can do." I tried to put an authoritative note of finality in my voice, to close the conversation for good, but I felt as though my willpower had been snapped with poor Princess Leia's neck. Unfortunately, I could feel irrational anger stepping in to take its place. This day had pushed me about as far as I was willing to be pushed.

"There's plenty we can do," Hector said stubbornly. "We're not going to let them make you into some kind of scapegoat."

I opened my mouth to reply, but his words cut me deep. They wanted to protect me as much as I wanted to protect them. Maybe I wasn't as alone in this as I felt.

Someone knocked on the mall door at that moment, sparing me from having to say something sappy.

It was Donald. Great. I trotted to the door and turned the locks. Donald swallowed repeatedly as he waited, and when I opened the door, he stepped through sheepishly, his hands thrust in his pockets, looking as out of place as a *Twilight* fan at a *Buffy* convention. "Hello, Autumn," he said.

"Donald." Frost rimmed my voice. I would not forget his failure to stand up for me in the morning's meeting.

"I see everything has been cleaned up out in the hallway," he said lamely. His eyes scanned the store, taking note of the hastily rearranged shelves, the items stacked on the floor, the dust bunnies holding court where a large shelf had once stood. "Did the police get what they needed from in here?"

"I think so."

Bay and Hector lingered at the register. Bay's eyes were wide, but Hector's narrowed visibly as he took in Donald's uncomfortable appearance.

"This whole thing has gotten—ugly."

"I'll say. It's cutting into my business now. We've been closed since it happened."

Donald cleared his throat. "About that."

Shit. I knew this was coming. Panicking, I said, "Why don't we step into my office?" At least I could spare Bay and Hector an argument they wouldn't win.

Donald nodded. He followed me around the mess. I tried to give my employees a reassuring smile as I opened the office door, but it came off more sickly than confident. I stepped into my small, messy office. Donald followed, looking painfully awkward.

"You want me to close," I said.

"Not permanently," he said defensively. "Just—for a week or so while the police finish their investigation."

I crossed my arms over my chest. "Why, in particular?"

"You'll find in your lease, there's a clause about maintaining safe conditions in the space. It gives me, the landlord, permission to close your store if—"

I waved a hand. "No. I mean, why. Why now? What pushed you to make this decision?"

He swallowed convulsively. "Well, the vandalism."

"Now that I'm a victim, you want me to shut down?"

"It's not that—well, people hear rumors, and there's always been animosity between you and Meghan—"

I threw up my hands. "So, naturally, everyone assumes I vandalized my own store to make myself look innocent." I realized I was pointing at myself, and I dropped my arms to my sides, clenching my fists to keep myself under control. "You actually think, Donald, that I would do something like that? Why does no one think Meghan did it, that I'm the one being framed here? One of my customers, my friends, is dead."

"I've thought of that," Donald stammered. "Believe me. That's what I mean, about the safety of the store. If you are being targeted, that means more things could happen—you and your customers are not safe!"

I took a long, shaky breath. "Donald, I won't be safe if you shut me down, even for a week. This was supposed to be one of my best months this year, and you're cutting my business altogether. I will sink. Especially if word gets around that I've been shut down because you—and the police—think I'm going around threatening people, abetting murder." Really, his opinion

mattered as much as the cops' did. Donald ran the White Lake
small business community: he headed the Chamber of Commerce, he organized the studio walks and craft fairs, he hung
the Small Business Saturday banner across Main Street every
year on Black Friday. Without his support, I was dead, no saving
throw.

"I'm sorry, Autumn. You know I don't want to do this, but
I'm under a lot of pressure—" He broke off, swallowing. "You're
not the only one who will suffer," he told me again.

I wanted to punch him, but instead I counted to five, slowly,
in my head: one-Mississippi, two-Mississippi. As I fought
to stifle my hissy fit, though, I sorted through the situation.
Donald was under pressure. Meghan didn't have to close her
store, even though she'd been threatened, too. Our little private investigation had been busted by the cops. Someone had
threatened me, my business. The committee kicked me off the
grant program. And now Donald was forcing me to close up, to
get out of the building until things settled down.

Someone was covering something up, and I needed to know
what. Maybe I'd come too close to something. Maybe Wes had,
too. Hector was right: there was plenty more we could do, and
scapegoat wasn't quite ready to be spitted for the fire.

"What about the memorial?" I kept my voice calm.

"Hmm?"

"We were planning a memorial for Wes. I'd hate to cancel
that. It seems disrespectful."

Donald hesitated, then shook his head. "I don't think it's a
good idea under the circumstances."

I nodded. "Okay." That was all the permission I needed. "I
guess that's that."

"I hope you understand, Autumn. I am doing what I think is best."

"I know you are." I opened the door to let him out. "We'll just clear up the mess here and then take a few days."

"Good, good. Hopefully things will move quickly, and you can reopen soon. I'll stay in touch."

"Thanks, Donald." I couldn't keep a note of sarcasm from my voice, but I walked him out like a good girl. He apologized the whole way, even when I shut the door in his face. He could apologize to my hastily scrubbed door if he wanted, see if it understood any better than I did.

When I turned back to the counter, Bay and Hector looked livid.

"They're shutting us down," Bay said.

"Yep."

"For how long?"

"Indefinitely—a few days, a week? It's in my lease that Donald can. He says it's for the safety of my customers."

"Bullshit," Hector said. No one said a word about the swear jar.

"What are we going to do?" Bay asked.

"We're going to close," I said. "Sort of."

"Sort of?"

"We have other things to do—people to investigate, leads to follow, a memorial to throw."

Hector's face lit up. "We're going to keep trying."

"Damn skippy," I said.

"Are you sure this is a good idea?" Bay looked like she wanted to be excited, like she wanted to jump on board, but she also looked like she feared I'd been possessed by a demon.

"No. But I think something bigger is going on, something we didn't know about." I told them what I'd realized, that everything seemed connected: the grant, the murder, the vandalism. I was at the center of it, but not for the reason the cops thought. Our little attempts to investigate had pissed someone off, and that told me we'd been doing something right, even if we weren't doing it well.

"You think all of this is about the grant money, then?" Bay said.

"Maybe. Not necessarily, but maybe. They say money and sex are behind most murders, right—well, there's money mixed up in all this." Not that twenty-five thousand dollars was enough to murder someone over, but it was more than enough to make or break a small business. "I've been thinking—Donald has been mixed up in all of this since the very beginning. And he was here the night of the murder. So was Meghan. What if, somehow, they met, and they were talking about trying to fix the grant process or something? Donald wants the money for his building. We know from Craig that he's wanting to make some other investments. What if Wes overheard the two of them—Meghan and Donald—conspiring?"

"Meghan and Craig were arguing that night, too," Hector said. "Maybe it was them."

I shook my head. "No, we know Craig left. Max saw him."

"He saw Donald, too," Bay objected.

"Yeah, but no one else saw Donald that night, remember? He lives alone. And he goes everywhere in this building. He has keys. Max just saw him on the main floor. He could have left and come back or taken the maintenance elevator."

"I'm not sure that hangs together." Bay bit her lip. "Look, Autumn, I'm all for figuring this out, but I just don't see how Donald could have committed the murder. I know he's giving us a rough time, but he's no Voldemort."

"Maybe Meghan did it, and Donald's helping her cover it up," Hector said, ignoring her. "He's the only one with access to the building at all times. And he's always here—he could have vandalized the shop at any point."

"We don't need to prove he did it," I said. "Just that he had motive, remember? And he's been weird about this stuff from the beginning."

"What do we need to do?" Hector asked.

"Well, I have some ideas. We need to check into Donald's whereabouts that night. I'll ask Craig if he actually saw Donald leave. And we need to get into Meghan's store—she definitely didn't want me in there. Maybe she's hiding something."

"Do we need to worry about you getting arrested?" Bay's tone was light, but her eyes were serious.

"I don't think so—Jordan can protect me. Anyway, you guys know I didn't murder Wes. I was here the whole time. I'm not really a suspect. Detective Keller just wanted to scare me." I was totally bluffing. Jordan wouldn't be able to protect me without jeopardizing her job, and I wouldn't ask that of her. And Detective Keller had succeeded in scaring me—but that was before Donald pissed me off. I wouldn't let an old bully cow me into submission, especially when my store, my dream was on the line.

"You still want to have the memorial?" Bay said.

"More now than ever," I said. "We need to invite everyone, talk to everyone. And it'll be a good cover for doing some investigating. If we have it during late business hours, someone could probably sneak down to Meghan's shop later in the night."

"Donald will be pissed."

"Yeah, but he won't want to upset people by saying we can't have a memorial. Everyone would hate him, and that's so not what he wants."

"We should invite Cody," Hector said.

Bay and I both turned to stare at him. "Why on earth would we do that?"

Hector shrugged. "I still think he's up to something. Maybe he's the one working with Meghan if Donald isn't. He could be doing the vandalism. And no one knows where he was when Wes died. Plus, he's just weird. Sneaky-like, you know?" He narrowed his eyes suggestively.

"Um . . ." Bay and I grinned at each other. "How about you pursue that lead?" I said. Hector nodded, oblivious to our mockery.

"So, first, we plan that memorial for tomorrow. After that, we pursue Meghan and Donald—and Cody, I guess, since Hector wants him to be a villain."

"He *is* a villain," Hector said. "I'm telling you. Ever since that game, he's been acting even shadier than usual. And whoever has been vandalizing the store knows how to mess with us. Donald wouldn't know a *Spellcasters* card from a birthday card. Plus, he never gave anyone a solid alibi."

There was a long pause as Bay and I both stared at him. She turned to me and said, "He may have a point, actually."

"You're right," I said. "Good thinking, boy wonder. Ask him more about that night. See if he gets nervous."

"I bet he'll come if I invite him," Bay said. "He's mad at you two, but he might listen to me. He gamed with Wes for a long time, after all. He should be there."

Hector grinned, pleased we had listened to his idea. We fell into planning mode, our heads together, working out the best way to honor Wes's memory and the best ways to cover up our mischief.

We had hope again, and that changed everything.

13

THE NEXT NIGHT, MUSIC blared from the stereo Bay had set up in the back corner of the store. Her partner, Allison, was DJ, and Wes's parents, a quiet, shell-shocked looking couple, had brought a selection of their son's music. The gentle, loving memorial should have suited Wes. We had his music, his friends, his favorite games, his favorite foods. We tried to throw a party he would want to go to, not a party that would have bummed him out.

But in spite of our forced cheer, it wasn't a very good party. Unfortunately, it wasn't a very good memorial, either. Paige lurked, red-eyed, in one corner while everyone else avoided her. Bay had actually persuaded Cody to show his grumpy face at the gathering, and he and Hector glowered at each other over a plate of cupcakes decorated with paper TARDISes on sticks. Nick had not shown, which must have contributed to Paige's woeful mien.

Wes's death was the elephant in the room. Everyone wondered if someone present had killed him. No one wanted to discuss the things he loved, because he had loved Ten Again and gaming with his friends, and, to all appearances, those were the very things that had gotten him killed. Add to the mix the fact that this might be the store's last hurrah, and you had the world's saddest party.

"I wish Nick had come," I muttered to Jordan over the bowl of potato chips I was painstakingly arranging.

She took a chip and crunched it in my ear. "Why? Isn't this weird enough? We've got a bunch of sad, socially awkward people with nothing to say to one another standing around a doomed venue on a Tuesday night. We're one disco ball and some balloons away from a sixth-grade mixer in hell."

"Not helping," I said. "It doesn't look good, him skipping out on this. Like he's guilty or something."

"He probably is guilty." She took another chip. "And believe me, you don't need that hanging around, especially when you're already going to piss off half the town leadership by throwing this party."

I rotated the bowl of chips another six degrees. "You guys aren't going to arrest me, are you?"

"Nah." She didn't elaborate.

"What about our plans to investigate?"

Jordan rolled her eyes and gave me a sideways glance. "What plans?"

"Right."

She took a fistful of chips and sidled toward the dip. She had made it clear as a broken window: no more amateur sleuthing for her. She couldn't know about it, couldn't help, couldn't even acknowledge that I'd spoken about it. I let her off the hook and moved toward Hector and Cody, still eye-wrestling over the desserts.

"You have no idea what you're talking about," Cody said. He tossed back the dregs of a can of soda, refusing to meet my eyes when I joined them.

"No?" Hector said. "You can ask around—no one saw you that night. No one but Max, downstairs. You left the release party. Where were you?"

"I went to talk to Paige and Nick. Ask her."

"Yeah, but that didn't take the whole time. We know you went after Wes."

The soda can crunched in Cody's fist. "Stop saying that. You don't have any proof."

"Yes, I do."

"No, you don't."

This was the world's most pitiful interrogation. Over the speakers, an angsty hipster sang to an acoustic guitar. I heaved a sigh.

"How did you leave the building, then?" Hector persisted. "You didn't come through the store."

"I went out the back. The service exit."

I blinked. "Wait—you went out the service exit down the hall on this floor? The cops were down there."

"Not when I left, they weren't."

"Did you see anyone else down there?"

"No." He still wouldn't meet my gaze.

"You're lying!" Hector snapped.

"I didn't see anyone."

"Not even Donald? I—heard he was down there sometime before Wes died."

Cody shook his head. "Nope. The only person I saw before I left was that security guard before I went downstairs."

Donald's story was weakening like it had been hit with a Klingon disruptor beam. He told Craig he went downstairs, but Max saw him leave on the main floor. And no one could say when he had left or where he had gone before then.

"Did you talk to Wes before you left?" Hector asked Cody.

Cody put his can down hard enough that it made a metallic crinkling noise. He clenched a fist and shoved it in Hector's face. Hector took a step back. "I have answered these questions for the cops, like, fifty times. If my answers were good enough for them, they should be good enough for you."

Jordan appeared as if Cody had pulled her out of a hat. "Easy boys," she said. She wasn't in uniform, but she took the square-shouldered cops' stance that made her look sturdy as a linebacker. She could take Cody out, and he knew it.

He stepped back, breathing thickly. "I'm sick of this guy's questions. Wes was my friend, too." He shouted this last, looking toward Wes's parents, still standing with Bay in the corner.

Wes's mom put a hand over her mouth. Bay muttered something to her, and I could see Mr. Bowen nodding. Apparently they weren't fans of Cody, either. I wondered if they'd gotten angry phone calls about his character's death just like we had. Around the room, people were shifting and looking at the four of us with wide, frightened eyes. The last thing we needed to liven up this particular occasion was a fistfight.

"Let him be," I said to Hector. "We're all here for the same thing." I looked at Cody as I said this.

He nodded grudgingly, then took another step back. Jordan let him pass, and we watched him disappear back into the crowd.

"That guy." Hector shook his head. "He's hiding something."

"Maybe," Jordan said.

We both stared at her, shocked. She shrugged. "Call it a gut feeling or just training. He's hiding something, but I'm not convinced it's murder." She made a finger gun and pointed it at Hector. "Good work, kid."

Hector flushed, pleased. If I could have, I would've elbowed Jordan to shut her up. We did not need Hector thinking he was good at this little cops-and-robbers game we seemed to have invented. Join the Ten Again LARPers, solve murders, put away the bad guy—but we play for keeps, so someone has to die before we can get started.

I moved away from them before Hector could start quizzing Jordan on the best ways to distinguish between gut instincts and mere biased suspicions. I thought, idly, that I would go talk to Wes's parents, try to reassure them that not all of our customers were rage-filled weirdos who couldn't separate a character from a friend. I'd been where Cody was, losing a character, betrayed by a gaming group, misunderstood and full of woe.

The difference was, I could separate the game from life. Cody wanted the fictions to be the realities, and when he couldn't rewrite his life, reroll the dice, he tried to make everyone else feel like a loser, too. Poor guy. I almost pitied him.

At that very moment, when the tide of my sympathy was at its highest, I saw Craig standing outside the mall door, peering into the window like Oliver Twist. I almost dropped my own plastic cup of soda when I spotted him.

When he saw me, I waved, too shocked to think of a rational response to seeing my ex crashing the memorial of a kid he didn't know. And Craig didn't even game anymore, so it wasn't like he was supporting the community.

He beckoned me. I made my way through the crowd and closed the door behind me.

"What are you doing here, Craig?"

He looked sheepish, standing there with his hands in his pockets. "I wanted to warn you—Meghan heard you guys are doing this. She's on the warpath."

"She called Donald?"

"I think she called the cops."

My jaw dropped. "Are you serious?" Donald may have asked me to close for a few days, but as far as I knew, I wasn't doing anything illegal. The wake wasn't even loud. There was no alcohol, no one in the hallway, nothing to complain about beyond our very presence.

"Yeah. She's upstairs. I got there a few minutes ago, but I heard her talking to a dispatcher, I think."

"You think?"

"She said, 'Yes, they're here,' and 'No, I haven't talked to them,' and, 'Could you send a car?'"

"Well, that doesn't sound too promising." I grimaced. "Thanks for the warning."

"It seemed fair. I know you guys aren't up to anything." He looked over my shoulder, peering into the party. "It's a nice thing you're doing. Paige has been devastated."

"Yeah. Thanks, I guess."

"Everyone says he was a good kid."

"The best." I gave him a half-hearted smile. "This is the least I could do."

Craig leaned sideways against the window, still looking in. "Do you ever think of just . . . throwing in the towel?"

"What?"

"Just giving in. You've got a great crowd. I know your customers love you. And that poor kid . . ." He looked at me. "You could just move across town. Get out of the building, give it up. You'd do just as well closer to campus or even in that new retail district on the other side of town."

"Are you . . . trying to sell me property?" I asked, a sour taste in my mouth.

To his credit, Craig's jaw dropped. "God, no, Autumn. You just looked so . . . worn down . . . standing in there. I want you to be happy. And you've been doing nothing but fight this place for months now. First the grant, now this. Aren't you sick of it?"

The brutal honesty of his question caught me completely off guard. It took me a moment to find my voice. "Yes," I said. "Yes. I'm sick of it." It hurt to say it.

"So why keep fighting?"

"I—"

I didn't have an answer. Not an easy one, and not right away. He was right. It had taken me ages to get Donald to even agree to my grant application, and from the day I'd started that process, I'd been fighting against my very nature. And back when I rented the store, Donald had been dubious about my role in Independence Square Mall. I wouldn't do well, he said, there was no market in the building for a game store.

On the other hand—

"What else am I going to do?" I said.

Craig smiled. He reached out a hand like he wanted to touch my face, thought better of it, and tucked his hand into his pocket. "You could just run your store. Game tournaments. Swords and sorcery. No grants, no politicians, no investigations."

"I could," I agreed. "Always assuming there are no murders on the other side of town."

He didn't laugh. "You should think about it."

"I will." That was a promise I could keep. I might have no choice but to think about it if Donald got his way.

The awkward silence that always fell between us hung thick in the air. Craig's hazel eyes traced my face, as if he could read my thoughts written in my skin. I didn't know what to think, what to say.

"I should go try to talk to Meghan," I said. "Or at least call Donald."

"I'll talk to Meghan," Craig said. Before he took a step to go, though, he froze, looking in the store window. "Is everything okay in there?" he asked, pointing.

"What?" I looked over his shoulder. Inside, I could see that a crowd had formed near the center of the store. Hector stood at its outskirts, his cell phone to his ear, while Bay was at the register, the store's phone in her hand, her other arm in the air, waving toward me. Mrs. Bowen stood behind her, crying. Jordan stood in the middle of the crowd, one hand holding tight to Cody's arm, the other extended toward—

"Damn it, Nick," I muttered. I pushed the door open and strode back into the store.

Nick drew back his arm, preparing to swing at Cody. "You did this to us," he shouted.

"Come on, son," Mr. Bowen said. He grabbed Nick around the chest, surprising me. He hauled his son's friend backward, but Nick was younger and had the strength of anger on his side. He broke free, pushed Jordan aside, and hit Cody in the face. Cody fell backward into the table of refreshments, sending him, the table, and the desserts crashing to the floor. Someone shrieked as cherry filling, red as blood, gushed everywhere. Nick dove for Cody. His head met Cody's chest with a thud, and Cody grunted before he sagged backward into the cookies. Jordan was a mere instant behind Nick. She slugged him in the gut, and he crumpled, wheezing. She grabbed him by the collar of his shirt and dragged him off of Cody.

"Stop!" I shouted, slower to react, and shoved my way through the crowd. Someone stepped on my heels as I moved forward. I staggered into Mr. Bowen, who held me up, looking shocked.

I'd missed the first hit: Nick was bleeding from a cut in his eyebrow. He wiped at it angrily as Jordan released him. Paige rushed to his side with a wordless cry.

Cody staggered to his feet. He wiped his mouth with the back of one hand. It came away bloody, and the sight of the red streak under the store lights seem to further incite his temper. "You did this to yourself." His eyes never left Nick's face. "Both of you."

"You're sick," Paige said. "This is all your fault."

"What are you talking about?" Mrs. Bowen cried. Tears ran freely down her face. "What do you three know?"

Bay's partner, Allison, put an arm around the other woman's shoulders. Wes's dad reached for Nick, but Nick jerked his shoulder away from him.

"What's going on?" Craig asked, his voice low under the uproar.

I turned. He was standing at my shoulder. I hadn't realized he had followed me in—he must have been the one crowding me. "I have no idea. Paige and Nick are suspects. Maybe."

"Really? Paige? My assistant, Paige?" His eyes widened.

"I know." I raised my voice, shouting into the crowd. "What's going on here?" I asked, echoing his question.

"He had the nerve to show his face here, that's what," Nick said. He jerked his chin at Cody. "Asshole."

"You're the one with nerve," Cody sneered. "Everyone knows you two killed Wes. The cops are just waiting for a warrant."

"They won't get one," Paige said. "We didn't do it."

"You're accusing us?" Nick said. "When you—"

Cody lunged for him. Jordan caught him again.

"Enough!" I shouted.

At the register, the mini gong sounded, ear-splitting as thunder in the confined space. Everyone in the crowd flinched, and Cody slowed long enough for Jordan to drag him out of the crowd, murmuring threats in his ear. Mr. Bowen had hold of Nick again, though Paige's expression said she wouldn't mind hitting Cody herself. I looked up and saw Bay, white-faced, the striker in her hand.

"Enough," I repeated. "This is supposed to be a memorial for Wes, not some sick kangaroo court."

"I think," Mrs. Bowen said, her voice trembling. She licked her lips and tried again. "I think we'd better call it a night, Autumn."

I nodded. So much for my grand heal-the-wound plans for this party. It had gone from awkward gathering to guilt-fest. "I'm sorry," I said.

"It's not your fault," Mr. Bowen said. He had released Nick. Around him, the other guests looked sheepish, as if ashamed of themselves for relishing in the drama. One by one, they began to trail out, many with backward glances of sympathy and poorly concealed curiosity. I let them go without a fight.

For Wes, for me, for all of us, the party was over.

14

THE POLICE ARRESTED NICK and Paige early the next morning. The local news station sent a reporter to watch them take Nick, and they replayed the footage on the eleven o'clock news, but I'd shut off the TV, not needing to see a friend shoved headfirst into a cop car. Again.

At noon, my stepmom brought me a latte and a bowl of sliced cantaloupe with yogurt. When I answered the door in my Wonder Woman bathrobe, Audrey gave me a sympathetic grimace and a careful hug, one hand held wide around me to keep from spilling the to-go coffees she had in a fast-food tray.

"Hi," she said. "I heard about last night. I thought you might want to see a friendly face."

I followed her down my front hallway to the kitchen. She made herself right at home, putting dirty dishes in the sink, hunting out a clean plate and spoon, and serving the cantaloupe and yogurt to me at my own table as if I were still fifteen and headed off to zero hour marching band. She ignored the time, ignored my messy kitchen, ignored the fact that I was at home, wearing my pajamas, in the middle of a Wednesday.

"Were you really cleaning icing out of your carpet in the store at midnight last night?" she asked, putting my latte—now in a real mug—in front of me.

"Yep," I said. I dug the spoon into the yogurt and took a big bite. "How'd you hear?" I asked around my mouthful.

"Alice called me from City Hall this morning. I guess Donald was telling the Economic Development Commission people this morning."

"Oh." I made a face at the cantaloupe. "Naturally."

"He said the police had to go and break up a fight."

"Uh-huh."

"Those two they arrested—they were your customers?" She asked, but it wasn't a question. Dark eyes shining with concern, she perched on the chair opposite me, coffee in her hands.

I nodded. "Friends, too. Paige especially. She's a sweet girl."

She nodded. "I'm sorry."

I pushed my breakfast away, suddenly nauseous. "How'd it happen?"

Audrey shrugged. "The boy fought a little, but I gathered from what I heard on the radio that the arrest was a long time coming. They said the police found a new piece of evidence that made it pretty clear."

"A new piece of evidence? Did they say what?"

"No. Your father said the police wouldn't have told the reporters." She gave me a small, tight smile. "I knew you'd ask."

"You know me well." I gave up on all pretense of uncon- cern and lowered my head to the smooth, cold surface of my kitchen table.

Audrey patted the back of my head. "I'm sorry, hon."

"Was I stupid to try?"

She didn't ask what I meant. "No. You always have to try. And I know those kids mean more to you than anything else in the world."

I rolled my head to look at her, one cheek smashed flat against the wood. "Do you think I'm a slacker?" I asked.

"No." She didn't hesitate, but a line appeared between her brows, and she smoothed her hand down the exposed side of my face. "Why would you ask that?"

I shrugged, scooting my face up and down the table. "I flunked out of the grant thing. I couldn't keep the store open. And I can't prove that some of my customers aren't killers, even when I know they're innocent."

"Do you actually know?"

"Yes."

"Then you had to try. And you should keep trying."

I sat up. "Why? They've been arrested. There's 'new evidence.' No one cares what I think, and if I keep going, I'll probably get arrested myself or at least get put out of business permanently."

"You won't go out of business." She smiled wryly. "My firm does your taxes, so I've seen your profit margins. You definitely won't go out of business."

"So what should I do?" I asked. I was whining, and we both knew it, but sometimes whining was part of my process. I needed to do it, so I could move on.

"How should I know?"

I sat up. "You always know what to do." I smiled as I said it, so she would know I was kidding.

"Your problems are a little bigger than they were in high school," Audrey said. "If you were having tax trouble, or you needed to have someone audited, I could help out."

I snorted. "No. None of those problems, thank goodness." Those were about the only problems I didn't have—though I would if I had to keep my business closed for much more than a week.

"Well, what sort of help do you need?"

"I could use a new landlord, to start," I said. "Maybe a more forgiving public perception of gamers. An excellent criminal defense attorney to get Nick and Paige out of trouble. Come to think of it, I'd better have a lawyer for myself in case the cops still want to say I'm an accomplice." I paused, drumming my fingers on the table. "And some sort of evidence that someone else killed Wes. Preferably Meghan."

"Meghan?" Audrey said. "How on earth did you cook that up?"

"Oh, she heard Nick and Paige arguing with Wes the night he died. Paige works for Craig, and she was afraid Meghan would point to her as a suspect. Which, evidently she did. But apparently some of the LARPers, including Wes, heard Meghan and Craig arguing that night, too."

"Not a good night for interpersonal relations."

"Clearly not." I toyed with my coffee, and some of it sloshed out onto my kitchen table. I blotted it with the sleeve of my robe before Audrey could get up and hunt out some paper napkins from my pantry. "Anyway, Meghan was there, and she had motivation. You know how she hates for people to see her off-kilter. And then the vandalism. I guess I'm more worried that she's trying to frame me for some of it, or at least direct enough suspicion my way to get me kicked out of the grant competition. Which she did. I guess she wins again. I couldn't even get anyone but my employees to suspect her."

"You don't have much to go on," Audrey said doubtfully. "Would she even have the upper body strength to move a fully grown man, let alone a dead one?"

"Probably not. She would have needed an accomplice—but I have one of those figured out, too." I reached for my yogurt again, taking the spoon in one hand. I pointed at Audrey with it. "Donald."

"Donald. Your landlord." When I nodded, Audrey smiled. "You just want to think it's the people causing problems for you."

"No! I swear, Donald was there that night, too. And we have no idea when he left or anything—his story doesn't add up. The security guard said Donald left when Craig did, but Craig said that wasn't true, that Donald went down to the basement after Craig left."

"Why would he have killed the boy?" Audrey asked. She loved solving mysteries more than the eponymous monster loved cookies, and I had given her a puzzle. I could always count on her, more than anyone else, to help me with my problems.

I pointed with the spoon again. "I don't know." I let it drop into the bowl with a clatter.

"What was he doing with Craig?"

"Talking real estate, I guess." I made a vaguely confused gesture with my now-free hand. "Something about comparable properties with green upgrades."

"That's odd."

"Not really, Craig will talk real estate with anything that sits still long enough."

"No, I mean, it's odd that Donald was asking about it," Audrey said. "He's not doing well financially."

"Are you serious?"

She bit her lip. "I really shouldn't—"

"Audrey, come on."

"Fine." She sighed and put her elbows on the table, rolling her cup between her palms. "My firm has been auditing him—he owed a lot of money for taxes, and I guess he wanted to see if he could come up with a better financial plan to keep it down next year. But it's not something a financial plan will help—there are just too many empty spaces in that building, and there's not enough cash coming in to keep it afloat. That's probably why he let you pursue the grant, actually. Any injection would help, and your proposed changes would lower his bills, right? I think he was hoping for it to happen."

"Why convince me to drop out, then, if he needed the money?"

"I have no idea. I told him your plans would help him out tremendously, and he seemed pretty receptive to the idea."

I frowned. "That is so weird. I wonder—"

"What?"

I shook my head. "It's pretty far-fetched. But what if, somehow, Meghan's remodeling plans would get the money to the building sooner? Like, if Meghan got it, Donald could use the money to pay his bills or something."

"That would be fraud." Audrey took a calm sip of her coffee, unmoved by my suggestion that her client might commit a crime to stay in business.

"And worth killing someone over?" I couldn't keep the note of excitement from my voice.

"I think you're reaching, honey. You have no evidence that Meghan and Donald are—colluding."

"No, but maybe Wes did," I said. "He was in the building with Meghan and Donald that night. When I overheard them, the day my store was vandalized, Paige and Nick said something about him knowing some information I would care about. And Meghan and Craig were arguing, too, something about Craig not doing something she needed. Getting the grant, even if it was rigged, even if it meant giving the money to Donald, would be in her best interest." In my excitement, I scooted my chair across the kitchen floor with a loud screech. I stood, making my bathrobe flutter around me. "All the pieces fit—Wes overheard, and he told Paige and Nick. Now Meghan and Donald are framing them and getting me out of the way in the process!"

Audrey looked alarmed. "Slow down, Autumn," she said. "I just said he needed money."

"But I already had all the other clues! This is the thing that ties it all together. I'll bet you anything that Wes overheard Meghan and Craig talking about her plans with Donald. Craig went to talk to Donald, Meghan found out that Wes had been listening, she got word to Donald, so Donald doubled back when he walked Craig out, and then they killed Wes and made it look like one of the gamers did it. That has to be what happened." I fumbled in my bathrobe pockets. "I have to call Jordan."

"Wait, wait. You have zero evidence of any of this—how did Meghan contact Donald? Wouldn't the police have a record of that? Why haven't the couple who got arrested come forward if they know about the collusion?"

"Well, Meghan has set them up, hasn't she? She and Donald look squeaky clean, and it would just seem like they're trying to get themselves off the hook by accusing the woman who gave evidence that they were fighting with Wes."

"Why wouldn't they have told you? You're their friend."

"Well . . ." I paused. That one was tough. They knew I wanted to prove they didn't do it. Why would they keep information like this a secret? Then it occurred to me. "Paige works for Craig—she would be worried about losing her job!"

"Going to prison for murder is a bit worse than losing a part-time job as a secretary at a real estate agency. And that doesn't explain why they were there the day your store was vandalized."

"Maybe they were just . . . there," I said lamely.

"Maybe. But if you want to get the police to believe this, you'll have to answer those questions. And that's not even the biggest hole in your story. You have no proof whatsoever that Meghan and Donald were colluding to get the grant awarded to her."

"Donald's on the committee—he'd be able to do it."

"That's not evidence."

"No. But I could find evidence."

"I don't think you should go evidence-hunting, especially knowing the police wanted to arrest you for interfering with their investigation. And for helping their suspects." She spoke as if this was a completely normal situation for me, like, "Oh, Autumn got detention again!" It was part of why I loved her so much. Nothing fazed her. I beamed at her, even as she continued trying to talk me out of my grand plans for Paige and Nick's redemption. "You should just call Jordan," she said. "Tell her your theory, and she can look into Donald and Meghan's phone records, or whatever she has to do."

"You're probably right."

I walked her out at the end of her lunch break, toying with my cell phone. Like perfectly arranged dominoes, all the elements of the conspiracy tumbled into place, one after another. If Wes had stumbled into this mess unwittingly, I could see how bewildered and angry he must have been—he would have gone to tell someone, to do something, but Meghan or Donald had found him first. I wondered if Meghan had been the one to stab him—anything to stop him from running. And then another wound to make it look like a vampire bite, and a trip over the balcony to seal the deal.

I shivered. I hated Meghan, and it was hard to like Donald, but it was a long leap between petty high school feud and vengeful murder scheme. This might even stretch the limits of Jordan's belief, though I knew I could trust her to hear me out.

But I did not dial her number.

She was my best friend, my greatest ally, the smartest woman I knew. But she was a cop, too, and there was no way she could approve of what I wanted to do. As a cop, she needed evidence and warrants and all those legal things that would slow down even the most intrepid of Scooby-wannabes. No, what I needed were people who were creative, motivated, open-minded, and dedicated to following a narrative to its bitter end.

I needed the LARPers again.

15

BAY AND ALLISON MET me that afternoon at Independence Square Mall, José and Olivia in tow. Allison looked excited—she didn't often hang out with our crowd, which was why I'd requested her presence. Hector, dutiful child, had a lab on Wednesdays and, with his wish to pin the murder on Cody, was not the most promising candidate for entrapping Meghan and Donald.

"What's the plan, boss?" Bay asked.

We sat around one of the little tables on the bottom level, the fountain's cheerful babble muffling our voices.

"Well, we need to get into the office of Chic and the office of our landlord, Donald." I glanced at José and Olivia to try and gauge how the prospect of breaking and entering would fit into their preferred hobby list. Neither of them seemed fazed, so I kept going. "We'll need people that aren't familiar to Meghan and Donald—that's why Allison is here."

She nodded eagerly, tucking her blonde hair behind one ear to reveal dangling spiral helix earrings. Bay gave her a nervous look, as if her girlfriend's enthusiasm for a life of crime had taken her by surprise. "What do you want me to do?" Allison asked.

"Well, I thought we'd tackle Donald's office first. He's here, so the door is open, but he's in a meeting with someone on the fourth floor. We'll need you to distract his secretary so that we can get in and out without being seen."

"What should I do—fake a fall, or something, and threaten to sue? Oh, or I could say I saw someone shoplifting, and—"

"No," Bay said. "Nothing that might bring the cops here."

I cleared my throat. I'd underestimated Allison's enthusiasm. "Uh, a fake fall might work," I said. "Or maybe you could try to sell her something, or ask for directions . . . ?"

"Don't do something too out of the ordinary, or you'll be more memorable," Olivia advised. "You run into that in RPGs—sometimes it's better to keep your head down and be discreet. If you make a big fuss, the villagers are more likely to remember you, or—"

"We only need a few minutes," I said, cutting in before she could go into the finer points of heroic character development.

"What are we looking for?" José asked.

"Financial and phone records," I said. "If we have time, emails from Donald to Meghan." I'd settled on those three things as the most likely to help. I doubted he would conveniently leave his cell phone behind for his meeting, but a girl could hope. Financials might be easy to find, and photos could be taken of emails with no problems.

"You've thought this through," Bay observed.

"I've learned a thing or two from Veronica Mars," I said, grinning. It was no joke, though—we needed a paper trail, but financials were the simplest thing to track. Plus, email was just obvious. Donald at least was clueless enough to have sent Meghan something about their collusion on the grant. While I doubted either of them was dumb enough to have admitted to murder online, I might get lucky proving their guilt elsewhere.

"I'll take the computer," Bay said.

"We'll go with Allison," Olivia said, indicating herself and José. They would "help," I had no doubt. Donald's secretary would have no idea what had hit her.

"Do you want help searching the office?" José asked.

I shook my head. "No, I think it's best if Bay and I are the ones breaking in." I couldn't ask any of the other gamers to risk jail. Bay would never let me go alone, so I didn't even try to stop her, but at least I could protect Olivia and José. Lying to a secretary wasn't a crime, and I doubted the cops would charge them with accessory to a trespassing as wimpy as this one.

Probably.

"Will we do the same for Meghan's office?" Bay asked as we all stood.

"More or less. She's there, though, so we'll have to be more careful."

"I'll create a scene," Allison said happily.

Her excitement didn't fill me with much confidence.

When we got to Donald's office on the main floor, I was relieved to see that Max had gone off on one of his rambling perimeter checks of the building. He strolled through about once an hour, looking in on the shops, peeking into bathrooms, and generally lurking. If he wasn't so old and nonthreatening, he would have been arrested for loitering decades ago. He did a thorough job, though, and that's why everyone in the building put up with him.

Luckily for me, he was off haunting one of the other floors.

As planned, Allison went toward Donald's office first while José and Olivia disappeared around the corner. Bay and I lurked, stalker-like, at the balcony railing, looking down toward the fountain below.

Allison rushed through the open doorway of Donald's office, panting as if she had run up three flights of stairs. We could see into the office over her shoulder as she gasped something to Donald's secretary, who stood, alarmed. Together they rushed back through the doorway and around the corner to the scene of whatever fake emergency our coconspirators had concocted.

"Damn," Bay muttered as they disappeared. I looked at her, alarmed, and she grinned. "I never thought she'd be so into role-playing. I'd have suggested it ages ago."

"I do not need to know about your sex life." I tugged her shirt. "Come on, we won't have long." I trotted ahead into Donald's office, Bay hot on my heels. His secretary's desk was abandoned, and there was no one in the closet-sized waiting area. Luckily, the inner door to Donald's private sanctum was unlocked. I left the door ajar behind us, so we could hear when Donald's assistant and Allison returned.

"Hurry, hurry," I muttered, mostly to myself, as Bay slid into his computer chair and grabbed hold of his mouse.

I turned in a circle. Donald's office was tiny, even smaller than the one I had in Ten Again, and he kept it in regimented order. If the man did anything here besides sit in the chair and stare at the computer, there was no physical evidence of it. At the computer, Bay frowned as she read something.

I spotted the filing cabinet then, a short standard-issue steel box sitting in the corner behind the desk. I squeezed around Bay and wedged myself up against the cold metal. The top drawer slid out with an angry screech of neglect. The first folder I saw held a lease agreement for the café on the ground floor, the next the lease for the gift shop, and on down the line. I snagged the folder for Chic, thinking it might be useful, and tossed it on the desk next to Bay.

The second drawer had the contracts for the janitorial staff, utility bills—I'd seen those before, for my grant application—and a folder marked "Banquet Hall Plans." Not helpful.

The third drawer had financial documents: two-year-old bank statements, an ancient purchase contract, and a thick stack of copied rent checks.

"There's nothing here," I said.

"That's because it's all here," Bay said. I stood up, banging my head on the top drawer pull in the process. I swore, and Bay shushed me as I moved to stand over her shoulder, my eyes watering. "Look," she said. "He has everything digitized. Financial records, messages from your stepmom's auditing firm, everything."

As my eyes cleared, I saw that she was right. He used the same sort of accounting software that I did, but nothing was password protected. Everything was there, from his monthly revenues to his projected earnings. I swore again when I saw the number, bright red and ominous.

"Shut up!" Bay hissed. She glanced wildly at the door. "They'll hear us."

"Well, copy the file!"

"What? How?"

"I don't know, you're the computer chick—"

"I'm not a super spy, Autumn, just take a picture with your phone!"

I did as she told me, snapping photos of several of Donald's account statements, as well as his high-level financial plan for the rest of the year. None of it looked good. Donald would be more than broke by the end of this year unless some serious cash came his way to cover some of the building's bills.

Bay clicked back over to his email, pulling up one from Meghan with a subject line that read, "funds required."

"Look," Bay said.

There was an incoming message from two months ago, just before the semifinalists for the grant had been selected.

Hi Donald,

I've attached the projected final figures. It looks like $18,000 should cover it. I know it seems like a lot up front, but you'll bring in a ton of money as a result. I think this is a great plan.

Let me know what you think,

Meghan Kountz

I snapped a photo. "Quick, pull up the attachment," I said. Bay started the download, but her phone buzzed at that moment. She looked down at it.

"That's Allison with the wrap-it-up signal," she said. "Damn."

"Well, we'll look at Meghan's computer, too."

She closed the open windows and hurriedly stopped the document from downloading. I bounced on my toes, waiting, until she released the mouse and stood. "Come on!"

We darted out of the office and back to the balcony railing. I gripped the smooth wood, my heart racing. "We did it," I hissed. "We found proof."

"Easy there," Bay said out of one side of her mouth. "We're not done yet."

At that moment, Allison and Donald's secretary reappeared. The secretary looked ruffled but not angry. Allison gave us a thumbs-up behind the woman's back, and I could see Bay's muscles relax. "One down," she murmured. The secretary nodded to us as she passed, and she disappeared back into Donald's office.

Exaggeratedly casual, we sidled over toward Allison, then began strolling down the hallway toward Chic.

"That was amazing," Allison squealed in a low voice. Bay shushed her, too, but I could see they were both smiling. When we were out of the secretary's sight line, José and Olivia popped out of a shop entrance, grinning.

"Did you get what you needed?" Olivia whispered.

I nodded a yes, and they high fived quietly in response. We marched down the hallway toward Meghan's store, our fabulous five, and I felt like we needed to be in slow motion with a killer soundtrack to reinforce our awesomeness—but there was only silence and the sound of Allison's super-cute heels on the tile floor.

"On to Meghan's?" Bay muttered.

"Yup," I said through gritted teeth. "This will be the difficult one." I stopped in front of the gift store and looked at Allison. "What's the plan here?"

"She's alone in the store?"

"Best I can tell."

"Okay, good," Allison said. "That means her phone is there, and you might get access to some things her employees wouldn't know about. Anyway, we'll distract her again—same basic play, and you guys can slip in." The woman was diabolical, but she had a point; Meghan being here alone might mean she'd left her guard down, and we would have the opportunity to take a look at things she didn't want other people to see.

"It's a smaller space, so we'll need to move faster." I nudged Bay, who was staring at her girlfriend with open surprise. "I think we'd better just go straight for the computer and hope for the best. Hopefully she has it up and running."

She nodded. "You got it."

We stepped aside while Allison, José, and Olivia went ahead to Meghan's store. We could see them through the glass wall, José trailing after Allison and Olivia as they moved into the store, pausing occasionally to look at a price tag. Meghan emerged from her office, a bright smile plastered on her face. She moved toward Allison instinctively, Stylish calling to Stylish. Olivia and José drifted deeper into the store, out of our sight.

I glanced at Bay. "This is going to be tricky."

She looked up from the display of little carved wooden angels in the gift shop window. "No joke," she said. "I was just thinking . . . are you sure you want to do this?"

"What?"

"Well, with Donald, if we got caught, you'd probably be able to get away with saying you were looking for him or something. But with Meghan . . . you two aren't exactly friendly. If she catches us, it's not going to end well. You could get in real trouble."

"It's a little late to be getting cold feet," I said, annoyed. I was more annoyed at myself for being annoyed at all than I was with Bay herself. The woman was always right—that was why I hired her—and if we were on different sides, then it might mean I'd finally crossed the line between enterprising and delusional.

"I could text Allison and call it off," Bay said. She had a pleading tone, and when I looked into her eyes, I saw she was serious.

"I—" I wasn't sure what I was going to say, but it didn't matter. At that moment, I saw Allison and Meghan rush toward the front of the store. Whatever distraction they'd planned was underway. I let go of my doubts and plunged ahead. "Come on." I grabbed Bay's sleeve and dragged her into Chic.

We could see Meghan and Allison hovering over José and Olivia. Olivia appeared to have faked a faint, and Allison was hysterical at the sight of her prone body. Bay and I slipped between the clothing racks as we approached the office stealthily along the store's back wall. We could hear Allison's voice, high pitched and nervous, and Meghan's shrill replies.

The office door, marked EMPLOYEES ONLY, was shut but unlocked, and we slipped in without a problem. The office was also a storage room, much larger than the office in my own store. A computer sat on a desk to one side, overlooking the rest of the unfinished space. A dozen boxes were stacked on the bare floor along one wall, several of them half-unpacked, and plastic-wrapped clothing spilled out of its packaging onto the floor.

Bay went right for the desk. She moved a packet out of the chair, perching it precariously on the desk, and I saw that it was a bubble-wrapped stack of earrings. Somehow the expensive accessories looked cheap and gaudy, seen in their cellophane wholesale cocoons. Bay ignored them and squinted at the screen as she slid the mouse around the desk.

"No luck. The accounting software is password protected, and it's not open," she said almost immediately.

"We just need the email." I stood behind her, one hand on the back of the chair. "Look, she left it pulled up." I pointed at the screen.

Bay navigated to the email hosting client and pulled up Meghan's in-box, a swamp of orders, business communications, and even some personal messages. She scrolled the messages, making my eyes cross as hundreds of them whirled by.

"There's nothing here from Donald," Bay said. "She must have been using a personal account." She turned to look up at me. "Pull up the photos on your camera. Maybe she left her web browser logged in. If we know what service she uses, we can pull it up."

I pulled up my image gallery, but the photos didn't make the address clear. "Crap," I muttered, scrolling through. "It's not here."

Bay swore. She pulled up the browser and began typing in the names of several popular email hosts in separate tabs. I tucked my phone back into my pocket and looked around the office for anything else that might help—a filing cabinet like Donald's, a murder weapon, a to-do list with "Commit fraud with grant money" scribbled on it. I didn't find any of those, but I did spot her cream-colored leather purse tucked under the desk. I snatched it with a wordless cry.

Her phone was right on top, with a flashing text message indicator. "Yes," I muttered, scrolling through. "I can see if there are any calls to Donald—"

I unlocked the screen: no password. I guess she distrusted her employees more than she did her friends. The new message opened up. It was from Craig.

Congrats, babe! You're one of the last three finalists!!

I felt the blood drain from my face. They'd announced the final competitors for the grant competition, then, and Meghan was one of them. If Meghan and Donald had tried to fix the contest, it had worked. She was in. It didn't help us, though.

"Weird," Bay said.

"Hmm?" I murmured, distracted, staring at Meghan's long line of messages from Craig. There were affectionate, lovey-dovey messages and prosaic couexpley messages, a living record of their relationship. And it culminated in Craig's congratulations for her success—success over me, again.

I took a deep, shaky breath. I needed to focus, not wallow in regrets for a bizarro life I didn't have and didn't want. I pulled up the call logs, then, and began thumbing back to Friday night. If she'd made a call to Donald between eight thirty and nine at night, then maybe I could convince Jordan to listen to me, to consider the possibility that Paige and Nick were innocent, and the cops might consider looking into Meghan's whereabouts the night of Wes's death. I frowned as I scrolled through the records—there were a lot. Apparently Meghan spent as much time on the phone as she did preening.

The records ended abruptly at one minute past midnight on Saturday. The history had been deleted.

"Crap," I said again, interrupting Bay as she took a breath to speak.

"What is it?" Bay asked.

"She's deleted the call logs. Hiding something."

Bay twisted in the chair, looking up at me. "Are you okay? You look weird—"

I shook my head. "I'm fine." I dropped the phone back into her purse. "We should go, there's nothing here."

"Actually, there might be—"

The office door, which we'd left ajar, thumped open, bouncing off the wall. Meghan stood in the doorway, her eyes wide. Allison peered over her shoulder, waving frantically at us.

"What the hell are you doing here?" Meghan asked.

"I—uh, I can explain."

Bay pulled her hands back from the computer.

Meghan smiled. "You are so going down." She pointed at her desk. "Pass me the phone—I'm calling the cops."

16

"No, you're not."

My heart almost stopped. Visions of Detective Keller with handcuffs, an interrogation room, criminal lawyers, and newspaper headlines danced across my blackening vision and faded into a puff of relief when Craig stepped out from behind Meghan.

I sagged backward against the desk. I never thought I'd rely on Craig MacLeod to be my knight in shining armor, but here he was to save the day, and I was grateful.

Meghan turned on him. "Oh, yes I am. I am done with this shit. She's been trying to sabotage me since we both applied for the grant, and now she's actually trespassing on private property to do it! The cops need to know she's behind all of this—"

"*I'm* trying to sabotage *you*? Are you insane? You've been working with—"

"We're not really in a position to make accusations here, boss," Bay cut in.

I rounded on her. "Excuse me . . ." I trailed off. She widened her eyes at me, clearly trying to send me a psychic message of some sort.

She had a point. I shut my mouth and turned back to Craig. I smiled in a sickly way, half-apologetic, half-sheepish. "It's not what it looks like?" I offered.

"This is insane, Autumn," he said. "Meghan would be perfectly justified in calling the cops. You shouldn't be here, whatever it looks like."

"Shouldn't be here? She's committing a crime! Trespassing! Breaking and entering!"

"I didn't *break* anything," I grumbled. She was right, though. Even if they didn't arrest me for trespassing, Detective Keller would probably say I was obstructing justice or interfering with an investigation, and I could end up with some actual jail time—and something told me I wouldn't last five minutes behind bars. LARPing a tough-as-nails character was one thing, and standing up for what was right was another; but wearing an orange jump suit and taking communal showers . . . nope.

"What are you trying to prove, Autumn?" Craig asked.

"That she and Donald were working together to fix the grant."

"That's ridiculous," Meghan scoffed. "You have absolutely no idea what you're talking about."

"And you thought you might actually find evidence here?" Craig's eyes narrowed as he studied me, as if he was surprised to discover that I'd put some thought into solving this mystery.

"Emails," I said. "It's possible." I lifted my chin. Bay was right to keep me from spilling the whole plot to Meghan or Craig. We needed those photos of the emails on Donald's computer, and there was no way Meghan would let me walk out of here a free woman knowing the extent of her crimes.

"She admits it, then," Meghan said, a note of Dolores Umbridge-like triumph in her voice. "Let me call the cops. They'll arrest her, and we'll never have to deal with her crap again."

Craig took a deep breath. "No."

Meghan recoiled as if she had stepped on a snake. "Whose side are you on?" she snapped. "This woman threatened me. She vandalized my store, and now she broke into my office. Do you honestly expect me to just let her walk away?"

Craig caught her arm in one hand. He lowered his voice, glancing sideways at Allison and José, who were watching their argument like newcomers to a pro-wrestling match. "Listen," he said, lowering his voice. "It'll look really bad for you, too, if you have one of the other grant contenders arrested, even if she's not in the race anymore. And you know Donald won't want the publicity. Wouldn't it be better to just let her go? You don't need to stress yourself out about it because you've already won. She's not in the race anymore."

Gee, thanks Craig. Bay moved to stand beside me and gave me a quick one-armed squeeze.

Meghan continued to stare at him as if he had suggested she let me pee in her lemonade. "You think letting her keep acting like a complete maniac is in my best interest?"

"That's not what I'm saying, and you know it. If you're actually worried, why don't we call Jordan? She's a cop; she can give Autumn a talking to."

"I don't need a 'talking to,'" I said, peeved. "Look, I'm an adult. I can walk away from this." I held up my hands, trying to look nonthreatening. "If you don't call the cops, I swear, I'll voluntarily stay away from this store until the day I die." Or until they arrested Meghan and Donald for fraud, anyway—then I would come in and do a Snoopy dance on the ashes of her stupid, overpriced merchandise.

I could feel Bay side-eyeing me. She, at least, could tell when I was being insincere.

But Craig had never been good at reading my mood. He looked at Meghan. "See? It'll be fine."

Meghan made a moue of dislike. "Well, call her friend, anyway. I want someone to know what actually happened here. That way Autumn can't pretend she was an innocent victim the whole time." She glared at me over her shoulder and narrowed her eyes at Craig, too, her expression contorting into a full-on grimace when he let her go and turned back to face me, his hands held out to me like he was approaching a wild Pokémon.

"Will you let me do that, Autumn? Meghan's right, she could call the cops. This is more than fair."

I drop my arms to my side in exasperation. It wasn't like I could complain, even though it felt like I was five years old and the kindergarten teacher was calling my mom on me. I *had* broken in, sort of, and I was definitely in the wrong. But if I could get away without an actual arrest record and with the photos we'd taken of the email Donald had sent, we might still be able to prove that Meghan was the criminal, not me. We clearly weren't going to find anything here, so my promise to stay away wouldn't hurt our amateur sleuthing, anyway.

"Fine. Whatever. I don't know what you expect Jordan to do or say, but fine."

I sent José, Olivia, and Bay home, seeing no need to subject them to whatever lecture Craig thought Jordan would give me. Craig, Meghan, and I stood around on the Chic selling floor, scaring away customers while we waited for Jordan. Meghan didn't want me in her office. She leaned against the cash register, watching me, until I wandered toward the mall entrance at the back of the store.

Through the windows, I watched a woman in the gift shop peruse the same tacky wooden angels on display that Bay and I had lingered in front of before we made our move. I wished I could trade places with her.

Craig tried once to engage me in conversation, but I refused to participate, staring at my scruffy Converse sneakers until Meghan snapped at him to stop encouraging me.

When Jordan appeared in the doorway in full uniform, I stood stunned, unable to speak or move: rarely did she wear her uniform when I could see her, and she looked like a total badass. I wouldn't cross her, not for a million dollars. She didn't look happy to see me, though, and I thought, for the first time, that I was seeing Jordan the way a criminal might. She held a cup of coffee from the café downstairs, and her face was creased with exhaustion. She was fresh off a shift, I guessed, and pissed at being called here before going home.

"What the hell is going on?" she asked without preamble.

"She broke into my store," Meghan snapped.

"What?" Jordan said, half-laughing.

I rolled my eyes. "I didn't break in. The store was open. But Bay and I let ourselves into the office—"

"Breaking in if I ever heard of it—"

"—the door was unlocked—"

"—ought to be arrested—"

"Shut up, both of you," Jordan said. She looked at Craig. "Why did you call me?"

He shrugged, looking as if he had begun to regret this plan. "Meghan wanted to call the cops, but I thought maybe it would be better to call you first, since—"

"Since I'm the only one who can control Autumn. Of course."

"Hey—" I said, affronted.

Jordan held up her hand, shushing me. I fell silent, oddly ashamed. She closed her eyes and exhaled deeply. When she reopened her eyes, she looked at Craig with a forced smile on her face. "Thanks," she said. "You did the right thing." She looked at Meghan, no longer smiling, and said, "Thank you for not calling the cops. I appreciate it, and so does Autumn."

Craig beamed at Jordan, and Meghan's lips parted like she wanted to say something. Craig took her arm, though. "The whole thing has gotten out of hand," he said.

"I agree," Jordan said. She opened the door into the mall and put a hand on my arm. "Come on, Autumn, let's talk."

I let her tow me out into the mall. The woman in the gift shop watched us with wide eyes, probably wondering if I was under arrest.

"Good luck," Meghan called. "She's a criminal mastermind now."

I turned to snap a reply, but the door had shut behind us, and Meghan was already rounding on Craig. It looked like she was yelling at him.

"Do you think she'll make Craig sleep on the couch?" I quipped.

"I have no idea." Jordan didn't laugh.

She led me back to Ten Again at full steam. I let us into the closed, locked store, my hand surprisingly steady for someone who was—technically—in the hands of the law. Jordan said nothing, sipping at her coffee in silence and exuding an air of star-destroying rage.

I probably deserved it. I still felt like a five-year-old, but it could have been so much worse. When she pushed me into my office, I bit my tongue and dropped into my chair to listen to my talking to like a good girl.

Jordan closed the door and leaned against it. But she didn't shout. "Autumn, what the hell were you thinking?" she asked quietly.

"I was trying to help Nick and Paige—"

She cut me off. "You broke into Meghan's office."

"It was unlocked! And anyway, it was just to prove that she and Donald were colluding on the grant—did you know Donald is in financial trouble? It looks like he and Meghan fixed the contest, so she would get the money, and maybe Wes found out—"

Jordan held up a hand. "I don't want to know!"

"What?"

"I don't want to hear it! Do you realize how much trouble you could have been in if Craig hadn't called me? Not just trespassing but also obstruction of justice, and maybe even some kind of restraining order from Meghan. And do you even realize how messed up it is that Craig called me on my cell phone—at work—to come pick you up? It's ridiculous."

"Well, he didn't want me to go to *jail*. Excuse me if I should have let him call the other number that gets you at work."

"That is so not the point," Jordan said, exasperated. "Are you even listening to me?"

"Of course I am."

"Then pay attention. Your ex-boyfriend called me today because you broke into his fiancée's store to find evidence that she, what, committed fraud and murder? And he saved your ass! Craig is a creep, and suddenly he's the one watching your back. Do you realize just how messed up this whole situation is?"

"I — I didn't think of it like that," I said.

"You need to drop this whole Nancy Drew act. You are not a private investigator. You are not helping Wes. You are getting yourself into trouble, and it could get a lot worse if you don't stop while you're ahead. Detective Keller already thinks you're hiding something, and believe me, you do not want her going after you!"

"What are you talking about? You actually think this case is being handled well?"

"Don't do that. Do not accuse us of not taking Wes's death seriously. You have no idea what has happened behind the scenes, what evidence we have, what our reasoning is. We did not just arbitrarily arrest your friends. A boy died. We are taking this very, very seriously," Jordan said. "Think about what you're saying."

I took a shaky breath, reminded that for Jordan not one bit of this investigation had been a role she was playing. This was her life. "Wow. I'm sorry, Jordan."

"You should be."

We stared at each other for a long moment. Our friendship was not one of long coldness or distance: we sailed a placid sea of loving acceptance. Even when we were at different colleges, one of us just had to pick up the phone and call, and it was as if no time had passed. There had never been a need for explanation between us. Whenever one of us got snappish, the anger that followed passed almost as suddenly as it had risen. I waited.

She exhaled. "I'm sorry, too. I'm not your mother. You don't need me to lecture you. Or you shouldn't, anyway." She couldn't help adding the last wry bit, but I saw her struggle to keep it in.

I gave her my best puppy dog eyes. "Are we okay?"

"Yeah," she said. "But I'm out completely—even if you don't drop this, which you should, don't tell me anything else, don't ask me for advice, don't tell me what you found, don't even speak my name when you're considering what to do." I opened my mouth, but she lifted a hand. "And don't text it or email it or ask for a hypothetical, either."

"Well, if I can't text you a hypothetical situation and ask for advice about it, there's really no point to our friendship," I said, smiling.

"Don't joke. You are so not out of the doghouse yet."

I nodded. "Understood. But—"

"No buts."

"Well, what if—"

"No what ifs! I'm serious, Autumn!" She stamped her foot.

I held up my hands. "Okay, calm down, don't shoot me. Police brutality is a serious issue."

"That is not funny."

I shrugged. "It was a little funny."

"Come on," she said. She put her hand on the doorknob.

"Wait." I hopped up. "I know you're out, but I wondered—"

Jordan sighed audibly and turned around. "What?" She crossed her arms over her chest.

I smiled prettily. "Well . . . if you could. Are Paige and Nick still in jail?"

"No. The judge set bail earlier and let them go. They're at home, by now, but they won't be going anywhere any time soon."

I nodded. "Fair enough. Just one more—what was the new evidence you guys found? That led to their arrest?"

"Oh." She waved a hand. "That will be public record sooner or later—we found the murder weapon."

"The—what weapon?"

"It was a pen."

"A pen? Like in that Batman movie?"

Jordan ignored the second question. "Yeah. Poor kid was stabbed twice in the neck with one of those fancy, sharp-tipped pens. There weren't any prints on it, but we got an anonymous call and found it in Paige's car. In the trunk."

"Just like that? You found a fancy pen in her car. And not even, like, on the backseat where this 'anonymous caller' could have seen it. In the trunk."

"It was convenient," Jordan admitted. "But we're not just basing this on one thing. You have no idea what else led up to this arrest."

"Was this caller a man or a woman?"

Jordan rolled her eyes. "Enough, Autumn." She opened the door. "Let it go. I'm out. Don't forget that. And now I want to go home and take a freaking shower. Can I trust you to go home and mind your own business without needing a babysitter?"

"Yes, ma'am," I said, feigning meekness.

I walked her back to the mall door. She gave me a last, lingering look of mingled affection and disgust before striding back toward the atrium and the elevators. I watched her go, standing idly in the door for a long minute, listening to the faint chatter from the café and people closing their offices on my floor—happier, more successful people who didn't have murders to solve or stores closed because of brawling customers.

When one of the office owners walked by, side-eyeing me, I sighed and went back inside, though I wasn't sure why since there wasn't much to do in a closed store. It was home, though, as much as any place was home, so I wandered through, straightening the knight in shining armor and reordering a messy display of pewter gaming figurines. I went to the front door to check that it was locked and nothing was amiss outside. I opened it briefly, letting the chilly March wind wash over my face.

The memorial for Wes was gone, I saw, all the little figurines and cards vanished. Someone had picked it up, one of my employees or maybe some police officer, taking it for evidence. I wondered where they had put everything.

Something glittering under the streetlights caught my attention. I bent and picked up another *Spellcasters* card from the step. It was a spell this time, not a creature: Aura's Folly. It showed a woman at the center of a magical maelstrom, a city blowing to pieces around her. She was on her knees. I knew from memory that she was weeping, but this card had the woman's face scratched off. Again. The blank white place where her tears should have been stared up at me, hateful and penetrating.

I shuddered.

If I had needed confirmation that Nick and Paige weren't behind the murder, I knew it now. The killer's little calling card disgusted and frightened me, but I didn't know what to do. Call the cops, so they could say I'd done it in a pitiful attempt to make my ridiculous behavior seem justified? Call Jordan back, who would come, I knew, even though she desperately needed me to let her do her job?

The card trembled in my fingers, and I realized I was shaking from head to toe. Whoever had killed Wes had been here, had known I was gone but would return. They knew our games well enough to make threats out of cards that brought people joy. They knew how to get under my skin, to frighten me. Why not just kill me, too, if I was such a threat? What the hell was with the foreplay?

I crumpled the card in my fist. I'd had enough.

17

THE MALL WAS EMPTY—EMPTIER than usual for a Wednesday evening—as I strode through it, my sneakers silent on the granite floors. I did not wait for the elevator but bolted up the stairs two at a time, heading for Chic. I didn't care if the cops came to arrest me for harassing Meghan, if everyone in town thought I was a deranged stalker woman, jilted in high school and unable to forget it. I needed answers, and Meghan could give them to me.

I yanked open the door to the main floor. It banged against the wall of the stairwell with a sound loud as an echoing crash in Moria.

On the other side of the frame, Craig threw his hands up. "Whoa, Autumn, calm down."

We collided, and I bounced off his chest. I flailed for a moment and then took a step back into the stairwell. He followed me, reaching awkwardly for me and then dropping his arms to his sides. The door slammed shut again.

"Damn it, Craig," I gasped. "You scared me."

"I'm sorry." He laughed. "I was just coming to look for you."

"Well, you found me." I glared at him, irritated at myself for letting him get to me and irritated at him just for existing. "What's up?"

"I wanted to see if you—if you were okay after what happened. I saw Jordan heading for the parking garage, but she didn't tell me anything."

I put my hands on my hips. "She's not my mom. I can speak for myself."

"I know."

"Why did you persuade Meghan to let me off?"

"I don't want to see you in jail for one," Craig said. "Plus, you know, the grant thing—she's been bitchy to you the whole time. I can understand what you were thinking, breaking into her office. What were you looking for?"

I ignored the question, refusing to be derailed. "Hey, did she and Donald fix the grant competition? Because it sure looks like they did. Donald needs cash, like, a lot. Did you know that? You're trying to sell him property, and he has no money." I paused. "Where the hell is he, anyway? I'd think he'd be here to kick me out of the building for good after today."

Craig blinked. "That was a lot of questions in a very short span of time."

"Well, I'm waiting for answers." I tapped my foot.

"You're on edge tonight." He leaned against the wall, as if his artful casualness would underline my own tension. The attitude snapped my already-tenuous hold on rationality.

I stepped forward and poked him in the shoulder. "You're damn right I'm on edge," I said. I poked him again. "I got kicked out of the running for a grant I really wanted, my land-lord made me close my store, I got arrested, a kid I loved died, and two of my friends have been accused of his murder." I emphasized each of my accusations with another poke, and he just stood there, looking bemused. My voice raised into a near-shriek. "Of course I'm 'on edge.' Hell, you should be more on edge—someone threatened your fiancée, and your freaking assistant got arrested. Why are you so—damn—cool about it all?"

I stopped, panting.

Craig lifted his arm and caught my poking hand in his fist. He forced my arm down slowly. "Easy there, tiger," he said. "You're dangerous with that thing."

"Shut up with your jokes!" I shouted. "Just—answer me!"

"Why am I so cool?" he asked. He tilted his head, pretending to think. "I learned from the best, I guess. Some girl I know taught me all about it when we were kids."

I deflated. "Ha, ha, ha."

"Do you feel better now?"

I nodded. "A little."

"Okay. So. Questions. Answers. I don't think Donald and Meghan fixed the grant competition, but I do know they're up to something. I know that Donald's having trouble with this building's finances, but I don't think he's as broke as you seem to think he is. And I have no idea where he is."

"What do you mean, Donald and Meghan are 'up to something'?"

"Exactly that—they have some plan, either for Meghan's store or for the grant money or for the building. They've been meeting a lot, talking on the phone. Meghan's my fiancée, after all—I know who she's been talking to, even if I don't know what she's been saying." He paused, studying my face like a book. "And I do know she didn't murder anyone, Autumn."

"You don't know," I said. "You left that night."

"I do know. Meghan does not have it in her to kill someone. She's a good person even if you can't see it."

"Oh, sure, real good. Steals other girls' boyfriends, fixes a high-stakes grant contest, calls the cops after a little harmless trespassing—"

"Are you listening to yourself? You're acting like a crazy person."

"I am not crazy. Craig, Wes is dead. There's no undoing that. And someone is threatening me, and someone is threatening your fiancée—" I broke off, shaking my head. "This isn't over."

"What do you mean, someone is threatening you?"

I held out my hand, the crumpled *Spellcasters* card sweaty and slick in my fist. Craig took it, frowning. "What is this?"

"I keep finding them. In the store, around the store. At first, I thought they were a remembrance for Wes, but they keep happening. Nick and Paige can't be doing it. And why would they threaten me, anyway?"

"Do the cops know about this?"

"Yes. They think I'm making it up." I laughed bitterly.

"Why?" Craig looked angry on my behalf, his hazel eyes sparking. Jordan wondered why I let Craig remain in my life: this was why. We had been and were still, after everything, friends. He cared about me. We had a history, a story we'd written together, and there was no undoing that. He had hurt me, yes, and he could be insensitive, but we were so much more than just a few months of pain.

"Because of the vandalism at Meghan's, and because I don't want to believe Paige and Nick killed Wes. They think I'm trying to interfere with their investigation."

"But Jordan is helping you, right?"

"No. Well, she was. But she can't anymore."

"Oh man. I'm sorry Autumn. It's got to be serious if she's not helping you."

"Yeah. Well." I rubbed my forehead with the back of one hand. "This whole week has been pretty 'serious.'"

"I think you should take off."

"What?" I took a step back and leaned against the metal railing. "What do you mean?"

"Take off—take a break, take some time. Or, better, just go—close up. You're already closed. Go stay with your mom in Madison. Open a new store there. Start over, try again. You don't need this little town, anyway. You never did."

"You're seriously telling me to uproot my life, move away, start over again—you're telling me this in a stairwell?"

"Does the location matter?" Craig took a step toward me. "Come on. Think about it. You never liked it here, always said you wanted to go somewhere else, do something else." He took me by the shoulders and shook me a little.

"Yeah, when I was like seventeen." I shrugged off his hands and pressed myself against the railing. "I'm a grown-up now, Craig. I like my life."

"You're not happy."

"This week is not a very good gauge of my day-to-day happiness." I sighed. "No. Tempting as it is, as it always has been, running away is not an option. This will pass, whatever happens.

The store won't be closed forever. I may have to move, but I won't shut down permanently."

Craig took a step back. He half-smiled at me, an odd little expression I couldn't read. "I guess you know what's best for you. I think you could be happier, though."

"Maybe so. Maybe not, though." I straightened my shoulders. "So why did you want to talk to me?"

"What?" Craig blinked.

"You were coming downstairs."

"Oh. Yeah. I wanted to talk to you about all this—ask you to ease up on Meghan, you know." He paused, looking like he was going to say something serious. He opened his mouth, and suddenly I didn't want to hear what was next.

As if I'd conjured them just to silence my ex, the fire alarms started blaring, the little lights in them flashing a blazing, brilliant white. The stairwell suddenly had the atmosphere of a rave, deafening us, the strobe-like lights distorting my vision. My hands went to my ears. "What the hell?"

Craig leaned toward me. "What?"

"I said, what the—" I broke off, shaking my head, and pointed at the door. "Come on—there's an exit on this floor."

Craig pushed the door open, and we entered the main lobby. The lighting was more tempered here, though the alarms still blared, and the flashing lights cast shadows that leapt across the floor and disappeared, creating random, dizzying patterns. There was no smoke, no evidence of fire, but no one occupied the lobby. Max's security desk stood empty.

A woman screamed down the hallway.

"Meghan!" Craig cried. He took off at a run.

Against my better judgment, I dashed after him. I couldn't see or smell a fire, but still, he might need help. I rounded the corner and saw a gush of white smoke pouring from the door of Chic. Craig stood at its outskirts, coughing and waving his hand in front of his face. The smoke had a chemical smell and billowed without a clear source. Distantly I heard sirens, but I still hadn't noticed any flames.

"What's happening?" I asked.

"I don't know—it's not hot. I don't think there's a fire. Meghan's in there!" He made for the door, but I caught his arm.

"Wait!" I said. "I hear the fire engines."

A figure appeared in the smoke. I took an involuntary step back, frightened, but the man approached, and I saw that it was just Donald entering from the street door at the other end of the building. His face was gray. "I don't see any flames," he said. "Why are you two here?"

"We need to get out of here!" Max, the security guard, had arrived. He panted as he approached, a hand pressed to his side.

A crowd of the other storeowners was forming behind us. Some of them were heading for the door, but others were making their way toward us, curious or frightened.

"Meghan is in there!" Craig said again. He shook me off his arm and plunged into the smoke.

"Wait!" Max cried, hoarse.

"Craig!" I shouted. The door closed, wafting some of the smoke toward us so that I was able to catch a glimpse into the store. I still didn't see any fire.

I swore and followed him in.

The smoke parted around me, thinner than it looked from the hallway. I groped my way through it to the door. My eyes burned as I patted the door itself gingerly, then poked at the handle with one fingertip. It was cool—if there was a fire, it wasn't burning anywhere near me. I pulled the door open and stepped into the store.

Smoke hung in clouds inside, and the place reeked of sulfur, but there were still no flames. The smoke seemed like something on a movie set, rising in tendrils and clouds from the ground itself. It dispersed, fog-like, along the ceiling, but nothing stirred it.

I saw as I approached that the source was smoke bombs: one of them smoldered on the floor a few feet away, thick white smoke rising from it like steam from a volcano, foul and chemical scented.

"Craig?" I called.

I couldn't see more than a few feet in front of me. I coughed, waving my hand in front of my face. The smoke was thickest ahead of me, near the office. A mannequin stood beside me, eerie and headless. I shouted again, not keen on venturing into the depths of the store blind. Even if there was no fire, the person who had dropped the smoke bombs could still be here, waiting to hurt me or whoever went looking for Meghan.

"Autumn?" Craig's voice came through the smoke. "Are you there?"

"Yes—where are you?"

The sprinklers came on and I shrieked as cold, stale water sprayed down from the ceiling. I heard Craig shout wordlessly, too, as the water hit him.

"In the office," he called. "You can come back. It's safe. I'll need help."

I darted toward the office, flailing my arms in front of me like a Muppet to keep from running into anything. Water dripped down my body, chilling me, and my sneakers squelched on the carpet. I found my way back, though, and pushed through the door.

Craig knelt on the floor over Meghan's prone form. I paused, stunned at the difference from the scene I'd witnessed earlier. Sprinklers sprayed everywhere, and the office was in shambles. The desk was soaked, and I could smell hot electronics. Steam rose from the computer. I saw a smoke bomb on the desk, still glowing even though spray from the ceiling fell all around it.

"Autumn," Craig said.

I shook myself and squatted beside him. "What do you need me to do?"

"I'll have to carry her. I think she's hurt—it looks like someone hit her. I just need you to lead me."

I could see the whites of his eyes, but his voice was calm. His arms were steady as he gathered Meghan up.

I nodded. "Okay."

Once he'd straightened, Meghan limp as a Beanie Baby in his arms, I held open the office door for him to slide through. He stopped once he had made his way out and waited for me to maneuver my way ahead of him. I lumbered on, guiding him, still waving my arms ahead of my body to make sure neither of us ran into anything on our way to safety. I banged my shin once on a low table that held expensive folded—now ruined—shirts, but Craig dodged it with ease.

Max was waiting for us at the mouth of Chic. We spilled into the hallway, coughing, and a solicitous crowd milled around Craig as he strode toward the lobby. I followed, solicitous hands guiding me toward clearer air. The fire department arrived just as we opened the front doors, and an ambulance pulled up to the curb. I watched, dazed, as uniformed paramedics swarmed Craig and Meghan. They produced a stretcher, took Meghan from Craig's arms, and laid her on the stretcher with expert hands. She started coughing, and one of the paramedics stepped forward with an oxygen mask.

"Are you all right?" someone asked.

I turned. A fireman stood beside me, looming large in his uniform. I nodded, though my throat burned, and my eyes stung from the smoke. My clothes were damp, and I felt like I'd been through a garbage masher. But I was fine—I was whole, unharmed. I hadn't confronted Meghan, but it seemed suddenly clear that she wasn't the killer. The paramedics were rushing around her stretcher, strapping things to her and peering into her eyes, and Craig held one of her hands while she looked up at him.

I'd been wrong.

I let one of the paramedics wrap a woolly blanket around me and push me to a seated position on the curb. She shined a light into my eyes and told me to take a deep breath, checking for some sort of smoke damage, I assumed. I waved her off irritably, not in the mood to be dragged to yet another tiny institutional room and asked questions I couldn't answer.

The paramedic fussed at me, saying that if I refused medical attention, I'd have to sign a form. I gave her my very best basilisk glare, then turned away, wanting to stew alone.

A crowd had formed around the building's entrance. Firemen rushed in and out the front doors, but no one carried hoses or buckets—there was, as I'd thought, no actual fire. Donald stood, stunned, beside a uniformed police officer, who appeared to be asking him questions. His sweater vest was dirty and his khaki pants smudged. I frowned at him. Why was he so dirty? And where had he come from? Max lurked at his shoulder, nodding to the police.

The paramedics and fire crew milled around me looking for other problems to solve. No one interrogated me—apparently I wasn't being accused of this particular act of vandalism. Someone pressed a bottle of water into my hand—I didn't see who—and I realized, dimly, that I must be experiencing shock or the aftereffects of adrenaline. The crowd, the smoke, the world all seemed very far away. I saw Meghan and Craig in sharp focus, though. The paramedics lifted Meghan's stretcher into the ambulance. Craig climbed in after her.

It couldn't have been her. She had been attacked, knocked out—she had a bloody wound on her forehead, I'd seen that much. The cops circled her, waiting to pounce, and I knew they would be reeling at this sudden act of violence. I was grateful that I'd been with Craig, though I wished someone else had seen us. There was no way he or I had done this, though, and if I'd needed any further proof that Meghan wasn't guilty of the vandalism, at least I had it now. I couldn't accuse her of attacking herself.

But Donald had been there. He could have been behind all of it—the *Spellcasters* card, which Craig still had, the petty vandalism with the dolls, the attack on Meghan, Wes's death, everything. It didn't make sense, though. I would have thought he had no insight into game or geek culture, didn't even know a game called *Spellcasters* existed. But he had motive and means. Maybe he was the one doing everything. I shivered and pulled the edges of the impersonal gray paramedic's blanket tighter around my shoulders.

I wished, desperately, that Nick and Paige had not already been arraigned. If they'd still been in police custody when this happened, maybe we could have settled it, finally and for good. I hoped they had an ironclad alibi for today's vandalism—and I hoped it had nothing to do with me or anyone else I knew. I was running out of energy for worrying about them, when it seemed I needed to be worried about my own safety, and the safety of the building itself. Someone bumped into me, jogging down the sidewalk behind me, and that seemed to emphasize the point: things were happening, and it had something to do with Independence Square Mall. And whoever was behind it would hurt anyone standing in their way.

I scooched myself closer to the street, trying to make myself smaller.

That's when I spotted Cody in the crowd, lurking near Max. He was watching me, his eyes dark, his shaved head shining under the lights. No one else seemed to see him—he looked like just one of the many rubberneckers who had stopped to see what the fuss on the square was. Neither Max nor Donald acknowledged him, and the policeman just kept talking to Donald, oblivious.

My stomach turned over, and I turned to the paramedic nearest me. "Maybe I do need medical attention after all."

18

I DIDN'T GO TO the hospital. The paramedics cleaned me up at the scene and sent me on my way, telling me to take aspirin if I felt any soreness, drink a lot of water to hydrate my lungs, and call my physician if I felt light-headed or disoriented.

Something told me my physician wouldn't be able to help with the kind of disorientation I felt now.

I sat at home, alone, as the clock ticked steadily on into the night, wondering if I should be alone. The vandal had targeted Meghan specifically, and that frightened me. She hadn't dropped the smoke bombs herself. Meghan might be willing to put on a show to win herself some pity, but she would never do anything to undercut her store's business—or permanently mar her pretty face. She was a horrible human being, sure, but she was also a good businesswoman. We had that in common.

It had to be about the building.

While I wanted to believe the grant was the connection, there didn't seem to be any involvement beyond Meghan and me. I'd looked it up: there had been no news about the other contestants applying for the grant, no reports of vandalism, no violence, no nothing.

Meghan was a target. I was a target. Wesley had died.

Cody was there, Donald was there, Craig was there. I didn't think it could be Craig, because I had seen his reaction to the attack on Meghan, and he had been with me the whole time. That left Donald and Cody—and while I could believe Cody would hurt Wes, I didn't think he would kill him, certainly not over a game. And that didn't explain why he would attack Meghan, unless he meant to cover his tracks. Maybe it was an elaborate set-up for Nick and Paige.

Or maybe, the cops were right, and Nick and Paige had killed Wes and that was the end of the story. I wondered if they'd been taken back into custody.

I gnawed my fingernails. Sitting bundled on my couch in a fluffy blanket had seemed like a good idea when I left the Independence building, but now I felt like a big, fat, target. I was probably safe at home, though. The killer had targeted people at the mall rather than out in the world, which pretty strongly suggested Donald was behind it all. The mall was his turf, his territory, and we were all in danger when we crossed his threshold.

If only the *Spellcasters* spells were real, and we could raise Wes from the dead for a minute or two to question him, like they do on all those TV shows where people, well, raise the dead so they can question them. But I didn't have any supernatural solutions. I was just a gamer with a stunning knowledge of how to green a building. I wasn't a private eye or a superhero or even a spunky heroine with more pluck than sense. My life would have been a lot more interesting if I had been one of those things.

The phone rang, and I shrieked. More horrified at the sound of my own voice than the thought of a phone stalker, I put a hand over my mouth as I picked up the receiver to muffle my own panting breath.

"Hello?" I said. I wondered if the caller could hear my heart pounding.

It was Bay.

"Hey. We heard about what happened—are you okay?"

"Yeah." I filled her in, describing the scene and my consequent worries.

"That's crazy." She sounded distracted, like she was eating or typing or both.

"What are you doing?" I asked, hurt. She should be worried about my safety or rushing to my side or something. I felt a little neglected by all of my people. Jordan was MIA, my parents were at home, Hector was off doing Hector things. And here I was, all alone, falling to pieces with no one to put me back together again.

"Just looking at those photos you took earlier."

"Oh, right." That mollified me a little. "Are they useful?"

"Maybe. The photos definitely show that Donald's having money troubles, and he and Meghan are up to something. But what's weird is what I saw that you didn't get a chance to look at before Meghan came in—there was an email from Meghan to Donald saying that the plan was off."

"What? Are you sure?"

"Yeah. It was really vague, and really short, but it just said that Meghan didn't think it would work well right now, and they both needed to focus on other things."

"Was there a reply from Donald?"

"I didn't see one—it was sent today."

"Why didn't we see it in Donald's email?"

"I have no idea. Maybe he deleted it. We didn't check his trash file."

"Deleting wouldn't accomplish much, anyway. You're always telling me that."

"Yeah, but Donald wouldn't know that. Maybe this whole fire thing this afternoon was to cover it up or to scare Meghan back into line."

I sucked in my breath. "Oh man, I bet you're right."

I could hear Bay typing furiously. "Too bad I don't have a photo."

"Meghan's computer was destroyed."

"Donald's wasn't, though." The typing stopped, and I could practically feel the heat of Bay's laser focus on me. "We should tell Jordan. I was thinking—"

My doorbell rang. "Oh, hang on, Bay, there's someone at the door."

"Be careful!" Her voice cracked. "Stay on the phone with me."

"You think I'm in danger here?" I stood, letting my blanket fall to the floor.

"Donald knows we were in Meghan's office! You might be."

"I think I could take Donald," I scoffed. For good measure, though, I stopped by my fireplace on the way to the front door and grabbed one of the pokers. I hoisted it in one hand and tucked the phone between my ear and shoulder. "I have a poker."

"Cold iron, that's good."

"What, in case it's a ghost?" If she was joking, she couldn't be that worried. But she was alert now, no longer dividing her attention between me and her computer.

"Well, it never hurts to be extra prepared."

"Right." I laughed, but the merriment felt forced. "I'm not sure my poker qualifies, though."

"What?"

"Yeah, apparently these days 'cold iron' is something special," I said. I kept my voice light as I padded up the hallway in my socks. My house was old and not well insulated. Whoever was outside would hear me before I saw them. They would know, at least, that I wasn't afraid. "Even a lot of iron pots aren't made of true iron. I doubt my hardware store fireplace tools would meet ghost-destroying standards."

"I don't think it'll matter if it's a person and not a ghost."

I tilted my head as I approached the front door. I couldn't see anyone through the rippled glass of the windows, but it was dark outside. I pressed my eye to the peephole. The door was cold, chilled by the outside air, and the rim of the peephole was foggy. I saw no one.

"There's no one there."

"Those damn kids again?" Bay asked, her tone light, but I could tell she was worried.

"Maybe."

I unlocked the door and opened it slowly. I peered out through the cracked opening, poker in hand, before I pulled the door open the rest of the way. "No one here," I told Bay. There was a manila envelope on the "Speak, friend, and enter," doormat, though. I stooped to pick it up. "Someone left an envelope."

"That can't be good."

"No." I stepped back in from the cold, shut the door, and locked it. With Bay still listening over the phone, I slid my finger under the edge of the envelope and ripped it open. I peered in before I stuck in my hand and saw a few thick squares of paper. "Photographs." I took them out—they were digital photos, printed off someone's computer.

They were photos of me.

One of me sitting on the curb, waiting for the paramedics. I was looking up at one of them, seen in profile in the picture, but my features were scratched bare, leaving a white place on the photo. I sucked in my breath.

"What is it?" Bay asked.

I didn't answer. I flipped to the next photo. Me, in my driveway. I was getting out of my car at home, bags in hand. My clothes were soggy—earlier that evening, just an hour or two ago. My heart pounded against my ribs. I heard a clang and jumped, but I realized that it was the poker from the fireplace—I'd dropped it. I flipped to the third photo. It was of my bedroom window. The blinds were closed, but I could see my silhouette behind them, a dark patch in the golden light.

This one had writing on it: *MIND YOUR OWN BUSINESS, BITCH.*

I realized Bay was calling my name, over and over again, but I could barely hear her over my rushing pulse. The photos shook in my hand, and I dropped them on the floor. They scattered over the cheerful, polished wood, one of them skidding into the kitchen, another toward the living room. My hands felt frozen, and my stomach heaved.

"I'm here," I said to Bay. "I'm alright."

"What was it?"

"Photos," I said. "Photos of me."

"Okay," Bay said. "I'm leaving right now." I heard noise, like her keys, Allison speaking in the background. "I want you to hang up and call 911 right now. Then get your cell phone and call me back. Allison will call Jordan, and we'll be there in ten minutes."

I nodded, though I knew she couldn't see me. I could feel my knees shaking. "Okay," I stammered. "Okay."

It took me two tries to disconnect, my fingers were trembling so violently, and when I finally did, I dropped the phone before I could dial again.

The doorbell rang, and I screamed.

"Autumn?" a voice called.

A female voice.

I put a hand to my chest. "Who's there?" I shouted. I bent, groping for the poker again, and picked it up with my still-shaking hands. I held it across my body like a fencer and took a step.

"It's—it's Meghan. Meghan Kountz. I need your help."

I staggered to the doorway. My vision had gone black around the edges, and I honestly thought I might faint. I pressed my hands against the door, leaning on it, and peeked out the peephole again. It was Meghan. She wore a bandage around her head and no makeup. Her hair was in a messy ponytail, and her jacket didn't match her pants. She looked like a crazy person.

"Please—" she said. "Open the door. I think someone's trying to kill me."

I laughed, my voice high and hysterical. "You do—there were photos, on my doorstep."

"What?"

"Is there anyone else out there?"

She glanced over her shoulder, nervous. "No, no one I can see. Should there be?"

"No." I opened the door and took a step back, the poker still brandished before me. "Come in, but show me your hands."

"Are you serious?" She took a hesitant step across the threshold. When she peered around the door, her eyes widened. "What's going on?"

"Show me your hands." I gestured with the poker, feeling a little ridiculous. She complied, holding both hands up to shoulder height. Her designer bag dangled from one elbow. "Drop the bag."

"Okay." She lowered it to the ground, then slid it a few inches away with her foot. "Is that better? Can I lower my hands?"

I bent, the poker still raised, and took her purse. I looked through it quickly, though I had no idea what I would do if I found, say, a gun or a bloody knife in it. There was nothing but a tablet and her keys and a lot of makeup. I closed it and handed it back to her. "Yes. Here."

We stared at each other in my dim hallway. I still had my poker, and she held her purse stiffly in front of her body. "What happened to you?" she asked.

I pointed the poker at the photos on the floor. "Someone sent me pictures of myself with the faces scratched off. I've been getting *Spell*—er, game cards with the faces scratched off for days now, but someone brought the photos to my house tonight." I looked her up and down. "What happened to you?"

"Someone attacked me from behind in my own store and then lit off a bunch of smoke bombs to destroy evidence."

I nodded. "Fair enough. Come on." I waved a hand and led the way back to my living room, stopping to pick up the phone from where I had dropped it. I left the photos on the floor—I didn't want to see them again, and when Jordan got here, I assumed she would want to take them as evidence.

Meghan perched on my couch, looking incredibly out of place. Her designer purse sat on the floor beside my polished tree stump end table. She glanced around, taking in my wall of DVDs, the anime poster, and the framed cross-stitched profanity sampler over the fireplace. I could see her absorbing it all in Sherlock-style, evaluating me as represented by my possessions, mapping my life and my place in the world. I didn't like it, and I didn't like her, but she looked so pitiful that I didn't have the heart to kick her out.

"Why did you come here?"

"I know you've been—uh—investigating what happened. I know you don't believe that your friends killed that boy. And I know you know bad stuff has kept happening, even after those two were arrested."

"Yeah. So?"

"So . . . I think there's more going on here than the police realize." She bit her lip, a vulnerable gesture that probably made men like Craig go weak in the knees. "I don't think it was just about their little game."

"Did you and Donald work together to fix the grant competition?" I asked bluntly.

"What? No!" Meghan's eyes were wide. "Of course not!"

"I saw the emails between you—that's why I broke into your office. And his. I know you were working on something together."

"Oh. Well—I guess I might as well tell you." She relaxed, clasping and unclasping her hands in her lap. "That was something else. We were working together on plans to convert the top floor of the building into a banquet hall—we were going to remodel it, and I was going to start working for him as an events coordinator to rent it out for parties and dances and conventions and things. He needs money, you know, and that would help to boost the building's income. The remodels from the grant would help to boost it, but the banquet hall was a separate project. We kept it quiet, though, because we weren't sure how it would affect my chances for the grant otherwise."

I sat back, stunned. "So—asking me to drop out, that wasn't because I was screwing up your plans?"

She rolled her eyes. "Well, yes, it was, but not in the way you've obviously been thinking. If you had to install solar panels and change the wiring and all that stuff, it would slow down our plans for the banquet hall."

"But Donald was interested in my plans—he wanted to save money on his utilities."

"He thought maybe we could do what you wanted to do as part of our remodel for the top floor. We could make it more efficient at the same time."

"Then the grant coming to me would have made it easier for you two, because you would have had extra money—"

"Not necessarily, because the expenditures for the grant money have to be tracked carefully, and it might have meant not getting to—"

I held up a hand. "Okay, this is so not the point."

She stopped, a funny look on her face. "You're right."

"Thank you."

"I'm sorry your customer died."

I stared at her.

She shifted in her seat. "Really. He was so young. And even though I complained about them, they never hurt my business or anything. They were a well-behaved group of kids."

"So why did you report them?" I asked. "Paige said you heard them arguing—it must have been your evidence that made the police suspect them."

"I did hear them arguing. I couldn't not tell the police that." She sounded miffed that I would even suggest she might consider hiding evidence, and I almost laughed. We couldn't help but argue, Meghan and me, but we weren't all that dissimilar. She told the truth, and so did I.

And we'd both been disappointed.

"I'm, uh, sorry I thought you killed Wes," I said.

Her eyes bulged. "You thought it was me? How could I have possibly killed him?"

"Well, I thought Donald helped you."

"Oh." She choked and put a hand to her lips as if to contain something more.

"What?" I said.

"It might have been Donald. But—" Her eyes filled with tears.

"What?" I said again, louder.

She looked at me, and the tears spilled down her cheeks. "I think it was Craig."

19

"ARE YOU SERIOUS?" I said. "How could it have been Craig? And why?"

"I don't know!" Meghan sobbed. She completely broke down, her hands over her face, her body shaking with the force of her tears. Her sobs clawed out from deep in her throat, raw and hoarse, and her face went bright red with the fury of it. I started to feel like a jerk, just sitting there staring at her like a deadbeat den mother, so I grabbed the box of tissues from the end table and moved to sit beside her on the couch.

I patted her knee. "There, there."

She looked up at me, and I held the box of tissues out. She took one, still sobbing. "Thank you."

After a few more minutes of wheezing tears and awkward reassurances, she started to pull herself together. "I'm sorry," she gasped. "I just hadn't said it out loud, yet, and I still don't want to believe it's true."

I tried again. "Why do you think it might be true?"

She shrugged and dissolved into tears once more. "Well, he—" she hiccupped and had to start over. "He was there that night. And then—he's been hiding things. And I know he's been talking to Donald a lot, threatening him. He's had secret meetings for months, but there have been more recently. And I—" she stopped, sobbing again. "I think the porch paint was blood."

I had to interrupt at that one. "Um . . . what?"

"The tin of porch paint—I think it was blood!"

"He has a jar of blood?" I said stupidly.

"Uh-huh." She nodded and snuffled into her soggy tissue.

"I think I need more information."

"And today—when I was attacked—he came in. I wasn't unconscious, not really, and I saw him—he saw me on the floor and then moved one of the smoke bombs, put it on the desk. After that, the sprinklers came on, so my desk was soaked, and he came over to me and—"

She melted into insensibility, sobbing and saying random words. From what little she had told me, it seemed possible— while I couldn't explain the jar of blood, unless it was stage blood, it sounded like Meghan thought Craig had been behind all of the vandalism and attacks. My mind reeled as I adapted to this suggestion. I couldn't begin to guess why Craig would do any of it, never mind why he would do so much damage to Meghan's store, but he had to have been pulling the strings. This would mean he attacked her and then came to find me as an alibi.

It was cold blooded, and I felt sick, thinking about how he'd just stood there in the stairwell, letting me poke his shoulder, while Meghan was bleeding on the floor of her office. If she was right, which was still difficult to believe, I was lucky he hadn't just pitched me down the stairs and fled the scene. The cops would have blamed, well, someone—it wouldn't have been my problem at that point—and he would have ridden off into the sunset.

But why orchestrate almost a week of violence and silly vandalism? Why kill an innocent boy—for what? A twenty-five-thousand-dollar grant that had nothing to do with Craig himself? No, we still didn't have the whole story.

I wanted to believe Meghan had solved it, but I couldn't quite bring myself to believe her over my old friend. Craig was—had always been—on my side, while Meghan had been my personal troll for nearly two decades.

"Why did you and Craig fight the night Wes died?" I asked.

"Because he never supported my plans with Donald to put a banquet hall on the fifth floor. He said it would split my focus." She broke down again in an ugly-cry born of days of fear and trauma.

At that moment, someone pounded on my door. Meghan froze. I leapt off the couch, my heart racing, and took a flying cat-leap for my poker, which I'd abandoned by the armchair. The pounding continued.

"Oh my god, oh my god, who is that?" Meghan cried.

"Autumn!" a voice shouted. "Open the door! Right now, damn it!"

It was Bay. "It's okay, that's one of my employees. It's fine."

I rushed to the door and found Bay and Allison. Bay's face was white, and Allison had her phone at her ear. "I've got 911 on the phone," she told me as soon as I opened the door. "They're sending a patrol car by."

"Wow. Thanks."

Bay pushed the door open. "When you didn't call back, we thought something horrible had happened." She froze when she saw Meghan standing in the door to the living room, tear-streaked and bedraggled. "Which . . . maybe . . . it did?" She looked at me, eyebrows raised.

"Boy, do I have a lot to tell you," I said.

The two of them sat down, and once Allison finished with the 911 dispatcher, I filled everyone in on the gory details of the story so far.

When I finished explaining Meghan's part in the day's drama, Bay clasped her hands in front of her, looking thoughtful. "It's wild to think that this whole time, he's been living with you, supporting you and being nice boyfriend-guy, when he was also threatening you and us and concealing a murder." She shook her head. "Goes to show that you never really know someone. But why would he do it?"

Meghan shrugged, morose, and I said, "That's the million-dollar question, isn't it? We don't have all the pieces of the puzzle." If we chose to believe Meghan at all.

"Jordan's on her way," Bay told us. "I called her as soon as I got off the phone with you. She said not to let you leave the house. She'll bring Detective Keller with her."

"Has there been any news about Nick or Paige, or about the smoke bombs in Meghan's store?"

"Nothing we've heard," Allison said. "But the 911 dispatcher wasn't well-informed."

Bay snorted. "They're like drive-thru operators, those people."

"That's not fair. It's an important job and with minimal training—" Allison objected.

"Hello!" Meghan shouted, cutting across their argument. "I just said I think my fiancé is a murderer, your friend found creepy stalker photos of herself on her front step, this is not the time to be arguing about our country's crisis response system!"

Bay and Allison broke off and stared at me. Bay's lips were parted in surprise. I blinked and felt a smile tugging at the ends of my mouth. "She has a point."

"Why are you smiling?" Meghan snapped. "Nothing about this is funny."

Allison giggled, and Bay started laughing. I felt a bubble of hysteria rising in my own throat, threatening to explode in a burst of inappropriate laughter. I forced it down, still smiling, and said, "I'm sorry, Meghan. We're all just a little on edge."

We pulled ourselves together before the police arrived in semi-full force, Jordan and Detective Keller striding up in street clothes, while a patrol car with lights flashing parked in my front lawn. They gathered in my hallway, the police using tweezers to collect the photos into plastic baggies. They questioned me about what I'd seen on my way home, who I'd talked to, what had happened, and Detective Keller dispatched a uniformed officer to quiz my neighbors about any strangers they might have noticed.

Throughout everything, Bay and Jordan stood at my sides, keeping Meghan and everyone else from coming near me. Jordan hugged me when she came in and squeezed my arm several times, apologizing, I think, for not taking my concerns more seriously. It wasn't her fault—it was no one's fault, and I could hardly blame the police for not accepting my half-baked theories. Even now, the argument against Craig seemed flimsy, and the officers interrogating Meghan looked dubious, to say the least.

Once the wheels were rolling on the new path of the investigation, the detective rounded on me. "I knew you weren't telling me everything," she barked at me.

"Ah—" I glanced shiftily from her to Jordan. "Well, before today, I thought that Meghan and Donald were colluding to fix the grant competition, you know, for the small businesses, and that they killed Wes Bowen because he knew about it, but now—" I looked at Meghan. "That doesn't seem so likely."

"You think your landlord was in on it then, too." In a thermal shirt, fleece vest, and jeans, the detective looked like she had walked out of an episode of *Supernatural*, and it made her even more intimidating than a uniform had. "Why do you think that?"

"Well—" Bay stepped in helpfully and showed Detective Keller the photos on her phone. The older woman studied them, a frown forming on her face. "We know we were wrong now, though. Meghan says they were working on something else."

"And Miss Kountz thinks her boyfriend, Craig MacLeod, might be behind the violence."

"Yes. But we thought Donald might be in on it, too. Bay saw an email from Meghan to Donald saying the plan was off—"

By the fireplace, Meghan's head swiveled toward us. "What?"

We all stopped, looking at her. "I saw it in your sent messages folder," Bay said. "But not in Donald's account."

Meghan shook her head. "I never sent that."

Detective Keller looked at me. "What does that mean?"

"I have no idea." I shrugged, looking at Bay.

"It might mean someone else sent it from your account," Bay said to Meghan.

"Someone like Craig!" Meghan cried.

"But why was it in the account that sent it and not in the account that received it?" Detective Keller asked.

Bay waved a hand. "He probably just deleted it, and we didn't see it."

"Deleted it," I said, "to cover it up, and then he attacked Meghan, trying to destroy her computer!"

"Craig tried to destroy my computer," Meghan objected.

"But they're working together!"

"Ladies, please," Detective Keller said. "You are jumping to conclusions. You have no proof of anything. We found the murder weapon in Paige Harding's car. She and her little boyfriend had means, motive, opportunity."

"What about the smoke bombs today?" I said. "And the attack on Meghan? And Paige works for Craig—he probably put it in her car!" If Craig was the DM of this sick little episode, Meghan had finally pulled back the screen, and now we could see him pushing us, the little painted pieces, around the board. I hadn't wanted to believe it, but it made so much sense, I couldn't deny it.

"Miss Sinclair, this man is your ex-boyfriend, and your behavior toward his current girlfriend has been outright suspicious. I'm not sure you want to keep making accusations against him."

Bay drew herself up to protest, and even Jordan looked uncomfortable at this assessment of my position. I waved them both off. "Well, why did you think I was hiding something? You know something in this case isn't adding up—you've known it for a while now."

"That does not justify your behavior."

Bay couldn't keep quiet anymore. "Someone is stalking her—she's not doing this!"

I shot her a grateful smile. "I'm not asking you to take my word for any of it," I said. "But I'm not the only one making the accusation. His fiancée thinks he's up to something, too."

Detective Keller looked at Meghan, then, her face somber. "Do you seriously think Mr. MacLeod has been behaving suspiciously?"

"I saw him," Meghan insisted, but she didn't sound certain. My heart leapt into my throat. We were losing Detective Keller—but she was here, and she was willing to listen. That wasn't something we could let slip through our fingers.

"Listen—we know that Donald didn't leave the building Friday night when Max, the security guard, said he did. He went to the basement. We found a witness who saw him. It's possible Craig didn't either. How much can we trust Max's word? He's not the brightest bulb in the box."

"He's your security guard," the detective objected.

"He's the Crypt Keeper's chatty older brother," I said.

"Say what you really think," Bay muttered.

"I know I'm being mean," I said, "but you have to see that there are holes in the story. Nick and Paige weren't the only ones there that night who could have killed Wes."

"Who was your witness?" Detective Keller said. "The one who saw Donald Wolcott in the building's basement after he said he'd left?"

"A guy at our store—Cody Patterson. He was there that night, too."

"Cody Patterson, the one who had an argument with the victim and our prime suspects?" Detective Keller said. "The one you wanted us to consider as a suspect? Listen to yourself Miss Sinclair—is he your key witness?"

"Well, I know he's not the most reliable, but you didn't find any evidence that he was the killer—"

"Oh, that's an excellent reason to trust him. We don't have any evidence that he's a murderer. Great." Detective Keller sighed. Her frustration was palpable. Clearly something was missing, but for all my efforts to help, I'd muddied the waters. No wonder interfering with a police investigation was a crime. I should remember that in the future. "Miss Sinclair, do you have any concrete leads for us?"

"Meghan," I said. "She's scared. What she saw, and what she knows."

Detective Keller turned to Meghan again. The cop who had been talking to Meghan took a step back, looking unsure, and Meghan herself looked like she wanted to disappear into the wall. "Miss Kountz?" the detective said, like she expected Meghan to produce video evidence of Craig moving the smoke bomb in her office, or lighting them off himself, or putting the murder weapon into Paige's car.

Meghan lifted her chin. I had to respect her for respecting herself, even if I didn't like her. "I told you what I saw," she said.

Detective Keller nodded. "Yes. Well, we'll follow up on that information." She turned to me. "Miss Sinclair, I suggest you and Miss Kountz stay with a friend for the time being, until we determine if whoever left these photos for you was stupid enough to leave behind a fingerprint or some other evidence." From her tone, I guessed she didn't think that would happen, that she half expected to find some confirmation of my own duplicity—Bay's prints in the ink or something to indicate I'd asked my employees to fabricate the threat.

"Will do," I said. "Thanks for your help."

The cops filed out as abruptly as they'd come in, Detective Keller trailing after them. She stopped at the doorway, looking at me. "I know you think I'm not taking you seriously," she said. "But there's a procedure to these things, and we have to follow the rules. We will investigate Mr. MacLeod, and Mr. Wolcott, as well, but I have to tell you, we've done thorough checks on everyone who was present in Independence Square Mall the night of the murder, and Miss Harding and Mr. Lawlis were still at the top of the list. We don't arrest people without cause. I would suggest you tell your friends to find themselves a good lawyer. If they're innocent, they won't go to jail."

"That's not very comforting," I said.

"Being comforting isn't part of my job description." And with that, she left.

Meghan, Allison, Bay, Jordan, and I all went to sit in my living room. A puzzled silence fell as the strain of yet another late-night emergency settled into our brains. Meghan sniffled into her tissue, and Bay looked like she was calculating numbers in her head.

"Now what?" Allison asked brightly.

I looked at Jordan. "Are you okay to be here?"

"Don't make me feel worse than I already do," she said. "Of course I'm here. Keller said I could help you out as much as you want, as long as I'm not on the clock."

"She said that?" Bay asked. "After her little speech about not arresting innocent people?"

"She's a good cop," Jordan said. "But she's right. The case against your friends is pretty strong. And she has to do what the law requires her to do."

"Of course she does," I said, trying to keep the peace. "But Allison's right, we need to figure out our next move. Staying here isn't a good idea, since whoever is behind all this—Donald or Craig—knows we're here and knows what we're doing."

Meghan flinched when I said Craig's name, but we all ignored her. She was the pretty pink giraffe in the room, and none of us wanted to face her issues or have to talk to her any more than was strictly necessary. I felt bad for her, sort of—it couldn't be easy to suspect your fiancé of killing a sweet boy and then trying to beat you into silence.

"We need to find real evidence against either Craig or Donald. Preferably both," Jordan said.

"We tried that—we broke into Donald's office, didn't we? And we found evidence, just not the right kind."

"Well, maybe we need to take a different approach," Jordan said, thoughtful. "Try confronting them openly rather than sneaking around."

"What good would that do?" Meghan sniffled. "They'll just lie."

"Consider their tactics, though—secrecy, and hidden messages, and literal smokescreens. Maybe if we force them out in the open, we'll be able to shock the truth out of them. It's role-playing one-oh-one: if we don't have high enough investigate stats to roll better than our opponent, we have to adopt a different tactic."

"It's not a bad idea," Bay said.

"How do we do it?" Meghan asked. Her nose was red, but she was starting to look irritable instead of sad. "Craig is impossible to corner. Just ask Autumn—the man can charm his way out of any problem." She gestured at me. The others looked my way, and I shrugged. It'd been ten years, and I wasn't going to spend the rest of my life acting as character witness for Craig, good or bad. I kept my face impassive.

"He's already getting violent," Meghan continued, "and he's been hiding things from me for weeks. He'll never even agree to hear us out, let alone publicly."

"Detective Keller's putting men on him, so he'll be trickier to confront, anyway," Jordan said. "So maybe it would be better to try and go after Donald—especially since we don't even know for sure that he's involved. Craig is the likelier suspect, but he'll be more difficult to entrap, too." She bit her lip. "I hope we don't scare him off."

"No!" I said. "We can't talk ourselves out of doing something before we even start!" I stood up, feeling like I should make a rousing call-to-arms speech, but when the others looked up at me, expectant, I started to feel silly. I sat back down. "Look, we just need to scare him. Where is he tonight?"

"At home."

Jordan shook her head before I could start. "No, the detective is going to talk to him tonight. If we interfere, she'll lock you up for sure, Autumn."

"Fine." I bit my lip. "So we need to go after Donald, and we need to confront him in a way that will knock him off guard and scare him into admitting he did wrong, preferably publicly so no one can doubt what we learn." A flash of inspiration hit me, and I grinned. "I have an idea that just might work.

20

MEGHAN STOOD BESIDE ME at the front desk of City Hall the next morning, unhappy at our plan and at having spent the night on Jordan's couch. Meanwhile, Bay and Allison had gone to keep tabs on Craig while we initiated stage one of Operation Prove Donald and Craig Are Evil.

Alice peered over the top of her desk at all of us, thoroughly bewildered at our presence in front of her desk at ten in the morning on a Thursday. "Do you have an appointment, Autumn?"

I stared at her, stunned by color. She wore another Wesley Crusher sweater, this one bright coral pink to match her lipstick.

"Uh, yes, I do." I nodded at Meghan. "I'm with her. For the grant committee meeting. They called everyone in, I guess."

"Oh, of course," Alice said. She smiled. "I'm not sure they'll want you there, though."

I shook my head. "No. Probably not. But . . ." I glanced at Alice, who was watching us like a rather interesting television program. She wouldn't rat us out. "I just need you to let me in, so I can talk to them."

"Well, it's not a normal meeting," Alice said. "It's an emergency session. Vanessa called it on Donald Wolcott's behalf. He had to close down his building because of the smoke damage, and now he wants to delay the official decision about the grant until later in the year." Alice turned her eyes on Meghan. "Was there a fire? What's going on?"

Meghan stepped forward. "Wait, he wants to delay? Why?"

"He wants the delay for you, I think, hon. With all the vandalism, you haven't had a fair chance. He says they need to reschedule so that you can be better prepared."

Ha. Donald really was trying to fix the competition for Meghan. I wanted to gloat, but it hardly seemed the right moment.

Meghan turned to look at me. "That means we're right, though—right? He wanted the delay, so he set off the smoke bombs."

"I don't know," I said. "Craig was the one who was trying to destroy your computer. You saw that yourself. But we still don't know who sent the email calling off your plans with Donald, or why either of them would do it. It doesn't quite add up."

"Maybe they turned on each other," Meghan said, her eyes wide. "Maybe Donald had second thoughts."

"Second thoughts about what?" Alice asked.

"We're not sure, exactly," I said to Alice before looking back to Meghan. "Maybe you're right, though, and they've turned on each other." I emitted a loud growl and pulled at my own hair.

Alice peeked over her desk at me. "I'm sorry, dear, but I'm going to need to ask you to keep it down."

"Sorry, Alice." I gave her an apologetic grimace. "We just need to figure out how to catch a murderer, and since he's here this morning, I thought we'd give it a shot."

"That's fine. You can make your illegal plans here, hon, but try to be a little more quiet. People are working down the hall."

"You got it."

"What now?" Meghan asked.

"Well, now we go accuse Donald of something in front of the commission, to try and get him to confess to something else."

This was the last straw as far as Alice was concerned. "Now, really, girls. You're going in there to stir up trouble?"

"Yeah, Alice, sorry to keep disturbing you."

"Don't worry about that." She put her hands on her desk and leaned across, her big eyes serious in her thin pixie face. "Is he really a murderer?"

"Well, yeah, we think so."

"Oh dear. I'd better tell my husband. He's in on Craig's investment plan to buy Donald's building, and if Donald's a murderer, he may want to reconsider."

I froze. "Wait, what did you just say?"

Meghan lunged forward and clutched at the edge of the desk. "Did you say Craig has an investment plan to buy Independence Square Mall? *My* Craig?"

"Well, yes — I assumed you'd know all about that. There's a development firm that wants to buy the place and remodel it, and Craig's been finding other investors to back the plan financially. I guess he'll be getting a big commission. My husband Tim's contracting firm was hoping to get in on the remodel, but I don't think he'll want to be a part of it if there's a crime involved. He was already getting cold feet when that poor boy died there. Bad press, you know—it doesn't look good to be the company remodeling the scene of a murder."

Meghan and I turned to stare at each other. Her jaw hung open unattractively. "An investment plan—that explains why Craig was never that supportive about the banquet hall plans. If Donald and I managed to get the building making money, Donald wouldn't need to sell it—"

"—but if you got the grant to refurbish the building, that might make it more attractive to the buyer." I shook my head. "He's been behind the whole thing. I bet Craig did all of it—sent the email, set off the smoke bombs, everything—to scare Donald into cooperating. If you guys couldn't go through with your plans because of all the bad things happening, maybe he hoped Donald would sell just to make it all stop."

"But why wouldn't Donald just come forward?" Meghan asked.

"If he was involved with Wesley's death, he couldn't, could he? Not without incriminating himself."

"Well, there's only one way to find out," Alice said.

"You're right." I tugged on Meghan's velour-covered arm. "Let's go."

"Good luck!" Alice called.

The grant commission was meeting in the same room where we made our presentations mere days before, though it felt like weeks, months, light-years. From the hallway, we could hear voices, low and urgent, Donald's worried tones strident over the murmurs of the others. Meghan hung back, looking unsure.

"Are we sure we want to do this? It sounds like Vanessa's in there, along with half the Economic Development Commission. There's no going back. I'll probably get kicked out of the running, and—"

"Does that really matter right now?" I snarled.

"Donald will probably just deny everything."

"Even if that's the case, we'll get our suspicions out in the open. He'll have to move against us, or Craig will, and the police are watching them now. They'll do something stupid, and that will get them caught."

"I swear, if this is just some stunt to make yourself look cool or some little *game* you're playing to make people pay attention to your store, I'll push you off a balcony myself."

I rounded on her. "You know what—you're hardly one to accuse me of trying to put myself in the spotlight." I kept my voice to a low hiss, not wanting to tip off the people in the meeting to our presence. "You're the one who sleeps with other girls' boyfriends. You're the one who sleeps with murderers and lets them act out their evil plans on my territory. You want to know what's typical? You. Getting hurt. Coming to me for help. You're completely incapable of solving your own problems."

"You're going to confront me now about things that happened ten years ago?" Meghan said. "What is your problem? You think everything I do is about you, when really my plans, what happens to me, my life—none of it has anything to do with you. You don't even factor into my view of the world. But somehow, when everything goes to shit, you're there, you're involved."

"I could say the same for you, you know. Everything would have been fine if you had just kept out of my way. But when things finally start going right, you just end up in the middle of it all, doing your best to ruin it."

We were inches apart, hissing at each other in the hallway like angry cats fighting over a dead bird. I took a step back. I would not be drawn into this fight—not today, and not by her. I was bigger and better than this now, and I wouldn't fight over a guy who turned out not only to be a cheater and a liar but also a murderer and a pathological creep. I took a step back.

Meghan had balled her hands into fists. She still wore her mismatched tracksuit, and her hair was gathered into a sloppy bun at the base of her neck. She was disheveled, red-faced with anger, her makeup half-done, and her clothing rumpled from our impromptu camp-out in Jordan's living room. But even in disarray and extreme distress, she was still very pretty. The bright-eyed cheerleader had grown up into a confident, driven woman who had managed to construct, brick by brick, the exact life she wanted. I didn't like her, but I did respect her.

We were the same person, deep down. I might not look like her or talk like her or think like her, we might not dress the same or act the same, and we might never agree on anything superficial, but when both of us started rolling twos, we would fight for ourselves and for our dreams. I might dress my world in starlight and magic spells, and she might drape hers with designer fabric, but we both did our best to shape our lives the way we wanted. We were strong, and right now we needed no one but each other.

That ancient crime, the theft of my boyfriend, had divided us, but it didn't matter, not now. Craig was the true villain, and while Meghan and I might never cross our long-standing divide, might never like each other, and would never be friends, we could, I thought, come to a place of mutual respect. But we could only do that if we put aside the old differences, right here and right now in this hallway, and agreed to work together to right a new injustice, one that had affected both of us and killed an innocent boy in the crossfire.

"Enough," I said.

"What?"

"Enough—of this," I waved my hand between us. "Enough of this feud. We have no reason to hate each other, not anymore. We're both better off without Craig, unless we want to end up dead, and it's time we start working on the same side. The grant money doesn't matter now. Nothing matters but stopping Craig and Donald."

Meghan stared at me for several heartbeats, her blue eyes glowing. "And saving our stores."

I paused, taken aback, but I nodded. "Yes. And saving our stores."

She put out one slim hand. I saw that her manicured finger-nails were battered and chipped, but her hand did not tremble. I took it, and we shook. She smiled. "Let's do this."

I pushed the door to the meeting room open, then, before I could lose my nerve.

Vanessa Cleary sat at the head of the table, Donald at her side, while two members of the Economic Development Com-mission and the assistant city controller sat opposite him. They all looked up when I opened the door and stormed in. Vanessa half-stood, and Donald turned in his chair, white-faced.

I took a shaky breath and tried to puff myself up like I was enraged and not shaking in my sneakers. I pointed at Donald. "This man—" I said dramatically. I looked at Vanessa, who stood all the way and gaped at me like a frog catching flies. "—has been lying and cheating to weigh the grant in his favor!" I gulped. We were feeding them half the truth and half a lie, accusing Donald of the things I'd suspected of him, to see if we could get him to confess to what he did. "He wants the money to go to remodeling Independence Square Mall, so he can sell it—he has investors lined up and everything. Everything he's done in this contest is a lie! He's been colluding with Meghan Kountz, and when I found out about it, they tried to destroy the evidence! She sabotaged me, and then they made it look like she was the victim!"

At this point, right on cue, Meghan threw open the door and stomped in. "It's a lie!" she cried. "He's been bullying me, blackmailing me—we had plans to do work on the building, but he's just been using me to try to get the grant money and sell the building for a huge profit! When I found out and tried to back out of our plans, he put smoke bombs in my store and attacked me!"

I rounded on her, my hands clenched at my sides. "You're lying! You undermined me, got me kicked out of the grant running—you killed my customer, hiding your plans!"

"He's the killer, not me!" Meghan shouted.

I whipped my head back to Vanessa. "Listen to this—they're turning on each other. I'm the victim here! I demand you stop this meeting, stop the grant competition altogether, until I've gotten some justice!"

That was overkill, maybe. I stopped ranting and gasped for air before I got carried away and said I needed to avenge my honor or something.

"She's insane!" Meghan cried. "Listen to her, she thinks the whole world is out to get her!"

"Enough," Vanessa said. She drew herself up. "I have no idea what's going on here, but neither of you has any right even to be here, let alone to be making wild accusations. You need to leave."

"I will not!" I said. "That man has destroyed my business and killed a boy and framed some of my friends, and all for what—twenty-five thousand dollars and an extra fifty thousand on his sale price? Are you going to let him get away with this? At the very least, you should care that he fixed your little contest to get the money for himself! We can report you all if you don't do anything about it." I wasn't exactly sure to whom I would report them, but the grant money had come from the state, and someone, somewhere had to regulate those dollars. It wasn't a toothless threat, even if it was beside the point.

Vanessa huffed, but everyone turned to look at Donald. "Is any of this true?" the city councilwoman asked.

Donald wheezed like a faulty bellows. "Of course it's not—I didn't kill anyone. I didn't fix the grant, not exactly—"

"He's been working with Craig MacLeod," I said, playing my trump card before he could deny the whole thing. "They have investors lined up to buy the building. He was never open to this committee about his financial situation—I have records to prove it. The entire mall is in the red, and Donald needed the grant money to repair the building before he could sell it."

Donald gaped at me, and I realized with a jolt that I must have hit on some piece of the truth. His face went pasty green and then bright red as his mouth worked, shaping words that went unspoken, and I could see the desperate search for excuses behind his eyes.

"Donald?" Vanessa said.

"Craig MacLeod—he's behind it all," Donald said in a choked voice.

"Ah-ha!" I said, triumphant, playing my role to the hilt. José and the other LARPers would have been proud. I felt Meghan stagger beside me, and I put a hand out to steady her. "What's the deal, then, Donald? You might still be able to save yourself."

"I didn't kill anyone," Donald said. "But Craig has been harassing me, bullying me, to sell the building. He knows I need money. He knows I'm struggling. I don't want to sell, but he won't take no for an answer. I thought if I fixed the grant for one of you girls, if I got the money into the building, the changes might help to save it." He swallowed thickly and looked at Meghan. "I didn't attack you, Meghan. I thought our plans were still on, but then Craig came to me the night the boy died—he told me to cancel our plans to start the banquet hall, or he would tell the grant commission about my money troubles, my plans to fix the grant."

So I'd been right—he had been favoring Meghan. He looked so sick, though, and Meghan was so gray-faced that my triumph died as quickly as it had been born. Had Meghan known about Donald's efforts? Was that why Meghan and Craig had fought, the night Wes died, and she'd just lied to me? Had Craig actually threatened Donald, or was this another lie, one meant to protect his slimy ass from prison?

"When the boy died," Donald continued, "I was scared. I think he overheard us. I thought Craig killed him. I didn't say anything to anyone, not even you, Meghan. I thought I'd be next—when the threats against you both started, I thought Craig was trying to intimidate me."

"Did you send the email from Meghan calling off the plans?" I asked.

"No—I got it, and I was shocked. But when Meghan was attacked, I assumed it came from Craig. I thought they must have fought, and he attacked her and then sent the email to cover his tracks. Our plans would be off no matter what."

"Why would he attack me?" Meghan asked. "And why send the email? I was in on Donald's plan, too, and I would know I didn't send it."

"So *you* wouldn't know he sent the email?" I suggested. "Maybe you would've been confused or assumed that you didn't remember? Or maybe all of this is just another lie, one to throw us off." I glared at Donald. "Nothing he says can be trusted."

Vanessa had a hand over her mouth, but she dropped it to her side and interrupted. "I don't know what's going on here, but I think we'd better call the police."

"Oh, don't worry," I said. "I've got one of them on speed dial. She can be here in minutes."

"I didn't kill anyone," Donald said again. "I'm a victim, too."

"Tell it to the cops," I said. I pulled out my phone. But I didn't make it to dialing.

21

I'D MISSED SEVENTEEN CALLS. Seventeen in the last twenty minutes.

Every single one of them was from Paige. And they'd stopped coming seven minutes ago.

I felt the blood drain from my face. Meghan's shrill voice, Donald's hoarse replies, and Vanessa's low, moderating tones all blurred together into meaningless noise. There was a message, too. My hands were shaking so violently I almost couldn't work the touch screen.

"Autumn," Paige's voice came through in a whisper. There was heavy static in the background, like she was standing outside in the wind or beside a running shower. "We need your help. He's here. He has us, and I'm scared—I don't know what to do. Craig—I thought he was my friend, my boss, but he's—"

The message cut off abruptly. I gasped for air, half-sobbing, half-feeling like I'd been punched in the gut. "Oh no."

"What is it?" Meghan asked. Across the room, the others had fallen silent and were staring at me with wide, frightened eyes.

I didn't answer but dialed Paige's number. Her phone didn't ring, instead sending me straight through to voice mail. "You've reached Paige," her cheerful voice said. "I'm out having too much fun to talk right now, but please leave a message and . . ."

I hung up. "I think Craig has gone after Paige. Maybe Nick, too."

"Why would he do that?" Meghan's voice cracked.

"I don't know—maybe to finish framing them? I don't know." I was frightened, repeating myself, but I felt trapped by uncertainty. It was just like the night Wes died, when Paige called me in tears—did she need my help this time? If I'd gone last time when she called me, would I have been able to make a difference? Was Craig after her now, too? Where was she? "I don't know what to do," I said.

"Call the cops," Vanessa said immediately. "Call your friend."

I nodded. Jordan would know what to do. This was her job, what she had trained to do for years. And yet—Paige called me, and time had passed since she had even been able to dial. We might already be too late to help. Wes had been killed in a mere span of minutes, and Paige's minutes might be up. But even if I had gone to help Wes, if I went to help Paige, what could I possibly do? We needed the cops.

"You're right," I said. "Of course." But I hesitated for one more second, then pushed my phone into Meghan's hand. It was so much like the night Wes died—so many of the same players, so much of the same uncertainty. And, it suddenly occurred to me, such similar circumstances—so close to the same setting.

"You do it. I think I know where they are. I'll go, and the cops will be right behind me—tell them to head to Independence Square Mall."

I knew where the rushing water was. How many of my own calls had been distorted by the noise from the fountain in the basement of Independence Square Mall? It was closed today, in preparation for cleaning up after the smoke bombs—empty and abandoned, the perfect place for a final crime, one that might wrap up all of the loose threads. If Paige and Nick weren't around to be proved innocent, they might just end up being the perfect scapegoats. And Craig might be desperate enough to try to end his problems with a final death.

Maybe.

I lunged for the door. Vanessa called after me, but I didn't stop. I dashed through the corridors of City Hall, down the stairs, and through the lobby. Alice stood up at her desk when she heard my steps, and I saw her mouth frame a question as I ran by, but I didn't stop. I flung the double doors open and hit the sidewalk at a run.

"Should I call a lawyer?" I heard Alice's voice echo through the lobby behind me, but I didn't slow down or take the time to laugh at the absurdity. The cold air seared my lungs as I ran the block between City Hall and Independence Square Mall. There were a few pedestrians, early lunch-goers visiting restaurants on the square and old ladies visiting the boutique shops sprinkled along Main Street, and I elbowed my way past the ones who had the nerve to get in front of me. A car honked as I charged through an intersection. I didn't care.

The mall, closed for fumigation after the smoke bombs last night, loomed dark and threatening over the street. I ran around the corner to the street entrance near my store, where the fountain's splashing echoed through the basement. My hands trembled as I fished for my keys, and I dropped them twice before my fumbling fingers managed to insert the right key into the lock.

I pushed the door open, leaving it unlocked behind me. It whooshed shut, closing me in the dim quiet of the basement. The stores were all dark, and the light from the doorway didn't carry far into the building. As my eyes adjusted to the dim light from the scattered windows on the basement level, I could see a fluorescent light glowing somewhere in the central lobby, near the fountain. The water echoed eerily in the empty hallway, muffling the sound of my sneakers scuffling on the tile floor.

I was alone.

I maneuvered my way toward the central lobby. I felt my heart pounding in my chest as though it were a moth trapped in a lampshade, and my palms were sweating. I wiped them on my jeans. After the week I'd had, I was starting to think that the life of a super-sleuth was not for me. I'd gotten caught snooping in the office of my nemesis, I'd found no legally admissible evidence, and I'd made myself—briefly—into a suspect. Not what I'd call rolling high. And now, I was alone at the scene of a crime, hoping to stop another murder using only determination, my charming smile, and the tube of lip balm in my pocket. It wasn't the best arsenal.

José would tell me to get in character, consider my stats. I wasn't off the charts in stealth, but I was reasonably fit and nimble, so my athletics had to be at least a little above zero. I may not have many points in investigation, but surely I'd leveled up in that skill line at least a little over the last week. I probably had a bonus or two for sheer insanity. No one would expect the humble shopkeeper to try to stop a murderer. And more than anything else, I had will.

I wouldn't let another of my gamers die. They were my tribe, my friends, my responsibility when they were in my store. I'd failed once. I would not do it again.

When I reached the central lobby, where the fountain bubbled and sprayed, I peered around the corner of the hallway. The chairs were all stacked on the tables, and there was no convenient flashing sign that said, "This way to murderer." I heard no voices, but I did see that the light was coming from the upstairs lobby, the main entrance where the security desk and Donald's office were.

If Paige and Craig were here, they'd left no signs.

I opened the door to the stairwell with as little pressure as I could, praying it wouldn't creak and give me away. I repeated my corner-check, looking around the doorframe in both directions to make sure no one would jump out of my blind spot to tackle me. People were always doing it in action movies, so I assumed it was a reasonable concern. I heard no one on the stairs, though, so I groped my way through the darkness up to the main floor.

It was brighter on this floor, where gray light filtered through the windows. A flat, stale chemical odor permeated the lobby, residue of the smoke bombs from the previous afternoon. The air felt thin and stale in my lungs. I wanted to cough but settled for breathing heavily through my mouth. When I looked around to scope out the scene, I saw that the light over Max's desk was on. There was a set of keys and a wad of cloth sitting on the surface of his desk but no one in sight. I crept toward it, listening with all my might to make sure nobody would catch me.

The keys were Max's or Donald's, I thought, or maybe a spare set belonging to the janitorial staff—there were dozens of keys on several sets of rings, tiny labels sticking up here and there to indicate which keys went to which floor. The cloth proved to be a canvas bag, which seemed either innocuous or really freaking creepy. I saw no murder weapons, no note indicating a killer's plans.

Craig was not making my job any easier.

Whoever had been here was nowhere to be seen. The desk was neat otherwise, Max's chair pushed beneath it, the computer turned off. Maybe he was just here to do a routine check. Maybe I was wrong, and there was no nefarious plot to end the cover-up of Wes's murder with a final killing.

A woman shrieked somewhere above me, her voice echoing down to the lower floors. The sound died quickly, as if she'd had something stuffed into her mouth. I hit the wall by the elevator, my heart racing, and gazed up the elevator shaft. It was too dark to see anything, and with the light from Max's desk shining in my eyes, I wasn't sure if I could trust what I thought I saw—but it looked like someone had a light set up on one of the upper floors.

I held my breath, listening, and a man's voice came echoing down to me, distorted with distance and the interference of the fountain's noise. He spoke rapidly in low tones, but the woman never replied. At least two people were up there—and I suspected one of them was Paige.

I heard another muffled shriek, and I knew I had to move fast. My trip up the stairs seemed to happen in slow motion, the sound of my feet hitting the steps almost as loud as my pounding pulse and rasping breath. I stopped at each floor to peer out, but I thought the lights I'd seen had come from high up—at least the fourth floor. Never let it be said that Craig lost his flair for the dramatic when he quit LARPing. I suspected he was going to reenact the drama he'd performed with Wes, maybe make it look like Paige couldn't live with the guilt.

He was in for a surprise, though. There was one player left in this game, and even if he knew I was onto him, even if he'd tried to scare me off, he clearly wasn't ready to kill me to keep his secrets safe. Killing Paige would be a cheap shortcut, and a rocky one at that. Craig had to be learning the first rule of adventuring: violence begets more violence, and trying to butcher your way out of a bad situation usually just causes more problems.

On the fifth floor, I opened the door a mere whisper and looked out with one eye. Sure enough, I could see a light around the corner and down the hall, near the balcony that looked down onto the lobby. The light glowed the eerie blue of a cheap LED lamp, one of those bulbs that lives longer than most people can hang onto a flashlight. Faint sunlight filtered through the office windows on this floor, and the lights over the emergency exit sign did little to dispel the gloom. It was a horror movie waiting to happen, but I was no nubile victim waiting for my turn to die.

I wished I'd had the foresight to bring a crowbar or a baseball bat or even just my phone, but I wasn't in the habit of stopping crazed killers, so I hadn't put a lot of thought into helpful supplies. I took a step back into the stairwell, considering my next move.

My eyes fell on the fire extinguisher, hung just inside the door. It was bulky and awkward, but it might do the trick. If I couldn't swing it, I could figure out how to spray it, and that might slow down Craig if he decided he wanted to attack me. I tugged the extinguisher free, staggering a little when it came loose. It was heavy, intended for use by someone much larger than me—and probably someone wearing turnout gear—but I could carry it menacingly across my body like a cross between a shield and a dwarven ax, and that was good enough for me. I tugged the pin loose and let it fall to the floor, the metal clinking noise deafening in the silence of the deserted building.

Thus armed, I nudged the door back open with one foot and stepped out into the hallway.

22

Near the base of the balcony railing, I saw a slumped form on the floor, legs sprawled out, head resting on the tile. I darted forward, fire extinguisher cradled in my arms, and dropped to my knees, skidding to a halt near the downed figure.

It was Nick, huddled loosely in a fetal position. My fire extinguisher hit the ground with a clang, but I ignored it, frantically searching him for signs of life. When I rolled him away from the railing, I saw that a gun lay on the floor beside one of his hands, and his arm stretched limply out toward it. I leaned over him, frightened, and nudged him with one finger. "Nick?" I whispered.

He mumbled incoherently, like he'd been hit across the head, but I saw no wounds. I wondered, looking at his half-lidded eyes, if he was drunk or drugged. He didn't seem in any shape to be shooting anyone—not that there was anyone to shoot. The LED lantern stood a few feet away, shining its cold blue light on us and the mirror-polished elevator doors, but there were no other signs of life. I glanced through the railing down toward the fountain, but it was too dark to see anything or anyone down below.

I shook Nick a little harder. "Nick, wake up. Come on."

He mumbled again. I grabbed his shoulders and tried to shift him upright, but he was much bigger than I was, and his inert form was heavy and limp as a sack of sand. He was way too relaxed to support himself, even if I could get him seated.

"Damn it," I muttered. "Come on, Nick." I nudged the gun away with one foot, scooting it back up the hallway with a metallic scraping sound. I pushed my fire extinguisher out of my path, then I grabbed his wrists and began to drag him toward the elevator. The lights were out, but if the fountain was running, the power was on. I couldn't get him down the stairs, but I at least needed to get him to the security desk so that I could call the cops myself.

I didn't make it far. He was too heavy, and I scooted him only about a foot before I managed to slip on the tile and fall backward onto my butt.

I swore again, then scrambled around to try pushing him instead of pulling. That's when I saw the blood on the floor, a slow ooze from his head that marked the path of where I'd dragged him. He'd been attacked, then. I shuddered and crab-walked backward a few inches.

"You're disturbing the scene of the crime," a voice said.

I turned so sharply I twisted my wrist, and, with a gasp of pain, I collapsed back onto my rear. "Craig?" I said. I squinted toward the lantern.

He stepped forward, and I saw that it was him. He was carrying someone—Paige, I realized. She was limp, too. Craig put her on the floor. I scooted back, frightened. I couldn't see if she was breathing or not. "The scene of a crime you made," I said. I rubbed my sore wrist, trying to be discreet. He didn't need to know I was hurt.

"I didn't do this."

"Yes, you did."

"No, I didn't. Paige called me. She was frightened, said she thought her boyfriend was setting her up. I tracked her phone here. I found her down the hall, unconscious, and this boy with a gun." He gestured at Nick and the gun on the floor beside Paige. "I surprised him, hit him in the head. I went back to see if Paige was okay."

"I don't believe you."

Craig gave me a quizzical smile. "No? Why not?"

"Why would you leave the gun?"

"It's not my gun." His smile looked too clever by half. He had an answer for everything—or wanted me to think he did.

"Donald told us everything," I said. "We know you've been harassing him, trying to get him to sell the building, and we know you've been heading up the investments to do it. What, you're going to use your commission from the sale to buy into it yourself? I'm not sure that's legal, Craig. And you killed Wes to cover it up! I called the cops before I came here—they know everything."

"That's quite a story." He bent and touched Paige's neck. He brushed her hair back from her face, and I could see how white she was in the dim light. She didn't stir.

"Is she alive?"

"Yes."

He straightened and looked at me again. "So, what, you rushed over here to save them from me? Autumn to the rescue, armed only with a fire extinguisher and her wits?"

"Something like that." I got my feet under me and hauled myself upright, my back to the railing.

Craig had the gun in his hand—he must have picked it up under the pretense of checking on Paige. My breath caught in my throat. I edged toward my fire extinguisher, though it wouldn't do a thing against a gun. Nick stirred at my feet, groaning. Craig moved toward him. I took the opportunity to move to the side and grab my makeshift weapon, though I struggled to hoist it up with my damaged left wrist. I braced its bottom on my left forearm and wrapped the fingers of my right hand around the trigger.

"You called the cops?" Craig asked conversationally as he rolled Nick to the side to look at his wound. "I hope they're bringing an ambulance. He's hurt pretty badly, and I don't know what he did to Paige." He glanced at me and gave me his fake-confused smile again. "Why do you have that, Autumn? I'm not going to hurt you."

"You hurt Meghan," I said. I aimed the extinguisher at him. "Someone attacked her, lit the smoke bombs. If it wasn't Donald, it must have been you."

Craig shook his head. "I swear, it wasn't me. Maybe it was him." He pointed at Nick with the gun, and I sucked in my breath.

"Put the gun down, please," I said. I tightened my fingers around the trigger of my fire extinguisher.

"Or what? You'll spray me?" He was still smiling. He started to stand, but when I flinched back, he froze, crouching. "Easy, okay? Look—" He put the gun down a few feet away and then straightened one vertebra at a time.

I relaxed but only a little. "You haven't convinced me."

"I shouldn't have to convince you—I didn't do anything."

"Meghan saw you move the smoke bomb to set off the sprinklers. She saw you destroy her computer. Why would you do that?"

His smile faltered. "She was hurt—she couldn't have seen anything."

"And Donald told us that Wes overheard you arguing. He overheard you threatening to tell the grant commission that Donald was trying to fix the competition unless Donald agreed to the sale." I scrambled for the right bluff—I just needed him to start talking. Hopefully I could keep him doing so until the police arrived.

But he wouldn't take my bait. My accusation had definitely shattered his fake smile, but he didn't start confessing, either. "Donald said that, huh? Well, you know he was fixing the grant contest for Meghan. Working with her behind the scenes to start their little party business, too."

"I know."

"Shouldn't you be accusing him of murder, then? He's the one who ruined things for you."

"I did," I retorted. "But unlike you, he convinced me that he's innocent. I could believe his story. Nick would never hurt Paige, not in a million years. You're the one that planted the evidence in Paige's car, aren't you? The pen that stabbed Wes—that was your pen, wasn't it? You kept it to hide it, but when suspicion fell on them anyway—I told you they were suspects—you thought you might as well frame someone else for your crime! And you almost got away with it!" I took a step back from him, appalled. I'd practically handed him Paige and Nick. It was my fault he'd been able to make the case against them so convincing. My mouth filled with hot saliva, and I wanted to hurl, but I forced myself to stay calm. "You took it one too far with the attack on Meghan. That was a mistake. You should have finished her off, too, but she saw you, and she came to me for help."

Craig said nothing. He stood over Nick's inert form, watching me. He tucked his hands into his pockets. Nick stirred. I flinched, but Craig didn't move. He just looked down at Nick, his face impassive. My wrist started to ache from the strain of holding my makeshift weapon, and I knew we couldn't continue our standoff much longer. Someone had to cave.

Distantly, sirens started to wail.

"You really did call the cops," Craig said. "I thought you were bluffing."

"They'll be here any minute."

"You think they believe your story?"

I nodded. "Why'd you do it, Craig? Why kill Wes? Even if he heard you threatening Donald, it wasn't the end. You still would have made your sale."

The gun lay on the floor between us, out of reach for both of us. I saw Craig's eyes dart toward it, but he didn't move. The sirens came closer, echoing as they entered the narrower streets of downtown.

"The sale would only go through if the developer could get the building at a bargain price. I had investors, but not enough, and even dilapidated, this building isn't cheap. If Donald got to make his improvements, we never would have been able to afford to buy it."

"He was just a kid." My voice, thick with tears, remained steady and even. "So are Nick and Paige. They're just children, finishing college, and you've ruined their lives."

"And mine wouldn't have been ruined? If it got out that I was playing the market, trying to make a sale I had a financial interest in, I would never work again. My boss would fire me. No one would ever hire me." He swallowed. "There's almost a million dollars on the line, Autumn. And I'll go to prison."

"A million dollars," I growled. "A whole million—is that what a life is worth to you?"

A few feet away, Paige whimpered. Startled, I almost dropped my fire extinguisher. She started to roll over, and I moved reflexively to check on her.

Craig lunged.

I shrieked and pulled the trigger of my fire extinguisher. The spray burst out from the nozzle and an explosive cloud of cold, cloudy white spread through the air. I heard Craig swear, but all I'd done was given him a blanket of milky fog to work in. I prayed it had obscured the gun, but I didn't wait to find out. I let loose another cloud of billowing, stinking carbon dioxide and then dropped the extinguisher, making a dash for the hallway and the stairs. I made it two steps before I felt Craig grab my legs.

I fell to the floor, coughing in the gas and kicking wildly with both feet. Craig grunted as I connected once, but I felt his hands reach for my torso and grope for my flailing arms as he tried to subdue me. Something hard hit me in the ribs, and I realized he had the gun in one of his hands. If he pinned me, he would kill me, of that I had no doubt. He managed to grasp one of my upper arms, his free hand tight as an iron band around my bicep. I could see his face now, red and livid with animal rage.

I screamed and raised one knee hard—I felt it pummel something solid, and he lost his grip on my upper body. Briefly free, I rolled to the side and continued kicking like Boba Fett trying to escape the Sarlacc. My foot hit Craig again, and he swore. He pulled back, and I heard the gun click. It fired, deafening at such a close range, and I distantly heard glass shatter. I huddled into a ball and rolled farther away.

The smoke began to clear off, and I spotted the fire extinguisher. I grabbed it, whimpering when my wrist screamed in pain, but I embraced the smooth metal cylinder with both hands. Though I was lying down, I put the force of my body behind it, rolled to the side, and swung the extinguisher at Craig. It hit him in the head with a dull metallic clang.

He collapsed backward. I gasped, my voice high and frightened. Craig went limp. I kicked him off my legs, dropped the fire extinguisher, and dragged myself to my feet. I staggered as I ran down the hallway for the stairs. The gas from the fire extinguisher had spread out, filling the air with flour-like powder, which veiled the entire hall in a ghostly half-light. My breath came in tearing gasps, and I hit the door to the stairs with the full force of my body.

I bounded down the stairs two at a time, half running, half falling as I scrambled for the safety of the first floor. I sobbed as I ran, terrified for Nick and Paige, terrified for myself, thinking of Wes's final minutes—had he been this frightened? Had he too tried to run from Craig? Had he been too slow?

I fell headlong when I reached the landing for the main floor, tasting blood and cracking my knee against the tile, but I bounced back up before I could feel the pain. The cops had to be here, someone had to have followed me, help was near, it had to be. I threw the door open—

—and ran smack into Max, the security guard. I screamed, an involuntary cry ripped from my throat before I could even register who I'd hit.

He caught me by the shoulders and steadied me. "Whoa, there," he said. "Autumn?"

I faltered for a moment, tears running hot down my cheeks. "Craig," I said. "Nick, Paige—he killed Wes!"

Max wrapped an arm around my shoulder and pulled me out into the still-dark hallway. "What's going on?" he asked. "You're not making sense." He guided me toward his desk.

"Craig—attacked me," I gasped, trying to put my words in order. "He has Paige and Nick upstairs—we have to get help. He killed Wes."

We reached his desk, and Max leaned me against it. He faced me, his wrinkled face concerned. "Did he tell you all this?"

I shook my head spasmodically. "No. I mean, yes. Sort of. He's trying to sell the building and use his commission to buy into the development. He blackmailed Donald." I felt like I couldn't get my thoughts into the right order. I could feel blood seeping hot into my mouth, and I desperately wanted to spit. My wrist burned with pain, and I could feel more blood oozing from my knee onto my jeans. My whole body shook.

Where were the cops? Was Craig unconscious?

Max moved away from me and went behind the desk. He dragged his chair out to sit at the end of his station, patted the seat, and went to take my elbow. I let him push me toward the rolling chair, and my legs gave out. I collapsed into the seat, rolling backward a little. Max stood beside the desk. I saw that the bag and keys were still sitting on the surface of his desk, and I wondered where he'd been when I was getting my ass kicked.

"Are the kids still up there?" he asked.

I nodded. "They need help. Maybe you should call the cops again—I thought I heard them coming." I glanced toward the phone and saw that it was off the hook. I looked up at him. "Did someone call?"

Max nodded absently. "Maybe I should go check on them." He wasn't looking at me but gazing steadily up toward the fourth floor, where the light from the camp lantern was dimly visible. "Might need help."

I rolled toward the desk. "I'll just . . . call . . ."

Under the desk was an open box of smoke bombs.

It took my brain a moment to catch up with my eyes, and I gaped at the box. Max—Max—our harmless security guard—he had access to everything, everyone in the mall. He had a new investment plan, something that would let him retire. He had an alibi, because he was always here, always at his desk. No one would ever suspect him. No one *had* suspected him.

I looked up at him. He had shifted to watch me, his rheumy eyes glinting in the dim light. "You?" I croaked. "You and Craig? Why?"

"I told you," he said. "I told you I had a new investment plan that would set me up."

"No. No. We trusted you." I swallowed. "You attacked Meghan, didn't you?"

"She was in the way with her little plans for the building. Craig couldn't see it. He sent an email from her to Donald, hoping it would persuade Donald to back out. He would take care of her, he said, but I knew it wouldn't work. I knew she needed to be scared off."

"But you screwed up. You guys did too much—it was obvious it wasn't just about Wes. When you threatened me and Meghan, we knew something else was happening."

"We would have pulled it off," Max said. "We would have made those two kids look like a murder-suicide, like they were trying to frame Craig. No one would have known I was involved."

"It's too late now," I said. "The cops are coming."

His teeth glinted in a feral smile. "You think so? When the security guard told them everything was quiet here?"

I shook my head. Denial was my friend. "They wouldn't believe that." Jordan would never get talked out of making sure I was safe. She would be here, if no one else came.

"So where are they?" He held out his hands, and we both fell silent, listening. There were no more sirens, no sounds of panicked people, no cops with megaphones demanding entrance. There was only silence. A dull roaring filled my ears, a whooshing sound of panic. I tried to shut it out, shaking my head, but it wouldn't go away.

I pushed my chair back and tried to stand, but my injured knee didn't want to cooperate. "Too bad your buddy's out cold," I said. I tried to sound confident, ballsy. "It's just us."

Max stepped toward the desk, reaching for the bag, and it occurred to me that I really didn't want to know what he had in there, what he had used to knock out Paige. I forced my feet under me and scanned the desk for something to use to defend myself. His desk was clear except for the smoke bombs, a newspaper, and a canister of pens, and I felt my blood pressure rise. It wasn't far to the door, and I only had to be faster than Max.

He lifted the bag—it was empty, I realized, as he shook it out. He had ropes, though, and a mean look in his eye. I struggled to my feet and caught myself on the desk. Max watched me, a little smile on his face, as I scrabbled for the cup of pens. I snagged something, drew it out and bared it like a lance—it was a wooden pencil, neatly sharpened. Max started to laugh.

I growled at him and did not lower my new weapon.

But at that moment, as I prepared for one last fight, I finally identified the source of the rushing noise.

Someone had called the elevator, and it had arrived on our floor. Max turned from me to watch it, and I lowered my pencil, horrified. The doors dinged, the lights turned on, and the doors began to slide open.

23

CRAIG STOOD INSIDE. HIS face was bloody, and the whites of his eyes showed brightly. He leaned against the wall of the elevator, breathing heavily, and my heart leapt into my throat. The gun dangled from his limp hand.

"Ah," he said. "You got her."

"Yep," Max said. "Was just about to tie her up. I figure we can make her part of the little scene upstairs—like she tried to stop Nick, got herself killed in the process."

I shook my head, mute. Craig smiled at me, made a tsking sound. "That hurt, Autumn."

"You think that hurt," I said. "Wait till you feel a good beating in prison."

"I'm not going to prison."

"No? This is too much," I said. "You kill me, and you'll get caught for sure. Four people dead, your own girlfriend injured in a stupid attack? There's no way you'll hide all the evidence, not even if you burn this place to the ground. Donald ratted you out, too—there were half a dozen witnesses. And Jordan will come."

"You always think your little friends will get you out of trouble. So trusting. You've never changed."

"Maybe not. But I'm glad I haven't changed if changing means turning into something like you. You're disgusting, Craig. You're a monster."

"Okay, okay, that's enough," Max said. He stepped toward me, bag held out. "You want to do this the easy way or the hard way?"

"Neither?"

Craig tightened his grip on the gun. He didn't aim it at me, but he did tap it against his leg. "Now, Autumn, we're going to need you to cooperate. We can't kill you here. I won't let you wreck another crime scene."

He took a step toward me, moving into line with Max. I stumbled back, tripped over the chair. I disentangled myself and stepped behind it, shoving it forward. He caught it and pushed it away across the lobby. I was cornered behind the desk, trapped like a rat. A really stupid rat who'd tried to hunt a cat without any help. Max loomed, bag in hands, and Craig took another step. I clasped my pencil in my fist but kept it at my side.

"Don't do this," I said.

"It's too late," Craig said. "It's already done."

I took a deep breath. I wouldn't go down like this, dragged to my death without even a struggle. I wouldn't make it easy. I would not stop fighting, not ever. I dove for him.

His instinct wasn't to fire the gun—he wasn't that corrupted, not yet. He caught me, the gun in his hand, but I was ready this time. I raised my arm as high as I could, pencil in a death grip, and drove it into the meaty flesh just above his collarbone. Craig roared, staggering backward.

I shoved my way free and began a mad, limping dash for the front door.

The gun fired. I shrieked and staggered, but I felt no pain. I ran for the door, ran for all I was worth, ran to save my life and hopefully Nick's life and Paige's—

It flew open before me.

Jordan stormed in wearing a SWAT vest, Detective Keller at her heels. They both had their guns trained on Craig. Half a dozen more cops followed them in, shouting at Craig to lower his weapon, to stand down, to put his hands in the air.

I collapsed to the tile floor, gasping and crying and laughing all at once. There was blood on my hand from where I'd stabbed Craig, blood all down my leg, blood on my face, blood pounding in my ears. My clothes were coated with dust from the fire extinguisher, and my wrist throbbed in time to my rushing pulse. But I was alive. I'd done it.

Jordan knelt on the floor beside me. "Are you okay?" Her voice seemed very far away.

Shock, I thought. That was a thing that happened when adrenaline ran its course. This was way more intense than LARPing.

I nodded. "Yes. I think so. Nick and Paige, though, they're upstairs—they're hurt, I think. On the fifth floor."

Jordan shouted something at someone, and a group of cops broke off and made for the stairs. Another group, headed by Detective Keller, had Craig and Max both in handcuffs. Detective Keller recited their rights in a tight, tense voice.

"How'd you guys know?" I asked. "Max said he sent you away."

"We were outside and heard the gun fire upstairs. It took us a minute to get geared up. We were never not coming in," she said, a funny smile on her face. "I wouldn't have left you in here."

"I know," I said. "I told Max that."

"Looks like you gave Craig what he had coming." Jordan's eyes were trained on him across the lobby. Blood ran freely from the wound in his shoulder, and dried blood crusted the back of his head and his face. "What did you do?"

"Um, hit him with a fire extinguisher. And then stabbed him with a pencil. He tried to shoot me."

"Wow. Good for you." We sat in silence for a moment, and then Jordan pounced on me. She squeezed me so hard I squeaked, her arms wrapped around me in a bone-crushing hug. "If you ever do something so stupid ever again, I will stab you with something way worse than a pencil."

I laughed, but my eyes overflowed and suddenly I was crying. "He stabbed Wes with a pen. Can you believe that? I knew he had a mean streak, but Wes was just a kid."

"Well, karma got him back—and you."

I nodded, blubbering. Jordan, one arm still wrapped tightly around me, waved at one of the EMTs, who trotted over to check on me. It was the same woman from the day Meghan had been attacked, and she clucked over me as she pulled me to my feet and towed me out to an ambulance. They tried to force me onto a stretcher, but I refused to lie down and instead perched at the edge of it, so I could watch the action in the main lobby.

Cops brought out Max and stuffed him into a squad car while he glared balefully in my direction. I gave him a little wave, which caused the paramedic taping my sprained wrist to make a disgusted sound in the back of her throat. I ignored her, waiting for my moment of glory—Craig came out on a stretcher, one of his hands cuffed to the metal frame. He protested as they forced him into an ambulance, and one of the police officers who had made the arrest hoisted himself up with him. I was glad to know they were taking his slipperiness seriously—even at the hospital, he would be watched.

My glee at his confinement faded when they brought Paige and Nick out on stretchers. I could see Paige's eyes fluttering open over her oxygen mask, but Nick seemed to be unconscious. I gave Paige a small wave, but I didn't think she saw me as they wheeled her into another ambulance. Nick disappeared into the same vehicle, and it took off for the hospital, sirens blazing.

Jordan reappeared. "The paramedics who saw them said it looks like they'll be okay, but they're worried about Nick's head injury. Paige was drugged. Both of them should be out of the hospital pretty soon, though."

"Thank goodness," I said. "Have they been cleared?"

"They will be once we bring the charges against Craig and Max." She turned to study my face. "You were right—but did you know about Max?"

"No way. I was shocked. That's how they almost got me."

"Everyone will be shocked."

"Did Donald make his statement?" I asked. "What about Meghan—did you find any evidence about their attack on her? And the pen that stabbed Wes, can you confirm it was Craig's?"

"I think you're in the wrong line of work," a voice said behind me.

I tried to turn, flinching when I wrenched my bad knee. The paramedic muttered threats of hospitalization but fell silent when Detective Keller stepped around to the front of my stretcher. I attempted a smile. "I'm not so sure. Catching murderers seems bad for my health."

"I'll say." She took in my bandaged wrist, my fat lip, and the paramedic swabbing at my bleeding knee. "You've looked better."

"Thanks," I said dryly. "And thanks for coming." I flinched when the alcohol made my scrape burn, but I didn't look away from Detective Keller's sober face.

"It wasn't a favor to you. Meghan Kountz called from City Hall and said you'd gone off after your friends. Right after, we got a call from Miss Harding's parents saying they thought she'd been abducted—there were signs of a struggle at their house."

"Did Donald tell you about Craig? Is that how you knew to come?"

"We knew to come because Officer Hansen here laid out your case. Mr. Wolcott's story helped, but it certainly wasn't the only thing that mattered." She gave me a sour look. "You sure were thorough. I'll admit, I thought you were nuts last night, but when the guys we had following Mr. MacLeod lost track of him this morning, we thought he might be up to something. He refused to answer any questions last night, you know."

"You were following him—you didn't see him attack Paige?"

"He's smarter than he looks." She didn't sound like she believed it, and her angry face said someone would have to pay for letting Craig get through her net. "He managed to lose our cops by hitching a ride out of his office with someone else. I'm betting it was your security guard."

"I never thought he was involved," I mused. We all watched as the police car with Max locked in the back pulled into the street and began to make its way, silent and slow, toward the police station. "Everyone saw him that night, but no one thought anything of it. We never thought anything of him being there."

"He was the perfect partner," Jordan said. "Practically invisible—no one ever thinks to suspect the person everyone trusts. Particularly when they seem so harmless."

I wanted to point out that her bosses had been quick enough to suspect Paige when she seemed perfectly harmless, too, but it didn't seem worth rubbing it in. Jordan had been right to chastise me for interfering, and I'd almost screwed things up for her—but she'd come through for me when things got dangerous, and even when I was stupid enough to put myself in danger, she had never stopped watching my back. We'd both done what we thought was right—had done what was right, I thought—and we'd caught the bad guys in the end.

"Will they go to prison?" I asked instead.

Detective Keller shrugged with one arm. "Not our problem. We've gotten enough evidence to arrest them and press charges now. Our part is done."

"That's not very reassuring."

She rolled her eyes at me. "What do you want from me, Miss Sinclair? It's not a police state—we can't just lock them up and throw away the key because we have half of an incriminating story."

"Right," I said. I wished I trusted them to get it done. Maybe Wes would get some justice. I wanted to believe it, but it had taken my efforts—and the work of my friends—to get the cops to stop focusing on a pair of innocent kids and start hunting for the actual monster who wore a suit and killed a boy with an expensive pen just for overhearing an argument about a lousy million-dollar deal.

"Still," the detective said. She smiled at me, but the expression didn't reach her eyes. "It'll be thanks to you if they do go to prison."

"Good," I said. "I'm glad."

This humble merchant had leveled up.

24

"Stop hoarding the jellies, Hector!" Bay cried. "You're keeping like half of them back for yourself."

"Am not." Hector ostentatiously licked powdered sugar off his fingers. "Autumn only got six."

"And there are only two out!"

"Don't blame me!" He pointed at me. "Autumn ate two."

"Did not!" I tried to wipe the jelly off my mouth.

"She totally did," Jordan said. She looked smug over her bowl of yogurt and fruit.

"Shut up, Jordan, geez!"

Bay reached across the table and took my plate. "No more for you."

"Hey, I paid for those donuts!" I reached for the remaining jelly on my paper plate, but Bay snagged it before I could. "You should respect your employer."

"Uh-huh. I'll respect you when you stop being such a jelly hoarder."

Right. Hector had eaten at least as many as I had. He grinned beatifically at me, his own hoard now safe. I stuck my tongue out at him, and he took a big bite of his donut, flaunting his successful diversion. I kicked his chair with my foot. He choked on his bite, and I smiled, satisfied.

"Shouldn't we open the doors soon?" Bay asked.

Beside me, Paige shook her head. "No. We still have twenty minutes before the draft is supposed to start." She patted Nick's head. He sat at her feet between us, a plate of fruit like Jordan's before him. They'd had to shave his head to stitch up the wound Craig had given him, and he looked like a tame Hell's Angel sitting at the feet of his mistress. He didn't speak but gnawed wordlessly at a piece of apple.

Today was the official grand reopening of Ten Again, and I'd invited my employees, Jordan, and a few friends over for a little pre-party party. We had breakfast for a dozen scattered across the cash wrap counter, and we'd set up the gaming tables for the *Spellcasters* draft we were hosting to take the place of the one that had been canceled. There would be a weekend-long tournament and a series of parties to honor Wes.

They'd set up the memorial on the front step again as soon as the building had opened after the fumigation and cleaning. I'd heard a rumor that Craig had left bloody handprints in the elevator, but I'd never tried to confirm it. I'd had enough murder-mystery for one lifetime, and I was willing to settle for stage blood for the rest of my theatrical needs.

Actually, I thought I'd stop carrying the stuff. Craig hadn't bought his stash from my store, but I saw no need to keep any more of it on hand after what had happened to poor Princess Leia on my doorstep. Meghan had been right about Craig's can of paint—it was actually fake blood. He'd been the one tormenting us. Max had been the one to actually set up the creepy tableaux and take the stalker-photos of me, and now that he was locked up, the police assured me that I should expect no more vandalism. For now, anyway.

But things were going back to normal. Independence Square Mall had reopened a few days earlier, though with a few changes: we now had a guard from a real security company, and cameras were being installed on every floor in spite of Donald's financial woes. Meghan's inventory had been destroyed by the smoke and the sprinklers, so she had yet to reopen Chic, but her plans to open a banquet hall on the fifth floor of the mall were in full swing. The last time I'd seen her, she was talking about starting an event planning business, as well.

The grant committee had been forced to call foul on the contest. If they were even able to keep the money, they would have to start over from scratch, and we would all have to reapply. Donald had been ousted from the committee, and I'd heard a rumor that he was being booted from the Chamber of Commerce, too. My stepmom said he was working hard to get his finances on track, though, so I suspected he would rapidly claw his way back to petty authority.

I was thinking of joining in on Meghan's remodeling efforts. We could jointly apply for the loan and work on the building together. It would mean a financial stake in the mall, though I felt surprisingly okay with it. I'd fought for this place, and I had a strange new territorial feeling about the space.

Ten Again was my home, and these people were my family. My feelings, I thought, were justified.

"Autumn?" Nick said.

I blinked. He'd obviously said my name at least once before. "I'm sorry. What?"

The others were still bickering about the donuts, and Paige was laughing along. Nick was serious, though, as he gazed up at me. "I have to tell you something."

I tilted my head. "What's up?"

"I need to apologize."

"For what? I'm the one who couldn't help you guys before you got hurt."

"Don't," he said. He looked so ashamed, I started to feel alarmed. Paige tuned back in. She put a hand on Nick's shoulder, and he reached up to squeeze it.

"We owe you our lives," Paige said.

"Come on." I ducked my head, embarrassed.

"We do," Nick said. "And after what we did . . ." He shook his head. "We don't deserve any of this."

"What?" I said. "Donuts?" I tried to laugh, but it fell flat. "What did you do?"

If they told me, after everything we'd been through, that they'd actually killed Wes, I would scream. And then I would find a pencil, since that seemed to be my weapon of choice, and I would stab them both.

"Remember how mad Cody was? About the RPG we kicked him out of?"

"Yeah," Hector said. He was watching us intently. Everyone was, in fact. The jellies were forgotten.

Paige blushed when she realized we had an audience. "Well, the night Wes died, Cody heard us arguing with him. After Wes died, Cody threatened to tell the cops about it unless we let him back into the game. We told him it wasn't just our call, so he made us start threatening you. He wanted to scare you into letting him back into the game. So we left the *Spellcasters* cards around for you and Hector. To scare you."

"I knew that creep was doing something!" Hector cried. "I knew it!"

"How on earth would that have gotten us to let him back into the game?" I asked.

Nick shrugged. "It might not have. But if he had something on us, and you were scared, we might have been able to talk you into it. I think that was his plan."

"That doesn't make any sense."

"That's because Cody is nuts," Hector said. "Now we can kick him out for good."

"He was mad," Paige said. "I think that was the real reason. He was using us to get revenge on you, by scaring you. Especially when we all knew there was a murderer around, and Craig was threatening you."

"What a complete and utter jackass," I said. Hector opened his mouth to protest my language, but I held up a hand. "No way. You know I'm just saying it like it is."

He shrugged. "Fair enough."

"Anyway," Nick said. "We're sorry. We never should have done it. We should have told you, but the cops were after us, and we were scared."

"Well, I forgive you. Cody, not so much. But you, definitely."

Paige beamed at me, and Nick relaxed visibly. One more mystery solved, I leaned back in my chair. I now knew what they'd been hiding, and as an added bonus, we had good reason to keep Cody from ever joining our games again. It had sucked to receive the threats, and I was sorry he'd drawn my friends into his sad little revenge scheme, but it felt good to have a legitimate reason to hate him. Sometimes a girl needs a grudge.

Bay stood and stretched. "We'd better get ready." She sauntered back to the register and began moving the platters of pastries from the cash wrap to the counter behind it. Hector joined her, and she slapped his hand away from one of the plates of muffins. "Save some for the customers!"

I grinned. Things really were getting back to normal.

Jordan scooted her chair closer to mine. "You look happy."

"I am. Everyone is safe, and we can mourn Wes now, knowing the guy who killed him is going to prison. The store is open again. Donald is off my back. Meghan and I have made a truce. Craig is out of my life for good. We're going to play *Spellcasters* for two days straight."

"And you have the best friends in the world." She grinned sideways at me.

"And I have the best friends in the world," I agreed. I nudged her with my elbow. "Especially when they join in the tournament."

"Do I have to?"

"You most certainly do."

Jordan groaned, and I laughed. She started to protest, but Bay shouted for me from the front of the store. "Autumn, someone's knocking on the street door! We still have five minutes!"

"No rest for the wicked," I sighed, but I smiled as I said it. I got to my feet and trotted to the door. There was a little crowd on the sidewalk, a sight to make my heart glow. José and Olivia stood together, and Wes's parents hovered nearby, looking out of place. Behind the familiar faces, though, were kids I hadn't seen since the night of Wes's death, parents in tow, and even some people I didn't recognize. Our customers hadn't abandoned us. My heart glowed.

I grinned at the crowd and held the door open. The parents hesitated a moment, the way adults do, but the kids pulled them forward, unabashed. I jerked my head to the door.

"Come on in, guys. Ten Again is open for business."

ACKNOWLEDGMENTS

From start to finish, this book took the proverbial village.

I owe a huge thank you to my agent Lisa Rodgers and to Joshua Bilmes of JABberwocky Literary Agency for helping me transform *No Saving Throw* from a manuscript into a book. To Mallory Soto and my editor at Diversion Books, Lia Ottaviano, thank you for taking a chance on a quirky book and then helping me make it shine. Thanks also to Jes Negrón, friend and former agent, who inspired this book and gave me great feedback on an early draft.

I have amazing friends and readers, and I'm eternally indebted to Shauna Granger, Brian O'Conor, and Evan Matyas for holding my hand, helping me polish, and supplying me with tons of great geeky references.

My dad, Bran McFarland, knows what a rough journey this has been, especially toward the end. Thank you for helping me through it.

And finally, my husband, Drew Buschhorn, has served as my unwitting muse and helped me level up in so many ways over the years. This book wouldn't exist without your support and encouragement. Thanks for everything, hon.

About the Author

Kristin McFarland has a Master of Arts in Journalism from Indiana University, which launched a short-lived but very exciting career as a reporter. She worked for various newspapers around the country, writing on topics that ranged from politics to prostitution to parades. Today, she lives in southern Indiana, where she spends most of her free time playing video games, scheming up trouble for her D&D group, and arguing with her very sassy pony.